Marcus pushed away ~~ ~~
and came toward her, stopping less than a foot away.

Reaching out, he tugged her face toward him with a blunt finger angled against her chin. "You're frightened of water. You're nervous about heights. You're terrified of me. Is there anything you aren't afraid of?"

She opened her mouth to speak, but one look into his mesmerizing blue eyes and she couldn't remember the question. "Wh-what?"

He smiled, his eyes going the color of the Caribbean Sea just before sunset. "Never mind. It's not important."

He started lowering his head. His lips were centimeters from her own when his earlier words came back to her.

In a desperate attempt to head off his kiss, she blurted, "I'm not afraid of water and I'm not terrified of you."

She was terrified of what he made her feel.

BOOK YOUR PLACE ON OUR WEBSITE AND MAKE THE READING CONNECTION!

We've created a customized website just for our very special readers, where you can get the inside scoop on everything that's going on with Zebra, Pinnacle and Kensington books.

When you come online, you'll have the exciting opportunity to:

• View covers of upcoming books

• Read sample chapters

• Learn about our future publishing schedule (listed by publication month *and author*)

• Find out when your favorite authors will be visiting a city near you

• Search for and order backlist books from our online catalog

• Check out author bios and background information

• Send e-mail to your favorite authors

• Meet the Kensington staff online

• Join us in weekly chats with authors, readers and other guests

• Get writing guidelines

• AND MUCH MORE!

**Visit our website at
http://www.kensingtonbooks.com**

LUCY MONROE

GOODNESS HAD NOTHING TO DO WITH IT

ZEBRA BOOKS
KENSINGTON PUBLISHING CORP.
http://www.kensingtonbooks.com

ZEBRA BOOKS are published by

Kensington Publishing Corp.
850 Third Avenue
New York, NY 10022

All Kensington titles, imprints, and distributed lines are available at special quantity discounts for bulk purchases for sales promotion, premiums, fund-raising, educational, or institutional use.

Special book excerpts or customized printings can also be created to fit specific needs. For details, write or phone the office of the Kensington Special Sales Manager: Attn. Special Sales Department, Kensington Publishing Corp., 850 Third Avenue, New York, NY 10022. Phone: 1-800-221-2647.

Zebra and the Z logo Reg. U.S. Pat. & TM Off.

ISBN 0-8217-7771-8

First Printing: December 2005
10 9 8 7 6 5 4 3 2 1

Printed in the United States of America

*For my dear friend and generous mentor
Theresa Scott,
a writer of talent and peaceful nature
who blesses all those she knows.*

Chapter One

Marcus Danvers hadn't had sex in eighteen months, two weeks and three days.

And a mere fifteen feet away stood the reason. Primal recognition roared through him as his nostrils widened, as if to catch her scent, while his body went taut and hard in places that had plagued him since her disappearance a year and a half ago.

Her slight body bent toward the marketing director of Kline Technology, and she leaned against the front of the man's desk, talking to him in a low voice. A voice that had haunted Marcus's dreams. The voice of the only woman he had ever considered making a permanent commitment to.

Veronica Richards.

She bent forward to pick up a stack of papers and silky brown strands swayed against her averted cheek. The blunt cut that ended just below her chin surprised him. A year and a half ago her hair had hit the middle of her back when it was down, although he hadn't discovered that fact until the first time they'd kissed.

She had kept a scrupulously buttoned-up appearance in CIS's office, which included wearing her hair in a severe twist on the back of her head. Her black-framed glasses, which somehow enhanced her soft gray eyes, had added to the picture.

She hadn't been buttoned-up when he touched her, though. She'd been full of shy passion and innocent ardor.

He'd worked with her for three years, assuming the ruthlessly efficient secretary had coolant rather than blood running through her veins. It had shocked him to discover otherwise . . . almost as much as learning that she had sold out his company's corporate secrets before skipping town.

His hand curled into a fist at his side. He wanted to stride across the distance separating them, grab her by the shoulders and spin her around to face him before demanding an explanation for the inexplicable.

She hadn't just betrayed her company; she'd betrayed her lover and he wanted to know why.

The one-word question had played in the back of his mind for the past eighteen months: why? Why after three years of being the perfect secretary, loyal in every way, had she sold information that soured a deal for CIS? Why after being his lover for two months had she left without so much as a good-bye?

Instead of acting on his almost overwhelming impulse to demand some answers, Marcus forced himself to turn to his client. George Kline, the president and owner of Kline Technology, had hired

Marcus to find an in-house mole. "You wanted to introduce me to the marketing director?"

"Yes." Kline nodded his gray head, the movement decisive. "His team and the project lead teams are the only ones with the kind of advance knowledge the person we're looking for has been leaking."

Ronnie turned slightly and Marcus saw that she still wore the black-framed glasses. Typically, her white shirt was buttoned up to her neck and tucked into a neat gray skirt. She looked prim and cool, not at all like the sort of woman who would sell out her boss and lover.

With a churning in his gut, he realized his investigation had probably just been made very simple.

"You said there are five people on the marketing team with access to the information that has been leaking."

"Yes," Kline replied, his green eyes lit with keen intelligence. "The department is a little over twice that size, but only my top people have open access to all our product information, including design team stats."

Marcus fixed his gaze on Ronnie's profile and asked, "Did you include admins in that number?"

Kline frowned and swore. "*No.* I didn't even think about our departmental administrative assistants. They've got access to everything."

"How many are there?"

Kline was briefly silent. "Marketing has three, the project design team has one and the sustaining team has two, but only one would be working with the engineers assigned to each product's launch."

"Is she one of them?" Marcus pointed to Ronnie, who had turned toward them, giving him his first full view of her face.

Kline gave him a speculative look. "That's Veronica Richards, one of the marketing admins. Came to work for us about six months ago. She has unhindered access to pretty much everything."

Kline's voice faded in Marcus's mind as his gaze clashed with Ronnie's.

He tried to maintain a detached air as he watched her react to his presence. He waited for first the recognition and then the shock to register. His company, CIS, had its headquarters in Portland and she'd left before he and his partner, Alex, branched out into corporate investigations. She probably thought she was safe in the anonymity of the larger city of Seattle, a good four hours north of Portland and across a state border.

As her gaze settled on him, recognition widened her eyes instantly. Soft lips that he had once kissed with incredible hunger parted as all color drained from the patrician features of her face. She swayed slightly, her mouth forming one word. He thought it was his name. She looked ready to faint. He cursed silently even as his feet pulled him forward against his will to come to her aid.

Kline reached her first. "Good afternoon, Veronica. I'd like you to meet Marcus Danvers. I've hired his firm to do some consulting for Kline Tech."

As Marcus listened to Kline give the cover story they had agreed upon to explain his presence, he couldn't help wondering how the older man could be oblivious to Ronnie's distress. Didn't he see the way her body had tensed? Didn't he notice the short little breaths that indicated her anxiety? Was he so blind that he saw only her face, schooled into an emotionless mask?

"We're looking at expansion?" Ronnie asked, her usually well-modulated tones tight with stress.

"Maybe," Marcus's client responded noncommittally.

Marcus turned his attention from her to Kline. "I think there's something you should know."

"*Marcus . . .*" His name came out like a plea.

He ignored it. No doubt she was afraid he would tell Kline about her betrayal at CIS. She didn't need to worry. Not yet. He wasn't ready to do that. If she was not guilty of the espionage he'd been hired to investigate, he didn't want Kline jumping to the conclusion she was and dropping the investigation, leaving himself vulnerable to the real culprit.

Besides, Marcus didn't think it would take him very long to find out if Ronnie was up to her old tricks.

"Veronica and I already know each other. She worked for CIS for a few years. She's very familiar with our information services to investment clients." He hoped Kline would pick up on his hint that Ronnie didn't know about CIS's corporate investigation activities.

Intelligent enough to build a garage business into a multi-million-dollar company, Kline got the message and the slightly panicked expression in his eyes faded. "I see. Then she'll be the ideal contact for you here at Kline Tech."

Turning with a swift movement, Marcus caught

Ronnie's reaction to Kline's suggestion. If she'd looked pale before, she looked green now.

She shook her head frantically, her almost abnormal control nowhere in evidence. "No."

Kline's gray brows drew together and his green eyes narrowed dangerously. "No?"

Ronnie's mouth opened and then closed without anything coming out. Her gaze skittered to Marcus and then away again.

"Do you have a problem working with Marcus?" Kline asked, his expression still grim.

Marcus could almost pity Ronnie, having to stand under that intimidating scrutiny. Almost. If a corporate spy deserved pity.

She made a visible effort to pull herself together. "It's just that I'm so busy right now with the new product marketing research for Cougar. I'm sure there's someone more appropriate to work with Mr. Danvers regarding investment strategies."

"On the contrary, I prefer having someone I know answer questions and point me to the right people. Besides, you already know how I work. That makes you a valuable resource." Marcus waited to see if she could wriggle out of that.

Her gaze flew to his and for a second he read hope in her eyes before it faded to wariness. "If that is what you wish."

He smiled, knowing that it did not reach his eyes. "It is. It definitely is."

"It's settled then. Veronica, you can begin by introducing Marcus around the marketing department. I've got some urgent things needing attention on my desk." Kline once again sounded like someone's jovial grandfather, all steely determination gone from his expression now that he had gotten his employee's compliance.

Kline walked away and Ronnie stood staring after him in complete silence for a full minute before Marcus spoke.

"It's been a long time, Ronnie."

Her head whipped up. *"Don't..."* She took a deep breath and expelled it slowly. "Don't call me that. Please."

"Why not?" he asked, with mockery, wondering at the pleading in her voice. If he didn't know better, he would think she was vulnerable to him. But she'd proved she wasn't when she disappeared without a backward glance. "It's your name."

Or at least the name he'd given her when their relationship had turned intimate.

"My name is Veronica. No one but you has ever called me Ronnie. I don't . . . I don't like it."

He wondered at her hesitation but chose to ignore it. "I *do* like it. It suits you, or at least it suits the woman I know you to be." Actually Benedict, as in Benedict Arnold, suited the woman he really knew.

She turned pale again and he almost felt guilty for baiting her.

Then her eyes narrowed and she said, "You don't know me, not the real me, and you never did."

He couldn't argue with her. Obviously he hadn't known her, or he would have realized what kind of betrayal she was capable of. "You're supposed to be introducing me around. We can save rehashing old times for later."

Her hand fluttered to her throat and she couldn't hide the panic his words caused her. Every second

he spent in her company convinced him more firmly of her guilt. She acted like a woman terrified of
being caught doing something wrong. Then again,
maybe she was just afraid her past had caught up
with her. Maybe.

And maybe she had found a pretty lucrative deal
here at Kline Technology selling secrets to Kline's
competitors. Was she afraid the gravy train was
about to end?

Marcus didn't know, but that's what he'd been
hired to find out and he was damn good at his job.

A bizarre dream. This had to be some kind of
really bad, really weird dream. Marcus could not
possibly be here at Kline Technology, his eyes cold
and hard, every speck of affection she'd once tried
to imagine in his gaze wiped clear.

What horrible act of Providence had led George
Kline to hire CIS as consultants on expansion? *Yeah,
right,* Veronica's mind taunted her, *like you don't want
to see him again. Like you haven't ached for his touch
every single day since you left Portland.*

How many times since returning from France
had she gotten in the car and considered driving
the almost four hours south on I-5 just so she
could see him? How often had she daydreamed of
hiding behind a bush outside his condo complex
to catch one teeny-tiny glimpse of the golden-haired
man she'd loved, the man she'd left?

She never fantasized about talking to him. Her
imagination didn't stretch that far.

She'd betrayed him and he would never understand or forgive that. Maybe if he had loved her,

she could have explained. But then if he had loved her, she would have gone to him and begged for his help with her problems. But their relationship had been based strictly on lust, at least on his part. He had made that very clear the first time they made love. No ties. No commitments.

Her reasons for doing what she'd done had centered on some very heavy commitments, responsibilities she couldn't walk away from . . . even if it meant losing the man she loved. And it had.

She tamped down the feeling of giddy joy bubbling up inside at his presence. It wasn't difficult, not when an almost overwhelming terror that he would learn her secret or expose her past had welled up to take its place.

She couldn't afford to lose this job. She needed the money and benefits to take care of her family. A family Marcus knew nothing about. He hadn't wanted to know the real Veronica Richards when they were lovers and she doubted that had changed in the past eighteen months.

In fact, he undoubtedly had even less desire to do so now. Because now he believed her to be a woman without honor, someone who would sell her loyalty to the highest bidder.

She gripped the report she held more tightly, hugging it to her like a shield. "Come this way and I'll introduce you to Jack. He's the director of marketing. He can give you a tour of the department and introduce you to the others."

Mockery burned in Marcus's blue eyes as he shook his head. "Oh, no, Ronnie. I don't think so. Kline assigned you the job of being my liaison and I intend to keep you to it."

Less than two years ago she had found the way his six-foot, two-inch frame towered over her own five feet, four inches exciting. She'd be lying to herself if she pretended it didn't have the same effect now, but the dread-filled panic skating along her nerve endings overshadowed even her body's usually overwhelming reaction to Marcus. *What was she going to do?*

She stepped back two paces and shrugged with what she hoped was cool indifference. "I'm aware that my boss insisted I accompany you around, but I assumed with our past history you would prefer a different escort. If that is not the case, then I will of course follow through on Mr. Kline's instructions."

Marcus's white teeth gleamed in his tanned face. She knew the tan was real and not from a tanning bed. He loved the outdoors and the well-defined muscles under his brightly colored shirt testified to an active lifestyle. The tacky Hawaiian shirt was his idea of self-expression.

He gave her a wolf's grin when he noticed the direction her gaze had taken. "Then, let's go meet Jack."

She nodded once, forcing herself to look at something besides his overly tantalizing body. She had a lot of practice doing that. She'd spent nearly three years as the invisible woman while he paraded through the office with a bevy of beautiful bimbos hanging on his arm.

She turned to lead the way to her supervisor's desk. When they reached Jack, he was on the phone. Though she had left several feet of space between her and Marcus, she found herself mere inches from his towering frame. The smell of his after-shave wrapped itself around her and she wanted to bolt, running from the memories it elicited.

Memories of the only passion she had ever known.

She tried to move away unobtrusively. It didn't do any good. He just followed her.

"What's the matter, Ronnie? Do I make you nervous?"

He'd used almost identical words to begin a flirtation with her at CIS. The flirtation had grown into something more and she had discovered a passionate streak in her nature she had never suspected. That he would be the one to bring out her woman's desires hadn't surprised her. After all, she had loved him since practically her first day at CIS.

What had surprised her, astounded her even, had been the fact that he had shared her physical reaction, if not her love. He'd wanted her and Heaven help her, she'd been unable to protect herself.

A twenty-three-year-old virgin, she'd fallen completely under his spell and given him more than her body. She'd given him her heart. He didn't know that, of course. He assumed she was as uninvolved emotionally as he was. She wished with all her tattered heart that had been true. Then leaving wouldn't have hurt so much.

His words did not seem flirtatious now. His tone was much too menacing for flirtation. Was he playing some kind of cat-and-mouse game? Heaven knew Marcus would believe she deserved to be tortured a little after what she'd done to CIS. She didn't harbor any illusions that she'd hurt him personally. He'd lost nothing more than a convenient bed partner, but CIS's reputation had suffered and for that he would never forgive her.

She saw no reason to hide the truth. It was obvious to him anyway. "Yes. You make me nervous. You have the power to destroy my life and you know it. I can only wonder why you haven't already said something to Mr. Kline."

Marcus's eyes widened at her honesty and he opened his mouth to answer, but Jack hung up his phone and turned his attention to them. "Veronica, did you need something more on that report?"

"No, Jack. I want to introduce you to someone." She indicated Marcus with her hand. "This is Marcus Danvers. Mr. Kline has hired his firm to do some consulting on possible expansion for Kline Technology."

She tilted her head so that she could meet Marcus's eyes. "This is Jack Branson, head of our marketing department."

Jack's freckled face creased with a charming smile and he extended his hand. "Marcus, it's a pleasure to meet you."

Marcus shook the other man's hand. "I bet you've got some ideas about the direction Kline should take in expansion."

Jack nodded his red head enthusiastically. "You bet I do. Maybe we can talk about them over lunch sometime this week."

Marcus made a noncommittal sound, but she didn't doubt he'd eat with Jack and listen to his ideas. Her supervisor could charm the tail off a rattlesnake. She ought to know. He'd turned that charm on her a time or two, looking for a date. It might have worked too, but her heart appeared to be stuck on one track . . . that of loving Marcus.

More the fool, her.

Besides, she had responsibilities at home, commitments that made a casual dating relationship almost impossible.

Marcus and Jack chatted for a few minutes before her supervisor got another call, and she led Marcus to the next cubicle in order to introduce him to one of the technical marketing people. It took her almost an hour to acquaint him with the entire marketing staff. With his easy humor, he made several conquests among the women in the department.

She worked hard at stifling any feelings of jealousy his flirtatious manner caused, but relief filled her when she saw that it was almost five o'clock and he had met the last member of her department. "I've got some things to finish before I can head home. I'm sure Mr. Kline is expecting you back in his office now that you've met the staff."

Marcus nodded, his hair shining gold in the fluorescent lights. Relieved that he'd taken his dismissal so easily, she turned to go. He put his hand out to stop her. His touch electrified her and she froze in place although his fingers rested only lightly on her shoulder.

"Have dinner with me tonight."

Shock slammed through her. "Why?" she croaked.

"We have things to talk about."

She shook her head. He was right, but she didn't want to talk about those things now. She couldn't. "No."

"Yes."

She stared at him, mute with a combination of longing and fear that paralyzed her mind and vocal cords. Finally she was able to force one word from her dry mouth. "What?"

"There's the little matter of your history as a corporate spy that I didn't share with Kline."

The statement sounded like a threat and she reacted to it as such. Terror washed over her, unadulterated fear that her efforts to rebuild her life would end up a heap of crushed rubble around her.

"I can't."

His eyes narrowed as his hand dropped away from her. "Why? Do you have a date already?"

She shook her head. Not unless she counted her nightly commitment to care for her baby son.

"Whatever it is, cancel it."

"I can't do that." Motherhood wasn't something you cancelled when the mood suited you.

She'd learned that the year both her parents died in a boating accident, leaving her sole provider for and caregiver of her younger sister.

"Can you afford not to? Don't you want to know if I plan to tell Kline about your little act of betrayal at CIS?"

Her heart constricted in her chest. "Are you going to?"

"It depends."

"On what?"

"On what you say over dinner."

He had her over a barrel and he knew it.

"I'll meet you at seven." She named a little seafood restaurant that overlooked the sound in west Seattle. She'd have to ask Jenny to watch Aaron. She just hoped her sister didn't have plans.

Marcus's eyes gleamed azure with triumph and she had a strong urge to wipe that smug look right off his face. He was so confident of his power over her, just as he'd been eighteen months ago.

All she'd have to do to send his arrogant humor on a trip south would be to tell him about Aaron.

Mr. No-strings-no-commitments would fall down in a dead faint to discover he was a father.

Chapter Two

"So, what's the story with you and my marketing admin?"

Marcus leaned back on the black leather couch in Kline's plush corner office.

Huge windows revealed Seattle's skyline against the backdrop of gray ocean waters. He let his gaze settle on the view for several seconds before answering. He found well-timed silences an effective technique for gaining the advantage in a conversation. Something he'd learned from his former boss and current partner, Alex Trahern.

"I told you she worked for us at CIS a couple of years ago."

Kline grinned, his expression both amused and pitying. "I see. Do you look at all your former employees with the possessiveness of a jealous lover?"

What the hell was Kline talking about?

If Marcus had worn any particular expression when looking at Ronnie, it would have been disgust, not possessiveness. He'd been pretty darn sure his face hadn't shown any telltale expression at all, though. Kline had to be guessing at a past relationship.

Marcus decided to brush off the older man's comment with a shrug. "Maybe."

"Why did she leave CIS?"

"I don't know."

It was the truth. He didn't know why she'd sold out her company to Harrison and he could only guess at why she'd left town without bothering to say good-bye.

He didn't feel guilty for not telling Kline the whole story. He was doing it for the man's own good. He'd learned early on when they opened the corporate investigations side of CIS not to share too much information with a client. It had a way of backfiring on him and his investigation, which he didn't like.

He'd developed a policy of telling as little as possible until he *knew* the answer.

"I got the impression you wanted to keep tabs on her, that maybe there was some unfinished business between you two."

Kline was an astute businessman, too smart to have been completely unaware of the undercurrents between Marcus and Ronnie. "You're right."

"Is working with her going to be a problem for you?"

"No." In fact, staying close to Ronnie was important to his investigation.

"You don't want to talk about it, I take it."

"I don't make a practice of discussing my past, my personal life or my predictions for the World Series on the job."

Kline smiled at Marcus's subtle humor. "Okay. Point taken. Did you find anything out today?"

Other than the fact that Kline had a former corporate spy working for him, not a damn thing. "I met your marketing staff. Your director wants to have lunch with me and discuss expansion."

Kline smiled. "Jack's a smart businessman. He's always got ideas for growing the company."

Marcus nodded. "That would make him a good marketing director."

"That and his charm. That man could sell a new operating system to Bill Gates." Kline's expression turned sly. "Veronica seems to think so, too."

Marcus restrained himself from demanding an explanation for the last comment. Barely.

"Are they dating?" he asked casually.

Kline shrugged. "I don't know. We don't encourage personal relationships among the employees at Kline Tech. Too much opportunity for sexual harassment lawsuits, but you can't police your employees in their off-hours."

Then why the hell had he said that about Ronnie finding her boss charming?

Kline went on, just as if Marcus's silence hadn't turned lethal. "I've seen them together in the employee cafeteria a time or two. Of course, that doesn't mean anything. She works for his department. Could have been a business lunch. It's what I told myself at the time anyway."

And just what was the man saying now? Marcus wouldn't give Kline the satisfaction of asking. He'd come to realize the older man shared his somewhat offbeat sense of humor.

He remembered the hard time he'd given Alex

about his wife, Isabel, before they got married and *almost* felt remorse.

Realizing the direction his thoughts had strayed, he put a firm mental clamp on them. His situation with Ronnie was nothing like that of Alex and Isabel. Ronnie had betrayed him and CIS, whereas Isabel loved Alex.

There had been a time when Marcus had wondered if Ronnie hadn't fallen in love with him too.

Instead of sending him packing like he expected, the idea had taken root and tempted him to think of a future. Until she had forcefully reminded him that love was an illusion and taught him his budding trust had been misplaced.

"Mr. Love 'em and Leave 'em is working for Kline Tech? I can't believe it!" Jenny's voice rose until she fairly vibrated with her agitation. "He wants to have dinner with you? Why? Did you tell him about Aaron?"

Veronica felt Jenny's disbelief and confusion beat at her already overburdened emotions.

"He isn't the one who left and he never said he loved me," she reminded her sister dryly.

Jenny snorted and her hazel eyes narrowed in skepticism. "He sure *liked* you enough. He gave you a baby."

Veronica's gaze skipped to the munchkin playing on the carpet. Oblivious to his mother's distress or his aunt's anger, her tow-headed son stuck the corner of a colorful plastic car into his mouth and drooled. She stifled the urge to grab it out of his hand and give him a teething ring. The pediatrician had assured her it was perfectly normal for a ten-month-old to be so oral.

She turned her attention back to Jenny. "*I know* he gave me a baby, but he doesn't."

And right now, she didn't want that to change. After leaving Marcus that afternoon, she'd rushed to her cubicle and hidden her pictures of Jenny and Aaron in a drawer. She'd also cleaned all the baby paraphernalia out of the car so that when she met Marcus for dinner later, the car seat and baby toys wouldn't give her away.

Jenny ran her fingers through her spiky brown hair. "Then why don't you tell him?" she asked, with exasperation. "It isn't fair that you work so hard to support Aaron while his dad doesn't even pay minimal child support."

"It isn't Marcus's fault I got pregnant." She was the one who had forgotten to take her pill.

She still couldn't believe that missing just that one day in her routine could have impacted her life so hugely.

She stepped around the kitchen bar and walked into the living room. Dropping to her knees on the carpet, she reached out and pulled her son into her lap, cuddling him close. The unique scent of baby filled her senses and indescribable love filled her.

She didn't have the father, but she would always have a part of Marcus and she couldn't regret that. She could not be sorry she had a son.

Jenny made a rude noise from the kitchen. "Yeah, like you got that way all by yourself. There's only been one Miraculous Conception in history and Aaron wasn't it. He definitely had a sperm donor."

Her sister's tenaciousness on this particular subject increased Veronica's sense of guilt.

She couldn't admit to her sister the overriding reason she hadn't told Marcus about the baby—her fear he would try to take Aaron away from her. He could be so hard and cynical. Why *wouldn't* he believe a woman who had sold company secrets would make an unfit mother?

Jenny didn't know the price Veronica had paid to come up with the money necessary for her younger sister's medical treatment in France.

And Veronica would never tell her.

That burden was hers alone to carry. Jenny's sense of right and wrong was as strong as Veronica's own. Her little sister would feel a crushing guilt to realize Veronica had chosen to ignore her own honor to provide Jenny with a chance at life.

Veronica herself was tormented by the thought that there must have been another way, but she still didn't know what it would have been.

She'd had no one else but herself to rely on since she was twenty years old and that hadn't changed when she and Marcus became lovers.

No ties.

No commitments.

No sisters dying from a blood disease that did not have effective FDA-approved treatments in the States.

As she looked at her sister, over Aaron's silky blond head, satisfaction washed over her.

The treatment had worked.

Jenny's disease was in remission and she had regained most of her natural vitality. At sixteen she'd been weak and so pale her skin had looked like

tracing paper. At seventeen and a half, Jenny was
fast returning to the feisty sister Veronica had grown
up with and ended up raising. Feisty enough to
argue the merits of telling Marcus Danvers about
his son.

"He told me he didn't want any commitments.
He never lied to me." Veronica didn't believe for a
minute the argument would halt her sister's tirade,
but she had to try.

It didn't. Jenny's eyes snapped with anger. "He's
thirty years old. It's time he learned that life is full
of responsibilities." She grew silent and her expression turned pensive. "Have you considered that
he wants to know about his son? Just because he
doesn't want a wife doesn't mean he'd turn his
back on his child."

Only all the time.

The possibility that she was denying Marcus a
relationship he might want with Aaron made her
heart twist with pain.

"That's a pretty smart observation for a teenager
to make," she couldn't help saying.

Jenny leaned on the kitchen counter and soberly
regarded Veronica.

She returned Jenny's look with understanding.
Her sister's wisdom beyond her years had come at
a heavy price for both of them and the knowledge
hung in the air between them.

Jenny had lost her parents at the age of thirteen
and been diagnosed with a potentially fatal blood
disease a year later. She'd spent her sixteenth birthday in a hospital bed, hooked up to machines, with
the knowledge that she might never go home again
hanging over her.

That had been the day Veronica had decided to approach Mr. Harrison with information about a hostile takeover that threatened his company. A takeover in which her own company, CIS, played a key role.

She'd tried to justify her actions by telling herself that Alex Trahern, the owner of CIS, had no right to destroy a company and the lives of hundreds of its employees to serve his own vengeance. He'd actually agreed with her when she called from France to apologize for the unforgivable.

He *had* forgiven her and assured her that he had no intention of taking legal action against her.

It was too bad she couldn't forgive herself.

She hadn't had the courage to ask how Marcus had taken her defection and had never called again.

However, knowing she didn't have the threat of prosecution against her, she had been able to bring her family home to the Pacific Northwest when Jenny got a clean bill of health from her French doctors.

They hadn't moved back to Portland. That would be pushing Alex's understanding too far, she had thought. Seattle had been the next best alternative. Only now it looked like it wasn't far away enough and Marcus wasn't nearly as forgiving as Alex.

Memory of the chilling disgust in his eyes when he had looked at her earlier that day settled in her heart like a lodestone. Her entire new life hung by a thread and she had a horrible feeling he would enjoy snipping it.

* * *

Marcus parked his black Jaguar outside the restaurant Ronnie had suggested. Scanning the lot for signs of her, he realized it was an exercise in futility. He had no way of knowing whether she still drove the decade-old Volvo she had owned when working at CIS. Hell, why would she? With the money she'd gotten from John Harrison for selling out, she could afford a new car to go along with her new life.

So, why was she working as an admin at Kline Tech? Surely her big payoff hadn't run out already. And where had she been for the past eighteen months? Kline said she'd only started working for his company six months ago. That left a year of time unaccounted for.

Had she developed a taste for corporate espionage? Had she been moving from one unsuspecting company to another, selling their secrets for cold, hard cash?

The scenario didn't ring true for the woman he had known her to be, but then neither had her betrayal. He swore under his breath, using a word he saved for times of utter frustration.

He had worked with Ronnie for three years before they became lovers. She had been honest and loyal that entire time. He would have staked his life on it.

And he would have been dead by now if he had, he reminded himself.

That bone-deep sense of integrity he could have sworn she possessed had been a sham and nothing more. Who knew how many tidbits of information she had sold over the years before making her big deal with Harrison.

Unfolding his legs from the Jag's driver's seat, he climbed out to stand next to the car and noticed a dark blue compact enter the lot. It was an older domestic model, a car with a reputation for being cheap but reliable. It took him a few seconds to recognize the driver. What in blazes was she doing driving that tin can? It was older than the Volvo.

She pulled into a spot near his and climbed out of the car.

She'd changed out of her business clothes into a pair of snug-fitting, sand-colored jeans and a loose, buttoned-up top the color of caramel. Her hair swung around her face as she turned after locking her car. It flirted with the pale skin of her cheek and he wanted to reach out and brush the silky strands back into place.

He controlled the urge with a self-derisive reminder that he was there to do a job.

"Don't tell me you went through all the money Harrison paid you already."

Her head snapped up and the rain clouds in her irises mirrored confusion. "Excuse me?"

"Harrison might be a damn savvy businessman, but you can't tell me that he didn't pay you enough to replace the Volvo with something nicer than this." He indicated her car with a scornful flick of his wrist.

Her expression closed. "I like it. It's reliable."

"So's a Mercedes. So why don't you have one of those?"

Her shoulders stiffened, but she didn't answer. Instead, she asked, "Are you ready for dinner?"

She wasn't avoiding his question that easily.

He snaked his hand out and grabbed her arm. "Tell me why you're driving that rattletrap, honey."

The endearment slipped out and he could have bitten his own tongue. She wasn't his honey, not anymore.

She wasn't even his friend.

She sucked in a quick breath, her face paling.

Damn, he was getting sick of her acting like a wounded doe every time he talked to her or touched her. If he didn't know better, he'd think he was the one who did the betraying and deserting, not the other way around. But he did know better and he wasn't buying it.

"Answer me," he demanded.

"I don't have a choice. I was very lucky to get a car with such a reliable engine for the money I had to spend." She spoke defensively, as if his attitude about her car offended her.

He tried to read her expression, but she'd closed up tighter than a clam just dug out of the sand. "What did you do, gamble away the money?"

He'd meant the question sarcastically. Ronnie didn't gamble. He'd discovered that when he'd taken her to one of the Reservation Casinos on the Oregon coast for a weekend. He felt sucker punched when she nodded.

"Yes, you could definitely say I gambled with it."

"And you lost." He didn't need her confirmation. Her current mode of transportation was evidence enough of her lack of luck as a gambler.

Is that why she was selling secrets again? Did she need another stake?

She pulled away from him. "It all depends on

how you look at it. I'd prefer not to hold this conversation in a parking lot. Can we go inside?"

Her soft voice washed over him like a breeze
in the desert. Man, he'd missed it. He'd missed
her.

The internal admission shouldn't have stunned
him, not when he'd gone without the horizontal
mambo for over eighteen months because of her.

He'd tried to tell himself it was just some down-
time. Everyone needed it, but his body was shouting that it was a whole lot more. It was the traitorous
woman standing there looking wounded, which
made him a world-class fool.

He stepped away from her with two long strides
and turned to lead her into the restaurant. "Yeah.
Let's go eat. I've got questions that are a lot more
interesting to me than what you've done with your
ill-gotten gains."

Like why she'd done it.

But he wasn't the one who started the ques-
tioning once they were seated in the chowder
house.

She laid her menu down on the table. "Why didn't
you tell Mr. Kline about what happened at CIS?"

Damn good question. He'd told himself it was
because he hadn't wanted Kline jumping to con-
clusions and putting himself in a state of false ease.

"Let's just say I decided to talk to you first."

Behind the black rims of her glasses, her gray
eyes mirrored wary hope.

Good. His job would be that much easier if she
trusted him. She had to trust him at least a little if
she was already hoping he wouldn't spill the beans
on her. Or did she think she could manipulate

him into staying silent? Either way, he would work it to his advantage and a speedy resolution to his case at Kline Technology.

"Wh-what did you want to talk about?"

His eyes narrowed at her uncharacteristic stumbling over her words. "I wanted to ask you why you did what you did, but I realize now that it doesn't matter."

She flinched, drawing her hands from the table and into her lap. "It doesn't?"

"No. Besides I think I can figure it out for myself."

"You can?" She didn't look like she believed him.

That irritated him because her motives were so blatantly obvious. "The money. You did it for the money, not that it did you any good."

"You're wrong, Marcus. It did me a great deal of good."

"You liked living the high life for a while? Too bad it couldn't last." Not that she wasn't already taking measures to increase her cash flow again.

And why in Hades was he baiting her? He needed her compliance, her trusting cooperation to find answers to his questions. He wasn't going to get it by pissing her off. And she was angry. Royally so.

Her gray eyes looked like a hurricane was swirling through them. "You know nothing about it, but that's no surprise. You were never interested in getting to know the real me."

Were they back to that again? The bitterness in her voice surprised him. Why was she so convinced he didn't know the real woman?

"You're wrong. I got to know you very well."

He let his gaze slide down her body and watched with interest as her skin flushed.

She glared at him, her face taut with strain. "That's not what I mean. You learned a lot about my body, but nothing about my heart."

She blushed as she said the word *body*, reminding him that she'd been a twenty-three-year-old virgin when they met. How many men had there been since then? How many others had tasted the passion that simmered under her cool exterior? The questions gnawed at him, making him harsher than he intended.

"What's the matter, Ronnie? You think I should have tried harder to see into your cold little heart and searched out your greedy desires for money and the high lifestyle it could provide?"

The chair scraped against the floor as she shoved it back and shot to her feet. "You *bastard*. I had reasons for doing what I did, not that you could ever understand them—not in a million years, not with your no-ties and no-commitment rules. I'm damn well not going to sit here meekly while you rip me to shreds with your tongue. It's a game I don't enjoy."

She spun on her heel and marched out of the restaurant.

The waiter, who had been approaching their table, made an about-face and walked back into the kitchen.

Marcus sat in stunned silence for several seconds. He had known Veronica Richards for three and a half years before she disappeared from his life, and in all that time, he had never once heard

her swear, had never seen her lose her cool like
she had just done.

Something about this scenario didn't fit and he
was going to find out what it was.

Chapter Three

Veronica's hand shook as she inserted the key into her car lock. *Darn. Darn. Darn.* Why had she lost it like that? She needed to find out if Marcus planned to tell Mr. Kline about her past. Losing her cool and storming out of the restaurant, not to mention calling him a name, wasn't going to predispose him to mercy. Not that she believed he intended to be all that kind anyway.

A brisk spring wind whipped at her hair and chilled her through the thin fabric of her blouse. She shivered as she tried to turn the key in the lock.

She didn't owe Marcus any explanations. She'd only betrayed him by association. It had been Alex's deal that got soured when she sold the information to Harrison. Alex had forgiven her, but Marcus never would.

The key would not turn. The lock was stuck. Again. She'd meant to get it fixed, but she couldn't

afford to make unnecessary expenditures, not when
Jenny would be starting college soon and Aaron
was growing out of his clothes faster than Veronica
could buy them.

Cursing at the stubborn lock, she yanked her
key out of it and rounded the car to unlock it on
the passenger side.

"Don't tell me your door locks don't work."

No. Why couldn't he have just stayed in the
restaurant?

Jamming the key into the hole, she twisted vio-
lently and was relieved to hear the muted click that
signaled an unlocked door. Ignoring Marcus, who
had almost reached her car, she yanked it open.
Climbing inside, she crawled over the gearshift to
get into the driver's seat. She had just inserted the
key in the ignition when the passenger door opened
again and six feet, two inches of devastating male
folded himself into her small compact.

She turned to glare at him. "Get out of my car."

"We aren't done talking."

She laughed, the sound harsh and grating to
her ears. "Yes, we are. We were *done* eighteen months
ago."

Darn it.

Why couldn't she be more reasonable? She had
to stop letting her emotions have the upper hand.
This was so unlike her, but then Marcus had always
been able to spark unexpected and mostly un-
controllable responses on her part.

"You walked out on me, so I suppose you see it
that way, but you'll have to excuse me if I have a
slightly different perspective." He sounded amused
and that infuriated her all the more.

And it hurt. Too much.

He found their breakup a cause for humor, while her heart was still bleeding from leaving behind the only man she had ever given her body to, would ever let into her heart.

"Get. Out. Of. My. Car."

So much for regaining her vaunted self-control.

He didn't react to the fury in her voice, or the fact that she'd practically shouted the order at him.

His mouth curved in a tiny smile, that darn sexy mouth that had once whispered raw words of sexual need in her ear. "I'm still hungry and you promised me dinner."

She wanted to scream but was afraid if she started she wouldn't be able to stop. Her sanity felt on the brink of extinction and she didn't know if she cared anymore if it went over.

She'd done what she had to do eighteen months ago, but it had lacerated her heart and her pride.

She'd been strong for Jenny while her sister faced death and the horrible side effects of the treatment for her illness. She'd managed to survive a pregnancy plagued with morning sickness, continual bladder pressure and the sensation of a bowling ball pressing down on her pelvis for the last three months, but she didn't think she could stand this.

She could not handle his amusement in the face of her pain. If he wasn't going to get out of the car, then she would.

Popping the lock up from the inside of the driver's door was no problem and that's exactly what she did before scrambling from the car. Then she started walking. She didn't care where she went, just as long as it was away from his mocking eyes.

He was the father of the son whom she adored and he hated her guts. She might deserve it, but that didn't make it any easier for her to deal with.

Her emotions had hit the breaking point and she hadn't even known she was close. She thought she'd been doing so well, staying strong for her sister and her son, when in reality she had been breaking apart into little pieces inside, and now she was about to shatter.

She wasn't going to stick around and let Marcus see it happen because she had the awful feeling he would laugh. He definitely thought she deserved whatever bad luck came her way. He would probably get a real kick out of watching her fall apart.

The bastard.

She didn't see the crack in the sidewalk, but she felt it—right before pitching forward. She tried to break her fall with her hands, but the impact was too strong and her elbows buckled. She landed facedown on the pavement.

The air whooshed from her lungs and she lay there in stunned pain.

She couldn't see the sidewalk any better close up than she had while walking. For one thing, it was getting dark. For another, her eyes were too bleary with tears to see anything. She shook her head, trying to dislodge the traitorous moisture. She hated crying. It didn't do any good.

Crying hadn't brought her parents back.

It hadn't made one iota of difference in getting Jenny treatment.

It hadn't lessened the pain of leaving Marcus.

It hadn't diminished the terror of giving birth alone in the same hospital that housed her sister's still-fragile body.

And it wouldn't help now, but Heaven above, she couldn't seem to stop. A sob welled up in her throat and broke free before she could muster enough control to stifle it.

She had to regain control.

She had to stop crying.

It was a litany in her head as she lay, strangely paralyzed, on the hard concrete.

"Are you all right, Ronnie? Speak to me, damn it!" She hadn't fallen that hard, but she was crying and hadn't gotten up.

What was wrong with her? Had she broken something? He didn't know what had happened in the restaurant. He'd set out to talk to her, to learn what he could about the possibility that she was selling corporate secrets again, and had ended up accusing her instead.

She'd gone ballistic in a way he hadn't expected. Neither her reaction nor his actions were going to help him solve his case. He cursed inwardly as he examined her in the fading light for signs of injury.

Her blouse had ridden up to expose the delectable curve of her behind in her jeans.

"Say something, Ronnie."

She didn't answer him but tried to push herself up.

He pressed gently but firmly against her shoulders, refusing to allow her to move. "Don't squirm, baby. You might have seriously hurt yourself."

She shook her head and pushed more insistently against his hands.

He didn't relent. "You shouldn't risk moving."

The subtle scent that was distinctly her wafted up and he wanted to brush his hands down her arms, caressing her soft skin through the thin cotton of her blouse.

She sucked in air and let it out again several times. With each successive breath the shudders that indicated her sobs lessened.

"I'm fine. Let me up."

Her voice was still husky, but she had gotten her tears under control.

Relief filled him. He didn't know what to do with her tears. They were so different from the usual cool demeanor she exhibited; they unhinged him a little. He shouldn't care that she was so obviously hurting, but he did. She might have done this to herself, brought about her own misery with her dishonesty, but he still didn't like it worth squat.

At the continued pressure against his hands, he let her up, cupping her shoulders as he helped her turn and rise to a sitting position.

Her expression was hidden from him in the fading light, but there was no mistaking the way she tried to move away from him. "Let me go."

He shook his head and tightened his hands on her so she couldn't leave. "You might need medical attention."

She laughed, the sound even more hollow than when she'd done it earlier in the car. Ronnie had not laughed often before, but it had always been genuine. The bitterness in the sound now made him wince.

"Your concern is touching. Unfortunately, we both know it isn't real. I fell down on the sidewalk because I wasn't watching where I was going. My knees are probably bruised and my hands feel like they're on fire, but I don't need a doctor's attention. I just need to go home."

She had herself completely under control again, no trace of the tears or her earlier devastation. He suddenly wondered where she had learned to control her emotions so quickly and completely. He'd taken it for granted before, believing she was a naturally cold person, but their time in bed together had taught him differently. Even her betrayal could not wipe out the image of her passion imprinted on his brain.

"I'll drive you."

She pulled away from him again and this time he let her.

Standing, she brushed off her jeans. "That isn't necessary."

He didn't agree. He didn't care how fast she subdued her emotions, he'd seen them and he didn't think she was steady enough to drive. "It is to me."

She crossed her arms under her breasts and moved away from him in a defensive gesture. Even after all that had just happened, the way her arms pressed the swell of her breasts against the caramel-colored fabric of her shirt turned him on.

He fisted his hands at his side, rather than let them reach out and touch her like he was aching to do.

"I'm not getting into a car with you."

"Why not?"

"You have to ask?" Her look and tone implied incredulity.

"Yes," he fairly growled.

He'd never done anything to make her believe she wouldn't be safe with him. He hadn't pushed her down, for cripe's sake. She'd fallen.

"I'm not going to spend twenty minutes in a car listening to you berate me. I already know you hate me. Isn't that enough?" Her voice was still husky with emotion, so unlike his cool little Ronnie that he peered through the gathering darkness and tried to read the expression on her face.

Hate? Did he hate her? It would be infinitely easier for him if he did, but his body still responded too strongly to hers to label what he felt for her hatred. He despised her betrayal, her dishonesty, and he'd been hurt by her desertion, but that wasn't hate.

"I don't hate you."

"Don't lie to me. There's no reason. I don't know why you didn't tell Mr. Kline about what happened at CIS, but I'm grateful. If I could make up for what I did, I would."

He had this insane urge to believe her. Was he going to let himself get sucked into the trap of trusting her again? No, damn it. He was not. He didn't react with the skepticism he felt, though. That wouldn't help earn her trust so he could finish his investigation.

Besides, he hadn't lied. Maybe if he *could* hate her, if he could get her completely out of his system, he would break his over yearlong abstinence. He despised her, but he wanted her too. Too blasted much. Man, what a fool! Suddenly a glaring truth stood out in his brain: he had to get this woman out of his system. To go on with his life, he had to exorcise his need for her.

He didn't know how, but while he conducted his investigation, he was going to find a way to stop wanting her.

He turned toward the restaurant parking lot. "Come on."

She followed him, a silent shadow in the spring night.

He stopped by her car. "We still need to talk."

She surprised him by nodding. "But not now."

"I'll call you."

"You don't have my number."

"Give it to me."

She bit her lip and then said, "I'll see you at work on Monday. We can talk then." She didn't want him calling her.

"Will your boyfriend object?" Was she dating her boss?

"I don't have a boyfriend."

He felt an annoying sense of relief at her quick denial. But she still didn't want him calling her. The knowledge shouldn't surprise him. She had every reason to fear him. Even she didn't know how much.

"We'll talk tomorrow. Give me your number."

She didn't answer but dug in her purse for a notepad and pen. After writing something down, she creased the paper and tore it neatly from the pad. "Here."

He took the paper from her outstretched fingers. "Tomorrow."

"Yes."

He waited until she had gotten inside her car, started the ignition and pulled out of the parking lot before pressing the automatic unlock button for his Jag.

Unwelcome anticipation at the thought of seeing her again plagued him as he drove the few miles to the furnished apartment Kline had rented for him.

Little baby toes squirmed in delight along with the rest of Aaron's body as he splashed in his bath.

Veronica smiled in reaction. She adored her baby son and he adored his bath. Sudsing the soft terry washcloth with baby wash, she carefully scrubbed the infant. Her hold on his forearm slipped as the soapy cloth made her son as slippery as a wet seal. He sounded like a seal too when he squealed in glee as he slipped from her to submerge to his neck in the warm water.

Using the opportunity to rinse him, she splashed the water over his churning limbs to be rewarded with a small shower of wet droplets against her oversized gray T-shirt. Aaron chortled with glee.

"You little imp. You meant to get Mommy wet, didn't you?"

Aaron splashed the water with his chubby fists, sending more moisture cascading over her. "*Mama.*"

Jenny came into the bathroom. "You have a phone call."

Veronica reached out and pulled Aaron from the bathtub. Wrapping him in a fluffy canary yellow bath towel, she asked, "Who is it?"

A sick sensation in her stomach told her she already knew.

"I think it's Marcus. He wanted to know who I was."

Baby-soft hands patted her face and Veronica smiled again at her son in spite of her feelings of misgivings. Typical of Marcus to think he had the right to demand that kind of information.

"Did you tell him?"

"Why? Are you planning to hide me too?"

Veronica's head snapped up at the unaccustomed censure in her sister's voice. "No. You just never came up before. Marcus wasn't interested in my life outside CIS or our relationship."

It had galled her to admit to her sister that she'd let herself get duped into a casual sexual relationship. An affair. But nothing but the truth would have sufficed once she had realized she was pregnant.

Her sister deserved to know the truth and Veronica had hoped knowing the sordid details would help Jenny to make different choices for herself when the time came.

Jenny's hazel eyes flashed and delicate pink stained her cheeks. "I told him that it was none of his business who I was. I don't like being interrogated by someone I've never even met."

Leaning over to unstop the tub, Veronica balanced Aaron on her hip. "Did you tell him that too?"

Jenny looked sheepish. "I may have said something along those lines."

Veronica could imagine Marcus's reaction to her sister's statement. She laughed and gave her sister a spontaneous hug that ended up including the baby. "Jennifer Richards, you are priceless."

Jenny hugged her back and planted a smacking

kiss on the baby's cheek. "I like it when you laugh, Veronica. I remember when I was little and you used to laugh at everything. Mom called you Sunshine. Remember?"

Not if she could help it. Going back in her mind to a time when she had been carefree and happy didn't make living the day-to-day existence of a single mother any easier. She didn't say that, though.

She just nodded and forced herself to say, for Jenny's benefit, "Yeah, I remember."

Her little sister stepped away, pulling Aaron into her arms as she did so. "Go talk to Mr. Nosy. He's been waiting for you long enough and he doesn't strike me as a patient person. I don't think he was in that great of a mood to begin with. I bet he's hopping mad now."

Great. Well, Marcus's mood couldn't be helped.

She turned to go but stopped in the bathroom doorway. "I'm not ashamed of you or Aaron, Jen."

Jenny smiled, all traces of her earlier impatience with Veronica gone. "I know. He just wasn't interested."

Maybe. And maybe, giving Marcus the benefit of the doubt, she had to admit to herself that she had hesitated to tell him about Jenny, not because he lacked interest, but because she feared his reaction to finding out the heavy load of responsibility she carried. She hadn't wanted to lose him. Coming to an inner decision, she squared her shoulders.

"I'm going to tell him who you are."

Jenny looked up from drying the baby, her expression somber. "I think that would be a good idea."

Veronica nodded and then went into the living room, where Jenny had left the cordless phone lying on the oak sofa table behind the couch.

She picked it up. "Hello?"

"What in the hell do you mean leaving me to cool my heels while you take an hour to come to the phone?"

Jenny had been right. Marcus didn't like waiting, but Veronica had already known that. "I'm sorry, Marcus. I was busy."

"Too busy to come to the phone in a timely manner? You were never that lacking in courtesy at CIS."

"I'm at home, not at the office and, yes, I was too busy to come to the phone immediately. Did you call just to harangue me about telephone manners?" she asked with exasperation.

He acted like waiting a few extra minutes for her was on par with a world energy crisis.

Heavy silence met her sarcasm. She waited it out. She knew this trick. She'd seen Marcus and Alex both use it to gain the upper hand in a conversation and she wasn't falling for it. She needed all the advantages she could get in dealing with him and knowing his foibles was one she intended to utilize to the max.

"Am I calling at a bad time, Ronnie?" he finally asked.

She wished he wouldn't call her that. It reminded her too forcibly of an intimacy that they would never share again. But she'd already asked him not to, pleaded even, and he had ignored her. She wouldn't ask again.

"No, I can talk now."

"Are you sure you don't need to go back to whoever it was who answered the phone? If you've got company, I can call back later."

She didn't fall for the polite routine either. She recognized a fishing expedition for information when she saw one. "She's not company. Jenny is my sister and she lives with me."

"You have a sister?"

He made it sound like she'd just claimed familial ties to an alien. "Yes."

"How long?"

"How long have I had a sister? Since she was born about seventeen and a half years ago." She knew that wasn't what he'd asked, but she couldn't help baiting him.

"I meant how long has she lived with you?" he asked, with barely checked impatience.

"Almost five years."

Marcus sucked in his breath. He must realize the implication. She'd had full responsibility for a teenage sister during the time they'd been together.

"Impossible. You never said anything."

"You never asked," she pointed out.

He was silent again. This time she sensed it was more out of consternation than any attempt at manipulating her. "Where are your parents?"

Where was this inquisition leading? She didn't really understand his curiosity. He'd never asked personal questions like this before, when their relationship had been a great deal more intimate.

"They're dead."

Ronnie's parents were dead? She had custody of a teenage sister?

"She never answered your phone before." It was a stupid thing to say, but it was the first thing that came to his befuddled mind.

"She was sick."

"For the whole time we were dating?" he asked, his voice registering the disbelief he felt.

"Yes."

He didn't like her short responses. He wanted to know more and she could damn well tell him. "What do you mean she was sick the whole time?"

Ronnie's voice came across the phone lines clear and soft. "She was diagnosed with a potentially fatal blood disease when she was fourteen."

Damn it to hell. Why hadn't he known? The simple truth was that she hadn't told him. It appeared Ronnie's job as a corporate spy wasn't the only thing she'd hidden from him a year and a half ago.

"How is she now?" The question felt dragged out of him.

His interest in the woman who had betrayed him and her life made no sense, but that didn't diminish his desire to know details.

"Better."

"Do you mean well?" he asked, probing because *better* could mean anything.

"Yes."

"I'm glad."

Why had he said that?

Of course, the thought of any child dying so young was abhorrent, but the surge of relief that had gone through him at Ronnie's answer had felt way too personal. He felt like cursing again. He didn't even know the girl and he didn't want to get wrapped up in Ronnie's life again. Not that he'd been all that wrapped up in it before, obviously.

Realizing how much of herself she had held back from him made him angry.

"Me too," she said, in reply to his inexplicable comment. "I'm sure you didn't call me to discuss my sister."

He gripped the phone tighter. How could she sound so soft and vulnerable one minute and so cold the next? "You're right. I called to set up our next date."

"Date?" She gave a mocking little laugh. "I'd hardly classify any meeting between the two of us as a date."

"Why? We were pretty good together before." He couldn't resist taunting her with the truth.

"*Don't.*" She didn't sound mocking now. In fact, she sounded a little desperate.

He smiled. "Don't what, sweetheart?"

He deliberately used the endearment, knowing it would irritate her.

"*Don't* call me sweetheart and *don't* pretend you want to renew our relationship. I'm not that naïve."

Desperation threaded her voice and that surprised him, but it didn't stop the churning need to keep pushing.

"What if I do?" he asked, with deliberate silky menace.

She wasn't the one who'd been naïve before. That had been him. He'd trusted her and look what it had gotten him. More than a year of celibacy and too many memories that wouldn't let him sleep at night.

"Come on, Marcus. We both know you aren't interested in me any longer. I was a temporary bed partner who betrayed the company you worked for. You are no more interested in renewing our relationship—if you could even call it that—than I am."

He could tell she was trying to sound cool, but her voice had wobbled there for a second. Maybe she wasn't as over him as she tried to pretend.

"What if I am interested?" he asked, driven by a compulsion that he could neither understand nor control.

But there was a burning need in him to goad her into losing her calm façade.

"You're not." Her voice was flat with finality.

"You sound so sure of yourself, *sweetheart*. It's always a mistake to be certain you know the mind of your opponent." Hadn't he made that mistake eighteen months ago when he had assumed he knew what Ronnie thought and felt? "Didn't it occur to you to wonder why I hadn't shared your past history as an espionage agent with Kline?"

Her sharp inhalation told him that he'd scored a point.

"Of course I wondered why you hadn't said anything," she said, her voice rising in agitation. "I asked about it, remember? But you refused to tell me why."

"What if I said I had a price for my silence?" He couldn't believe he'd asked that.

He would no more blackmail her than commit his own act of espionage. So, why had he said it?

"Don't be ridiculous, Marcus. Blackmail isn't your style and you know it."

She was back to sounding disinterested, almost bored, and that did something to him. He'd spent eighteen months pining for a spy and she acted like she'd never thought about him once, like the idea of sleeping with him again was a joke.

Something inside him snapped at her cool indifference.

"Maybe I learned something from you when you left."

"What do you mean?"

"How to play in the big leagues. What if I said that my price for that silence was for you to sleep with me?"

There was a split second of silence and then the phone clicked with ominous finality in his ear.

Damn. He'd said it. He'd actually threatened to blackmail Ronnie back to his bed. He couldn't believe he'd let it go that far and, worse, he couldn't believe how much the idea appealed to him. Decent men did not blackmail women into sleeping with them and virile men didn't have to. He'd always considered himself both.

The receiver in his hands started to beep.

Oh, hell. What had he done?

Chapter Four

Veronica stared at the green cordless phone in her hand and wondered if it would bite her.

No. Of course not. Phones didn't bite. It wasn't a dog, *or a man rabid for a taste of revenge.*

She'd been feeling on the edge of her sanity for a while now. Had she finally gone over? Or had Marcus actually attempted to force her back into his bed? She could not make herself believe that he had just threatened to tell Mr. Kline about her past if she didn't sleep with him.

She shook her head in denial of the euphemism. No, not sleep. Never sleep. He wanted sex, plain and simple.

When she and Marcus had shared a bed in the past, sleeping had been the furthest thing from either of their minds. Not that she would have objected to waking some morning in the security of his arms, but Marcus didn't do things that way. It was all part of the no-ties package. Sleeping, really sleeping, together might be construed as some kind of commitment.

Still, a carefree and easy bachelor who had a thing against commitment in any form was a far cry from a man who would blackmail a woman into his bed. Wasn't he?

She felt herself tremble and carefully laid the phone down on the sofa table before she dropped it.

The scent of beef stew simmering in the Crock-Pot registered at the same time as her sister's voice singing silly songs to Aaron in the other room. Mundane things . . . everyday occurrences that made it no easier to come to grips with the unbelievable conversation she had just had with Marcus.

The man had tried to blackmail her.

But it was more than that. He had shown more interest in her personal life than he had eighteen months ago, when they'd been lovers.

She couldn't understand it any more than she could comprehend the seductive feeling of hope curling up in her insides. Could she truly be hoping for some sort of reconciliation?

Only a besotted fool would be feeling hope after that conversation, she lectured herself.

The fact that Marcus was threatening her was bad enough, but what was beyond her comprehension, what made her shake with real fear, was how tantalizing she found the prospect of being intimate with him again. She'd missed him so much the months they had been apart.

Leaving him had opened a gaping hole in her heart that neither her son's birth nor the remission of her sister's disease could fill. She'd never had another lover, and if she were honest, she would admit she never wanted to make love with anyone but Marcus.

She sank onto the overstuffed green couch she'd gotten for a song at a garage sale from a retired couple intent on moving into a smaller home. She usually felt a certain satisfied gratitude whenever she sat on the comfy cushions, being reminded how lucky she had been to get good furniture at such an affordable price. She'd bought several other things from the couple, but right now gratitude for her windfall was the furthest thing from her mind.

Marcus's threats brought images that she'd tried hard to suppress over the past months rushing to the forefront of her mind. Memories of her first time with Marcus washed over her. They were so intense that for a second she imagined she could still feel the pressure of his lips from the simple kiss that went so far out of control.

They'd been flirting in the office for weeks. He'd cajoled her into going out with him a few times and had kissed her on the occasions she did, telling her in graphic terms how much he wanted her. She'd held him off, instinctively knowing they wanted different things from a relationship.

Namely, she wanted a future and he wanted a body.

But she couldn't stop seeing him, couldn't resist the seductive lure of the flirting and attention from the man she loved. Inevitably, the yearning and desires that she had kept in check the three years she had loved Marcus from afar broke through the tenuous hold she had had on her self-control.

And one night when he had kissed her, she had plastered herself against his body in mindless longing and need. Even in her innocence, she had recognized the signs that he was just as affected as she. She'd been amazed.

That alone had been enough to send her beyond common sense and she had said one thing she knew she shouldn't have. "Love me, Marcus. Please, love me."

Then, she had felt his hands on her face while his body stilled against hers. "Open your eyes."

She had obeyed him, though she hadn't wanted to. She had wanted to hide behind the darkness of her closed eyelids, but he wouldn't let her.

She'd known somehow that what he wanted to say was something she didn't want to hear. She'd been right.

His eyes had turned the color of the Caribbean Sea. "It's sex, Ronnie. Not love. I don't believe in that fairy tale myth that other people use as an excuse to make bad decisions. I'm offering you sex. *The best damn sex you've ever had.*"

She hadn't doubted that. Even if she'd ever had sex before, she would know that Marcus's brand of lovemaking would outshine any other man's for her. Because she *did* believe in love and she loved him. There was really only one choice she could make.

So, she had made it. "I want you."

He hadn't resumed his overwhelming touching right away but had fixed her with an intense look. "I'm not looking for permanent ties, Ronnie. You understand that, don't you?"

She had nodded, accepting that their relationship had no future. "No ties. No commitments."

She would have him in the present and right then that was all that had mattered.

"Right." He had smiled and then his expression had turned heated with blatant male desire.

She had worried that he would be angry when he realized she was a virgin and think she was trying to trap him with her innocence. Instead, his eyes had flared with surprise when he felt her body's barrier.

He'd stopped moving. "Baby, are you sure?"

She'd known he would withdraw if she said no.

She hadn't. She had wanted him too much, had desperately needed the brief time they could have together to stave off the fear and loneliness surrounding her life with Jenny at the time.

He had finished the joining, binding her to him in a way that had been both physical and spiritual.

For her, it had been an act of love so intense she still ached from the recollection.

For Marcus, it had been just sex.

He'd used a condom that first time, but she had insisted on going on the Pill. She hadn't wanted even that thin barrier between them. If she could only have him for a short while, she wanted every bit of him she could have.

It was a decision that had far-reaching consequences.

Any other form of birth control could have failed as well, and she'd refused to beat herself up about it.

Her son had not been an accident.

Regardless of how complicated her life had become, she considered her baby a blessed result of her love for Marcus.

The sound of Aaron's laughter and Jenny's

voice talking nonsense reached her from the other room, bringing her back to the present and the reality of her recent phone call with Marcus.

As she replayed the conversation in her head, she tried to understand why Marcus had attempted to blackmail her back into his bed. The man had too much integrity to resort to such base behavior; so much integrity that she had been sure her desperate actions at CIS would make him despise her forever.

Besides, he needed to blackmail a woman into his bed like a desert sheik needed to import sand. So, why had he tried to?

He couldn't really want her. Could he?

The idea was ludicrous. Marcus could have any woman he wanted. His blond good looks and sexy humor made him irresistible to the opposite sex. She'd seen enough of that the day before just introducing him around the marketing department.

He didn't need to resort to taking a woman to bed whom he despised to fulfill his sexual needs.

But he had implied that was exactly what he wanted.

What could that mean, but that he did want her?

Could his awful threat be his way of reestablishing intimacy between them, even if he did not consciously realize it? If she could have shaken herself, she would have.

Just as she had tried to convince herself a year and a half ago that she meant more than a casual bed partner to Marcus, she was now trying to believe his motives were somehow related to his feelings for her. Feelings he did not have.

With blinding clarity, she realized she had returned to the Pacific Northwest not just because it was home, but because she would be closer to Marcus. She was still chasing after rainbows, hoping to gain his love and trust once again. She gave a self-derisive snort. What an idiot.

The most likely explanation for Marcus's threats was plain and simple revenge.

She could just see him gloating as she agreed to go to bed with him, her heart all swelled with hope and wanting. Then he would turn her down flat and laugh in her face, or some such horrible scenario.

She was tempted to say yes just to get the torment of waiting over with. At least then she'd know what form his revenge would take. Something told her that if she called his bluff, even if Marcus rejected her, his own sense of honor would prevent him from turning on her later and telling Mr. Kline about her actions at CIS. After all, they would have a deal.

The question was: Did she have the courage to risk getting eaten in order to attempt declawing the lion?

Allison waited for Marcus Danvers to arrive for his morning appointment with George. She sat in her chair behind her desk in the anteroom outside the president's office just as if she hadn't woken feeling snuggly and sated in his bed two hours before.

At forty-five, single and a grandmother, snuggly and sexually sated were not emotions she took for granted.

George Kline had brought an element back into her life she'd believed gone forever when her first husband left her for his bimbette sales manager three years ago.

Sexuality.

She was a sexual being.

She was also a damn fine personal assistant and George appreciated both elements of her nature.

It flattered her. Such a dynamic and wealthy man could have his pick of young, nubile beauties, but he'd chosen her.

She smiled at him when he walked out of his office.

"Danvers here yet?"

"No, George, he's not."

He frowned, his pale eyes narrowing. "I told you to call me Mr. Kline in the office, Allison."

He was fanatical about keeping their relationship at work separate from their private life. Kline Technologies strongly discouraged personal relationships between employees. George believed in setting an example.

Sometimes she slipped up.

She didn't mean to, but it was hard to separate the two areas of her life completely when he played such a major role in both of them. "I'm sorry."

He nodded, brisk and efficient. No sentimentality to mar his perfect business image.

"When Danvers gets here, send him right in."

"Yes, sir."

He smiled, his approval warming her even though it was short-lived, and he disappeared into his office a second later.

Marcus Danvers arrived five minutes later and

Allison showed him into George's office with all the professional decorum at her disposal.

Okay, you can do this. Think lion tamer. Think safety for you and your family.

Veronica's short self-lecture did nothing to slow the pulse that had begun throbbing at the base of her throat at the first sign of Marcus's golden hair above the cubicle walls. He was obviously headed in her direction. She slid shut the file drawer she had been looking in and sat in her desk chair, trying to compose her features in a cool mask before Marcus entered her cubicle.

After several deep breaths and a few more bracing self-directives, she felt ready.

Right.

About as ready as a four-year-old to go toe-to-toe with a grown-up.

Marcus walked in, filling the small space with his distinctly male presence. Other men had been in her cubicle, dozens of them, but not one had dominated the enclosure as Marcus did.

"Good morning, Ronnie. I trust you slept well last night."

She'd tossed and turned in her bed for hours, gnawing on their conversation in her mind.

"Like a baby," she said and forced herself not to wince at the poor choice of words.

The last thing she needed right now was a reminder of the guilt she felt at not yet telling Marcus about their child. Even if he didn't want to know, she still felt guilty.

He smiled, his eyes mocking her lie. "I'm glad. I

wouldn't want to think you might have been upset about anything I said on the phone last night."

He knew she hadn't slept a wink. The rat. "About that . . ."

She *could* do this. Just call his bluff and it would all be over. She'd be safe at Kline Tech and he would have gotten the revenge he clearly needed. It was all very balanced, very logical . . . and very terrifying.

He shook his head with feigned regret. "Sorry. I don't have time to get into it now. I just stopped by to see if you could get me on Jack's calendar for lunch sometime this week."

She stared at him, feeling her mouth drop open in ridiculous amazement. The man was blackmailing her but didn't have time to go into it?

"You want an appointment for lunch with Jack?" She felt like she was strangling on her own voice.

"That about covers it." He thrust his hands in his pockets and leaned against the doorway. "Oh, I also wouldn't mind some help getting a temporary office set up. I should have asked Kline's personal assistant, but he got a phone call shortly after I arrived for our meeting this morning and I didn't think of it. Is that something you can do?"

"Of course." Hadn't Mr. Kline practically ordered her to help Marcus in any way he needed?

"So, what day do you think would work for Jack?"

Disoriented by the mundane question when she had psyched herself up for a confrontation, she forced herself to focus on the computer screen. She clicked into Jack's calendar. "Tuesday or Thursday would be best. He can take a long lunch either day."

"Let's make it Thursday. I'm still getting my feet wet around here and want to wait to meet with him after I have a better feel for Kline Technology's environment."

She nodded. He and Alex had always taken their consulting services very seriously. They didn't just steer clients to particular investments because of earning potential but took the time to match their clients with other strategic fits.

She entered the appointment into Jack's calendar and then turned back to face Marcus. "You're set. I'll send an e-mail to Jack letting him know I put you on the calendar for Thursday."

Marcus pushed away from the door and moved toward her. Mesmerized by the suddenly intent look swirling in his aquamarine eyes, she waited to see what he would do.

When he was just a couple of feet away, he reached out and caressed the line of her jaw with one finger. "You're pretty damn efficient, Ronnie. We miss you in the office. Your replacement isn't nearly as organized."

A short laugh of disbelief erupted from her throat as searing jealousy coursed through her at the idea of another woman filling her place at CIS and perhaps in Marcus's life.

"I'm sure she's a lot more fun," she couldn't help saying cattily, remembering Marcus's many jokes about her being a human robot.

She had never felt like a robot around him.

In fact, right now her body was reacting in a most human, most feminine way to the slight touch of Marcus's hand against her face. She should have slapped his hand away or, at the very least, jerked her face from contact with that clever finger, but the feel of his casual touch had sent a sharp ache of longing through her.

She wanted to reach out and grab his hand, bring it back to her face and let it rest there against her cheek indefinitely. How pathetic was that?

Marcus's inner laughter was even more blatant now. "Well, she's interesting. I'll give her that much, but you were definitely more fun."

What did he mean? Did he want to imply he'd slept with the new secretary too, but she wasn't as good in bed as her? Or did he mean that she had held out against his flirtations, unlike herself? The tormenting thoughts chased through Veronica's head and absorbed her concentration so that he had almost made it past the gray walls of her cubicle before she realized he was leaving.

"Wait," she blurted out before thinking.

He turned, his body already halfway into the corridor. "Don't worry. You can take your time looking into office accommodations for me this morning. I'll be busy getting a feel for a couple of other departments. I'll get back with you around lunchtime."

And with that he was gone. She stared at the open doorway and wished she had a real office, something she could shut herself up in and collect her thoughts without risk of interruption. That wasn't going to happen.

Besides, she had work to do. Not only did she have her own work to finish, an unending task, but now she had to find and furbish office space for Marcus. She picked up the phone to call a friend in space allocation. Even with Mr. Kline's personal approval, getting Marcus set up in an office that morning wasn't going to be easy.

Fifteen minutes later, she barely controlled the urge to slam her receiver in its cradle. The only office space available on such short notice was kitty-corner to Veronica's cubicle. For the time Marcus would be at Kline Tech, he'd be working mere feet from her. He couldn't have planned a more effective torment if he tried.

And the worst of it was that she knew he hadn't had a word to say about it.

Marcus tunneled his fingers through his hair as he waited for the elevator to reach the floor that housed the design team. Why had he teased Ronnie like that? He had decided last night to tell her that he hadn't meant the blackmail threat. He wasn't sure how he could extricate himself from it without losing some of his pride and she'd already walked all over his ego by leaving him, but he didn't want her back in his bed on those terms.

He shouldn't want her back in his bed at all. She was a spy, a liar . . . a thief of corporate secrets.

Telling himself that did not lessen the pleasure he'd felt at the evidence of her jealousy of CIS's new secretary one iota. He'd gone on baiting her just to see the way her soft gray eyes turned almost obsidian and her pale skin colored in her agitation. She'd tried to hide it, but he knew her responses too well.

He smiled inwardly. Her little comment about the new secretary being more fun couldn't be further from the truth. He liked Alex's mom a lot, but he wouldn't describe Priscilla Redding as fun. She'd loosened up since marrying again, but she still exuded good breeding and propriety.

The idea of another woman in his life had really flustered Ronnie, though. Did that mean she still cared about him?

More importantly, did that mean she hadn't replaced him in her life, or in her bed?

He had spent more nights than he cared to admit contemplating that very question. She'd been a virgin when they had started dating, but there was no denying that by the time Ronnie had left Portland, she had proved herself to be the most passionate bed partner he had ever known.

The thought that now that she had been initiated into physical pleasure she would look for other lovers had kept him awake more nights the past year than the ones he spent angry over her defection from CIS.

He didn't believe in love. It was a weakening emotion, an excuse that people used to hurt themselves and others.

He should know. He'd spent the first thirteen years of his life the despised bastard son of a big man in a small town because his mother *loved* his father too much to leave her life as the man's mistress and take her son someplace he wasn't known. Someplace where other people didn't care that his dad had not bothered to divorce his wife and marry the mother of his youngest son.

No, Marcus didn't believe in love, but this feeling of possessiveness he had toward Ronnie couldn't be denied. He had a strong sense that he'd be tempted to get violent with any man who tried to take his place in Ronnie's bed.

Even if he didn't want to be there himself.

Chapter Five

Veronica picked at the chef's salad she'd gotten for lunch from the cafeteria kitchen, her mind on Marcus's strange behavior that morning. At least it seemed strange to her.

After convincing herself that the only way to ensure the safety of her life in Seattle was to call Marcus's bluff, she'd primed herself for a confrontation with him when she saw him next.

Marcus, the wily man that he was, hadn't obliged. He'd known what he was doing when he asked her to arrange a lunch date with Jack instead.

The man was too darn adept at psychological warfare.

She rolled a cherry tomato in the ranch dressing on her salad and then popped it in her mouth, enjoying the way the tangy pulp exploded on her tongue as she bit down.

What was his game? Did he or did he not want to blackmail her? A more important question, one she had better figure out before calling his bluff would be: Did he or did he not want her back in his bed? In the very unlikely chance that this blackmail threat was about more than revenge and rejection, she had to tread very carefully.

Yet, they had to work through her betrayal somehow. And she had to know what he planned to do with the information about her past before she told him about Aaron. She'd like to think she was strong enough to risk a custody battle, but she didn't know if she was. She'd used up her emotional reserves during Jenny's long battle with illness.

Could she tell Marcus about his son with the risk that he might use that information to hurt her hanging over her head? Did she have a right to put her own happiness above that of Marcus's right to know about his child?

The thoughts were a confusing whirl in her head when a familiar voice sounded from over her left shoulder. "Is this seat taken?"

She looked up from her salad and forced her lips to tip in a welcoming smile. "No. Have a seat, Sandy."

The willowy blonde slid gracefully into a chair opposite Veronica, setting her plastic tray loaded with what appeared to be a very healthy lunch on the table as she did so. "Whew, it's been nuts trying to get Cougar launched. I'll be really glad when this product goes to market."

Veronica nodded in understanding. A technical marketing engineer, Sandy had a very hairy job toward product launch time, and Cougar had had more than its share of troubles.

"I still can't believe that information about

Cougar's problems with the new high-speed chipset got released to the press. It makes you wonder if we've got moles working in our department or for the design team."

Veronica shook her head, chewing another bite of salad before speaking. "More likely we've got some loose-tongued engineers who share info with their buddies from college over a beer after hours."

"Yeah, and when those buddies just happen to work for rival firms, our secrets get leaked to the press. It could happen that way, I suppose." Sandy laid her utensils out neatly and put her paper napkin in her lap, almost covering the short black skirt she wore. "But haven't you noticed how many times this past year we've had confidential information leaked to the press, or our competition has beaten us by less than a day in announcing similar technology advances?"

Veronica realized her friend was serious. "You really think Kline Technology has some sort of corporate spy in its midst?"

"It wouldn't be the first time such a thing has happened in our industry. Computers and their peripheral technology are a hotbed for that sort of game playing. Someone could make a lot more money selling secrets than their nine-to-five salary."

Chills of cold dread crawled up Veronica's legs and into her spine.

A corporate spy at Kline Tech? She didn't want to believe it could be true, but Sandy's words couldn't be denied. There had been a lot of information leaks over the past six months . . . since Veronica had come to work for the company, in fact.

Having worked at CIS for so long, she knew first-hand how easily information could be obtained by those who knew how to go about getting it, men like Alex Trahern and Marcus Danvers. She had never stopped to think that the wealth of information on Kline Tech's products might have an internal source . . . a leak.

She and Sandy ate in silence for several seconds while Veronica tried to comprehend the significance of her company's setbacks in the past few months and what it might mean to her newfound security.

From the contemplative expression on Sandy's beautiful face, Veronica thought the blonde might be doing the same thing. Only she undoubtedly wasn't plagued with the worry that she could be accused of the crime because of past actions.

Marcus's blackmail threat took on more sinister tones, and, for the first time, she contemplated running. Perhaps coming back to the Pacific Northwest had been every bit as stupid as letting herself fall in love with Marcus in the first place.

She took a small sip of her iced tea, wanting desperately to calm her own nerves.

"Is there room at the table for one more?"

At the sound of Marcus's voice, she inhaled and swallowed wrong, throwing herself into a coughing fit as her lungs refused the tea. Marcus dropped his lunch on the table and started slapping her back with strong, firm strokes until she stopped imitating a three-pack-a-day smoker after hiking to the summit of Mount Rainier.

"Take deep breaths, honey." Marcus had stopped patting her back, but instead of moving away, he stood there and rubbed gentle circles between her shoulder blades. "You need to relax."

Relax? She was supposed to relax when he was touching her and talking to her in that tender voice she hadn't heard since the last time they had been to bed together?

"Are you all right?" Sandy's concerned voice cut through Veronica's thoughts.

She stiffened, pulling forward, to let Marcus know he could stop rubbing her back, and instantly regretted the action when he did. Darn. She needed to get a grip.

"I'm fine. I just swallowed wrong."

Not that they required the explanation. It had to be pretty obvious what had happened.

From the thoughtful look in Sandy's eyes, Veronica knew that the other woman was speculating about *why* she'd lost her ability to control her basic drinking skills rather than what exactly had gone wrong. Feeling heat creep up her neck, she attempted to ignore Marcus's legs so close to her own now that he had taken a seat at their small table.

She consciously ignored the look of interest on Sandy's face as well.

"I arranged for your office space this morning. I can show you your cubicle after lunch, if you like." She turned to Marcus as she spoke, trying very hard to pretend she was no longer blushing.

His blue eyes, which had warmed with concern for that brief moment during her coughing fit, were now cool and unreadable once again. "That'll be fine, Ronnie."

She nodded, not knowing what else to say.

Sandy wasn't so handicapped. The gorgeous blonde always knew what to say around men.

"You certainly were quick to the rescue a moment ago. Did you take CPR classes or something?"

Marcus turned his lady-killer smile on Sandy and Veronica was surprised the other woman didn't melt into a puddle at his feet from the warmth of it.

"Actually I did, years ago, but when I heard Ronnie choking, I acted on instinct."

"Thank you," Veronica said, knowing it was expected of her and realizing she should have said it right away rather than bringing up his office space first.

The man had a way of sending her normally organized thought processes into chaos.

He inclined his head. "No problem."

"So, do you have any concrete plans for Kline Tech's expansion yet?" Sandy asked when the conversation lagged again.

Once again, Marcus smiled, this time with amusement. "I'm fast, but even I'm not that fast. It'll take a while to get a feel for the company and then I'll start doing preliminary information gathering on possible investments. Kline isn't sure if he wants to bring in new projects to his current technology line or branch out in different directions."

"I can't wait to hear what is decided," Sandy said, her eyes warm and compelling.

Was she interested in Marcus? She had every reason to be.

Veronica had gotten to know the technical marketing engineer rather well over the past few months and had no doubt that Sandy and Marcus would make the ideal pair. In fact, anyone seeing them together would think they made a fair imitation of Barbie and Ken. They were both fun loving, gorgeous and had many of the same interests.

She didn't know if she could bear to sit at the small table and listen to them discover that information for themselves.

She pushed her salad around on the clear plastic plate and wondered what excuse she could make to leave the two alone. Not that she wanted to.

As painful as it would be to sit and watch the friendship develop and know it would probably turn into more, she couldn't quite stomach the idea of just leaving them to it either. She knew she couldn't have Marcus, but that didn't mean she wanted to watch him find someone else.

"You'd better start eating that rather than playing with it if you're going to finish sometime before the next century," Marcus teased her.

She shrugged. "I'm not all that hungry, I guess."

Sandy shook her head. "You must eat your lunch in order to have sufficient energy to finish the afternoon with a clear head. The last thing you need to do is drink that caffeine-laden tea without eating nutritious food to counterbalance it."

Marcus laughed. "Don't tell me you're one of *those*."

Sandy's smile was definitely inviting. "One of those what?"

"A health food fanatic."

Sandy's laugh was soft and entirely too appealing. "You bet. You don't think I look this good without working at it, do you?" she asked, with guileless assurance.

As Marcus gave Sandy a flirtatious once-over, Veronica couldn't help comparing what he saw when he looked at the willowy blonde with what he saw when he looked at her.

At five feet eight, Sandy would fit Marcus to a tee, while Veronica's own five feet, four inches made her feel tiny next to his muscled height. Sandy also dressed in a way to attract men, with short skirts and bright, appealing tops that highlighted her blond hair and fair skin.

Veronica's own black skirt reached past her knees. She'd paired it with a plain silk shell, the color of Seattle's skyline—dull gray.

She felt like a drab little wren next to a peacock as Marcus winked at Sandy. "I guess there's something to be said for bean sprouts and granola."

Sandy laughed, obviously pleased by Marcus's compliment. "That's what I keep telling Veronica, but she won't even venture to low-fat salad dressing."

Marcus turned his attention back to Veronica and she braced herself for the critical comment Sandy had unwittingly set him up to make. She knew her friend hadn't meant to criticize her. Sandy's health food habits were a source of a running joke between the two of them, but Marcus didn't know that and even if he had, would it have stopped him from making the sarcastic comment she was sure was coming? She didn't think so.

"Ronnie looks pretty damn good to me. Regular dressing must agree with her."

Sandy sighed. "You may be right, lucky girl."

Veronica said nothing. She felt as if her vocal cords had been frozen by Marcus's compliment.

She hadn't expected it and was even less prepared to respond to it.

Then he shocked her further by taking her fork from unresisting fingers, filling it with a bite of salad and saying, "Open up."

She did so without thinking and then felt another embarrassing blush crawl up her face, as she realized what she'd just allowed Marcus to do. Sandy would think their relationship was much more intimate than it was.

He smiled.

The fiend. He knew exactly what he'd just done and was enjoying her discomfort.

She snatched the fork from his hand and concentrated on eating the rest of her salad while Sandy and Marcus discussed a sailing competition north of Seattle the following weekend.

"Well, I've got a one o'clock, so I'd better go. It's been a real pleasure getting to know you, Marcus." Sandy extended her hand toward Marcus, who had stood when she did.

He shook it and said good-bye before reseating himself at the table.

Veronica looked at her watch pointedly. "I've got things to do this afternoon, as well. Stop by my desk when you're ready and I'll show you your office."

"Okay, honey."

"Please don't call me that. I'm hardly your honey and I wouldn't want my coworkers to get the wrong idea." She sounded like a spinsterish schoolmarm from the 1950s.

Why couldn't she carry things off with Sandy's easy sophistication?

Marcus cocked his head to one side and studied her. "Just what exactly would be the wrong impression, Ronnie? That we once meant something to each other? That there's more to our relationship than the surface connection of Kline Technology?"

"There isn't more to our relationship. Not anymore." She realized it was the wrong thing to say as soon as the words left her mouth.

They sounded too much like a challenge and Marcus was too darn competitive to ignore it.

He gave her a wolf's smile. "Have dinner with me tonight."

This was it, then. The moment of truth. Did she have the guts it would take to call his bluff?

She didn't really have a choice. If there *was* a corporate spy, she had to de-tooth Marcus's threats to tell Mr. Kline about her past. She opened her mouth to say yes, but Marcus forestalled her by speaking.

"You owe me."

Shocked, she blurted out, "I don't owe you anything."

His blue eyes narrowed, deepening to the color of aquamarine. "I was your lover; you betrayed me."

The idea that he would have felt personally betrayed did not sit well with her. She had enough guilt to carry without adding that burden.

"I betrayed Alex and CIS, not you. The Harrison deal was his baby."

"You left me. You didn't even say good-bye."

She stared at him, her mind grappling with his words. "We didn't have a formal enough relationship to break off. Remember? No ties. No commitments."

He ought to remember the rules; he'd set them.

He leaned across the table until their faces were inches apart. She could see her own reflection in the black depths of his pupils. Her gaze lowered to rest on his firm, male lips. Did they still taste as intoxicating? Would they soften with desire if she gave into her insane urge to lean toward him until their mouths met?

"We were sleeping together almost every night of the week. I'd call that pretty damn formal, baby."

She shook her head, denying his words while trying to break the sensuous spell he'd woven over her.

"We never slept together. Not once. You didn't do the morning after, remember?"

Part of her, the rational part, was still conscious of their surroundings and could not believe they were having this conversation in the employee cafeteria. No one was sitting within hearing distance, but she still felt conspicuous with his body leaning so close to hers.

She could have moved away. She should have moved away, but she didn't. Because having Marcus this close to her felt too good, even if it was only due to his desire to set her straight.

"Stop arguing semantics here, Ronnie. You left me. You didn't say good-bye."

She watched his mouth move as he spoke, getting a peek at his straight, white teeth, the tongue that used to drive her wild. It took her rapidly melting brain a second to make sense of the words that had come out of that mouth.

"I left the note so Alex wouldn't suspect you," she couldn't help pointing out.

It had cost her a lot to leave that note. It was as good as a confession and had been a huge risk if Alex decided to prosecute. She'd taken the risk, though, because she couldn't stand the thought of Alex possibly suspecting Marcus of leaking the information to Harrison.

It was only later, when her mind had cleared a little, that she had realized her disappearance would have been confession enough. By then, the damage had been done. She'd written the note, confessing her sin to Marcus, and had left for France with her gravely ill sister.

She didn't find out what Marcus would have said in reply to her reminder because at that moment Jack walked up. "Hey, you two. Is this a high-level planning session or can anyone join?"

Marcus sat back in his chair, the soft fabric of his signature Hawaiian shirt—a different one from the day before, but just as garish—flowing against the muscled wall of his chest. His movement was both graceful and casual.

He didn't invite Jack to join them but smiled at her red-haired boss. "It's not a planning session at all. Ronnie and I were just talking about old times."

Jack's eyes widened and he spun to face her. "Old times?"

Irritated with Marcus for implying a personal relationship between the two of them yet again, she nevertheless felt compelled to answer. "I used to work with Marcus at CIS."

Jack's smile was all masculine speculation. "I see. Is he by any chance the reason you've turned down my invitations to dinner?"

"I turned down your invitations to dinner for

the reason I gave you. Kline Tech discourages personal relationships among members of the same department."

Not to mention the fact that she had other things to do with her off-hours time than spend them with Jack. She had a baby son and younger sister to take care of.

Of course, as a charming but fairly egotistical man, Jack would have a difficult time believing she just hadn't been interested in him.

Jack turned his attention to Marcus and gave him a man-to-man look. "She could transfer to a different department if she really needed to, but I doubt Kline would even notice."

And why should she be the one to transfer? Men could be so arrogant when it came to relationships.

"I like my job and at times I even like you, Jack. But I don't appreciate this conversation."

She also didn't like the look of gathering doom in Marcus's eyes. He hadn't liked her saying she liked Jack. Not one bit. Why was not important. She figured it had something to do with him seeing his prey possibly moving out of reach. If she had a relationship with Jack, Marcus couldn't very well blackmail her into his bed.

He never played around with women in committed relationships. It was a rule he adhered to just as strictly as the one about no commitments.

Jack shrugged and took a sip of his coffee. "Don't sweat it, Ronnie."

The subtle emphasis he placed on the shortened version of her name was not lost on her, nor on Marcus, judging by the narrowing of his gorgeous blue eyes.

He stood up abruptly, his jaw tight, then picked up her tray and his own. "You said you had things to do this afternoon, honey. I'll walk you back to your desk."

She nodded, getting to her feet. Now was not the time to take him to task for his abrupt manner. She might as well show Marcus his cubicle while they were at it.

Jack jumped up too. "Hey, I'll walk with you."

Veronica tried hard not to grind her teeth. The last thing she wanted was to walk to her cubicle with two testosterone-laden men vying for one-upmanship. She knew Jack's use of her nickname had been a deliberate ploy to show Marcus that he had as much claim on her as he did.

When in truth neither man had a claim on her at all. And neither wanted one either. This wasn't about her; it was about male competitiveness and she wasn't having any part of it.

Marcus returned from dumping their lunch trays. "Let's go."

She drew herself up. "You two go ahead. I need to stop by the design team admin's desk. She and I have some scheduling issues to work out regarding an upcoming meeting."

Issues that would be handled more efficiently on the phone with each admin having her department's calendars in front of her, but it was the only excuse she could come up with on such short notice.

"What about my office?" Marcus asked.

"It's kitty-corner to mine. There's a temporary nameplate with your name on it on the cubicle wall outside. You can't miss it." She smiled with smug triumph.

She had taken care of walking upstairs with the two men and given herself a reprieve from seeing Marcus again. All in all, she'd handled the situation pretty well, if she did say so herself.

Marcus's eyes narrowed. "I guess I'll see you tonight then. Let's say six o'clock at the same restaurant we met at on Friday. Maybe this time we can actually get around to eating dinner."

Chapter Six

Marcus watched Ronnie follow the hostess to his table with a sense of relieved anticipation.

After his parting comment that afternoon, he hadn't been entirely sure she would show. Storm clouds had already been gathering in her eyes when he'd decided to set Jack straight about Ronnie's availability.

However, he knew for a fact that if he'd made such a suggestive comment in front of Alex two years ago, the last place she would have shown up for dinner tonight would be a restaurant he had practically ordered her to meet him at.

The thought that she'd only come because of his threat to tell Kline about her past gnawed at his conscience.

The hostess led Ronnie to the seat across from him at the small table, giving her spiel about the night's specials as she did so. Ronnie listened with grave politeness, saying nothing even after the hostess took her leave.

"I didn't think you would show."

If he moved his legs just an inch or two forward, his knees would be touching hers. She had worn a skirt tonight and it was a tempting thought.

Those too-serious gray eyes fixed on him. "I didn't think I had a choice."

His jaw clenched. "We all have choices in life, Ronnie."

She'd made hers eighteen months ago when she sold out CIS and abandoned her lover.

"You're right," she surprised him by saying. "But sometimes our choices are all bad for us and we have no alternative but to pick the lesser of two evils."

Was she just talking about tonight, or was she trying to explain her actions down in Portland?

"Is having dinner with me really such an evil?" he couldn't help asking.

She looked at him, her eyes unfathomable pools of gray. "I don't know. I'm not sure of anything right now."

Her honesty surprised him, but then it always had. She'd never played emotional games with him. That was one of the reasons her actions with CIS and Hypertron had gutted him so completely.

"Tell me about your choices, honey. Make me understand."

The words surprised him, but they seemed to shock her even more. She picked up her napkin-rolled cutlery and carefully undid the bundle, laying each utensil in its proper place on the table before placing the burgundy cloth in her lap.

"I didn't realize you would want to. I guess I just somehow assumed you'd decided you hated me and that would be the end of it."

Didn't she care if he hated her? "And it didn't matter to you how I felt?"

She looked at him as if trying to read his mind. Finally, she spoke. "It mattered a great deal."

"But not enough." It hadn't stopped her from betraying him.

Her eyes filled with a wealth of sadness. "No, not enough."

His heart twisted and the pain he felt at her words was physical. *It hadn't mattered enough.* Whatever they had had together hadn't been important enough for her to give up her plans to make a fast buck.

"You said you gambled with the money."

The thought sickened him, only increasing his inner turmoil. He'd been closer to Ronnie than any other woman in his life and she'd given him up to make a gambling stake.

"I did. I gambled for my sister's life."

He didn't know what he would have said and was glad for the interruption right then by the waiter. The pimply-faced kid identified himself as Jason and proceeded to go through the entire list of specials again.

Marcus caught Ronnie's eye and winked. Her lips tilted and he knew she was biting back a rare giggle. Man, he wished she wouldn't. He'd love to hear her laugh again.

He and Ronnie gave their orders and the waiter disappeared, only to reappear moments later with their drinks. Marcus realized that any further private conversation would be impossible.

"I want to finish our discussion, but not here," he told her.

She bit her lip and then nodded. "Okay."

Looking for a less volatile subject, he said, "Alex told me you called him once."

"Yes."

"You didn't call again." So much for less volatile. His voice sounded accusing and he couldn't do anything about that.

"I didn't see the point. He said he'd forgiven me and wasn't pressing charges. I told him I was sorry and thanked him. I didn't know what else there was to say."

"You didn't ask about me." Damn. He might as well write his feelings in neon and let her know just how much her desertion had hurt.

She rearranged the condiments in the middle of the table. "I didn't want to hear how much you hated me. If I didn't ask, I could go on pretending you believed in me enough to know I'd had a good reason to do what I did."

"Did you?"

She sat up straighter in her chair, looking around the dimly lit restaurant and then back to him. "You said we'd talk about this later."

He bit down on his frustration as the waiter approached their table, two plates of salad in his hands. "Right. So, what do you want to talk about?"

She surprised him by contemplating his question much longer than he would have expected.

She tucked the soft brown strands of her hair behind her ear. "I don't know. . . . Why don't you tell me about CIS and how things are going there, or Alex and Isabel, or last year's Rose Festival."

He stared at her, struck by how much she must miss it all. She'd once told him she considered CIS like a family. The sentiment had really surprised him considering how unemotional she was in the office. He was beginning to see it would take a powerful motivator to send her away from the familiar. She'd said she gambled on her sister's life. That would definitely have been a strong enough motivation to leave.

"I'm a partner at CIS now."

"You are?" She smiled, clearly pleased for him. "I'm not surprised. You and Alex were always more like brothers than coworkers."

"That's what he said when he made me godfather to his daughter."

Her eyes filled with shock. "He and Isabel had a baby?"

"Yes."

"How old is she?"

Marcus had to think for a second. "About ten months, now. Hope's a doll. She just started walking. She's early. I told Isabel she'll probably be early at everything else too. She's a smart baby. I had to childproof my whole apartment after she started crawling."

"You baby-sit?" She sounded appalled by the possibility.

"Yeah. I'll never forget the first time Isabel dropped Hope off at my place. She said she wanted to surprise Alex with a couple of hours alone." He didn't know why, but it felt right talking to Ronnie like this, telling her stuff he hadn't told anyone else.

"Hope was about two months old and still breast-feeding. When I brought that little matter up, Isabel produced a bottle, a diaper bag and her assurances that everything would be fine. I was terrified, but by the time Isabel and Alex came later that evening to pick up Hope, I was in love. I get second dibs right after Priscilla."

Ronnie's eyes had opened wide as he spoke and now she stared at him as if she didn't know him at all.

"Second dibs?" she asked faintly.

"Yeah. As grandmother, Priscilla gets first dibs on baby-sitting privileges, but as Hope's pseudo-uncle and godfather, I get second."

Ronnie made an obvious effort to pull herself together. "That's Alex's mom, right?"

"Yes. She's also CIS's new secretary."

He waited to see her reaction to that piece of news and wasn't disappointed as two flags of color slashed across her lovely cheeks and her pretty gray eyes narrowed.

"*Alex's mom is the new secretary?*"

He smiled, feeling smug about the way he'd played her that morning.

She hadn't liked hearing about the new secretary at CIS and he was glad. He sure as hell didn't like knowing Jack was on the make and Ronnie was his prime target. He really didn't like feeling possessive about a woman who had betrayed and left him. It made him feel a little better to know that she might have left, but she still cared on some level at least. Cared enough to be jealous.

"Like I said, she's not quite as organized as you are, but her loyalty is unquestionable."

He bit back a curse at the look of hurt on Ronnie's face. He hadn't meant to say that last part, or for it to sound the way it had, like he was rubbing her nose in her own lack of loyalty.

"I didn't mean it the way it sounded."

She picked up her fork, obviously hurt, her gaze averted from him. "Maybe we should just eat our dinner."

He felt like a heel. "Sure."

They ate in silence for several minutes before he reminded himself that as interesting as his personal relationship with Ronnie was to him, he had a job to do. He was supposed to find Kline Technology's corporate spy.

"You said this afternoon that you liked your job," he said, by way of opening up a neutral topic.

She nodded, finishing her salad and pushing the plate away. "It's challenging and I like Kline Tech."

"Does Jack come on to you a lot?"

Where the hell had that question come from? Certainly not from his neutral list, but then maybe nothing could be neutral between the two of them.

She shrugged. "He's asked me out a few times. I never feel pressured to say yes and I haven't."

"Would you if you felt pressured?"

She took a sip of her water before answering. She set the water glass down and fixed him with a penetrating stare, like she was looking into his very soul.

"Are you trying to figure out if your attempt at blackmail is going to be successful?"

When you didn't know what to say to an opponent's question, you asked one of your own. "Why don't you tell me? Am I?"

"It doesn't matter. I'm not going to answer you, regardless of what your motivation was for asking."

She spoke quietly, in a tone he'd learned long

ago meant she was digging her stubborn little heels into the dirt and wouldn't be moved.

"Let's go back to Kline Tech. It's a good company. What do you think of Kline's idea to expand?"

She shifted in her chair. "I'm not sure expansion is the smart road to take in the current economic climate. Mr. Kline has a product that consumers want; his long-term marketing forecasts are good. If he tries expansion and it fails, his currently solid company would be put at risk."

"It's a solid company all right, but there have been a few setbacks these past few months. Competitors coming to market with similar products just before Kline Technology, the press getting wind of problems in design before they can be fixed—"

The sound of her glass hitting the salad plate cut him off. Water poured over the plate and onto the table.

She whipped her napkin from her lap and blotted at the rapidly spreading liquid. "That was so clumsy of me."

He signaled for their waiter and when the kid came asked for a towel to clean up the mess.

His stomach tightened as she darted a glance at him, her eyes wary, her face set. "You were saying?"

"It's just that with everything that's happened over the last six months, I can see where Kline might want to expand into something different to prove to stockholders that they still have the edge."

She nodded. "Yes. I see your point."

The stiltedness of her words undermined her attempt to put on a natural front.

Damn it. He hadn't wanted her to be guilty. The sick feeling in his gut made him acknowledge that fact, but did he need anything more than her re-action to his pretty innocuous question to con-vince him she was in up to her eyeballs again in corporate espionage?

George Kline reclined on Allison's sofa and let his worries about a corporate spy at Kline Tech-nologies take a back seat to what he was feeling, which was contentment. Allison was a very restful person.

She'd invited him over for dinner after work and he hadn't even considered turning her down. Hell, if he had a choice, they'd spend every evening together and every night. But they both had grown children and commitments they had to keep out-side of their relationship. But time with her gave him peace he didn't get anywhere else.

He didn't know what he would do if he didn't have Allison to decompress with.

The stress of running a multi-million-dollar company didn't control him when he was with her.

She made him feel good.

"Hey, darlin', why don't you come on over here and set a spell?" His southern roots came out when he was with her, but the rest of the time no one at all would have known he spent his first fifteen years in Texas.

She laughed, a soft, melodious sound. "You get that Texas drawl going when you want to make love and I know just what will happen if I come over there."

"I'll kiss you stupid and touch you until you moan."

Her breath hitched and she fumbled with the CD she'd been about to put in the player, almost dropping it. She managed to get it in the stereo and the play button pushed before turning around to face him, her eyes filled with sensual promise.

"Will you really?"

He put his hand out. "Come here."

She came and he pulled her down into his lap with more force than he'd intended, but she didn't complain.

Her body was open to him in a way no other woman's had ever been. Allison was a generous lover. And passionate.

Everything he could want and more. He tipped her head back and kissed her, his hand coming up to cup her breast with possessiveness he made no attempt to hide when they were alone together.

She started unbuttoning buttons and they kissed, touched and teased each other with the sound of George Strait singing in the background.

When they were both naked and she'd touched him until he thought he'd go crazy from the pleasure of it, he stood up and carried her into the bedroom.

He laid her on the bed and grabbed a condom out of the bedside drawer. "You make me feel like a teenager, Allison. I get so hot when I'm with you, I don't want to wait to put on protection."

She spread her legs in blatant invitation. "I don't want to wait either."

His hands trembled as he put the condom on and then he came over her, going inside her with the same feeling of rebirth their lovemaking always gave him.

It was almost mystical how he felt when he was with her.

Later, they lay together under the covers, their bodies entwined, her soft breathing indicating she was asleep even though it was still relatively early. It felt so right. Maybe he'd have to do something to regularize their situation after Danvers found the culprit who was giving his company the shaft.

Until then, he'd settle for nights like this that reminded him Kline Technologies wasn't the only thing in his life worth living for.

"I'll follow you home and then we'll go for a drive."

Veronica nodded in reply to Marcus's words. "All right." It made sense. They needed privacy to talk.

A half hour later, ensconced in the plush leather passenger seat of his Jaguar, Veronica silently waited for him to speak. She had expected demands for a complete explanation of her past actions as soon as Marcus had her alone, but he now seemed preoccupied.

She hesitated to bring up the topic because how could she explain her decision to sell secrets to John Harrison without telling Marcus about everything that had driven her to do so? She hadn't been just gambling on her sister's life; she'd had her own pregnancy to consider as well.

Perhaps she should begin with how it had all started.

"My dad was in construction. It's a pretty decent way to make a living, but self-employment is always risky and Dad wasn't very good at planning for the future."

Marcus's head snapped round and he focused on her for a second of startled silence before returning his attention to the road. "What happened?"

"He and Mom died in a boating accident the summer I turned twenty. I had just started working part-time for CIS. You were dating that blond bombshell at the time. I think her name was Cynthia."

Where had that come from? Did she really want him to know just how pathetic she'd always been? That she could name each and every one of his girlfriends over the three-plus years they had worked together?

He made a dismissive gesture with his hand. "I don't remember who I was going out with." His grip on the steering wheel tightened. "I also don't remember you mentioning your parents' deaths."

She looked out the window, the lights reflecting off the water of the sound as they crossed the bridge back into west Seattle.

"I didn't. I told Alex I had a family emergency and took the time off necessary to plan the funeral, but I'd gone into shock, I think. I was only twenty and suddenly I had responsibility for closing my father's business and taking care of my sister, and my grief somehow just got all bottled up inside. I had to keep doing normal things, like coming to work and going to my classes at the university, or I thought I would break apart."

Marcus exited from the bridge and drove up Harbor Avenue. The road winding along the cliff led to a lookout parking area, where he stopped the car.

"Do you want to get out?"

She answered by opening the door and stepping onto the pavement. Walking over to the lookout, she soaked in the sights of Seattle at night. She'd come to love this cosmopolitan city on the water. She had felt safe here, amid the amalgamation of different cultures and crush of humanity.

Hugging her sweater close to her body, she felt the spring wind against her face. It brought the scents of the ocean with it and helped to clear her mind.

Marcus came to stand beside her. He had slipped a well-worn leather jacket on over his Hawaiian shirt, the brown suede looking soft enough to touch in the evening light. "You said your dad wasn't good at planning for the future."

She dragged her thoughts away from the temptation of touching him.

"No. He didn't have life insurance and we'd gone without medical insurance for as long as I can remember. Still, with the house and selling dad's equipment, we did all right. I had enough money to continue college and I figured I could work to put Jenny through after I graduated and got a decent-paying job."

He put his hand on her arm, and even through the knitted acrylic protecting her from the spring chill, the heat of his fingers burned her. "It didn't work that way," he said softly.

"No."

"Jenny got sick."

She'd never thought of Marcus as a dumb man and he wasn't.

"Yes. I made it through a year, a hellish year, but

I made it and I thought everything was going to be fine. Alex offered me full-time employment and I took it, shifting my class schedule to work around my job. Jenny was in school and involved in sports, so she didn't need me home every night because she wasn't there. I tried to make it to her games when I could, but that wasn't often."

Marcus made a noise of disbelief. "You tried to do too damn much."

Not that it had done her, or Jenny, a bit of good.

"Maybe. It doesn't matter now. When Jenny got sick everything happened so quickly. Before I knew it, the hospital bills were piling up faster than I could hope to pay them. I had to sell the house and everything else of value. We moved to a small apartment and I tried to get on the Oregon Health Plan, but I made too much money to be eligible."

Marcus swore under his breath. A truly vicious word.

"It didn't matter anyway. Her illness wouldn't have been covered because it was a preexisting condition."

"What did you do?"

She hadn't been able to do *anything*. "I watched my sister get sicker and sicker. The doctors kept promising a miracle cure, a treatment that the FDA was supposed to approve for testing in the U.S. any day. It didn't happen."

"Damn it. You never said anything, not when your parents died, not when Jenny got sick. Why?"

She twisted away from him, needing more than the night's protection from his probing gaze.

"I told you; I couldn't. Talking about everything

would have just made it more real, made the pain too overwhelming to bear. I was always a private person to some extent, but something inside me changed when my parents died. The grieving, I guess, but I didn't want to share it with anyone. After the accident, I started acting like an automaton and that's how you and Alex treated me—like the robot secretary. I didn't mind. It helped me to separate my grief from my work. I had to keep that job to support Jenny. I couldn't afford to break down crying all the time, so I just didn't let myself feel at all.

"Later, when Jenny got sick, I was so used to handling things alone, I didn't even consider asking for help. Besides, Alex had changed since hiring me. He'd gotten tunnel vision about his revenge. I thought marrying Isabel would soften him, but he kept his plans to destroy her dad on track. I realized I couldn't go to him for help. He had no reason to care if my sister lived or died. I was just his robot secretary."

Marcus made a noise of dissent. "It wasn't like that. Alex would have helped."

She gave a harsh laugh at his words. "*It was just like that*; I was there. Besides what could my *boss* have done? Given me a raise?"

"What about me? Why didn't you come to me? I was your lover."

His words were like a slap in the face and she felt bitter resentment swirl up.

"Right. Face it, Marcus, you were no more my lover then than you are now. I was a temporary bed partner for you, nothing more. You'd made your feelings on ties or commitments of any kind very clear. But I had commitments, in the biggest way. My sister was dying and I couldn't stop it."

She spun away from him, away from the view of lights across water. "They were having a lot of success with treatment of her disease in Europe. The FDA was scheduled to approve test programs of the drug in the U.S., but the approval date kept getting pushed back. Jenny spent her sixteenth birthday in the hospital in France, hooked up to monitors. No sweet-sixteen party. No boyfriend. No new car. I couldn't afford new shoelaces at that point, much less a new car for her birthday. Not that she could have driven. I would have done anything to stop my sister from dying."

He grabbed her shoulders, pulling her back against the heat of his body. "Including selling company secrets." His voice sounded strangely charged.

She couldn't afford to relax against him, couldn't let herself show that kind of weakness, but she wanted to. So much. So very much.

"Yes."

"Tell me about it," he demanded, not letting her go when she tried to pull from his grasp.

"I stayed up all night that night, trying to come up with a way to get Jenny treatment. I could only think of one alternative." And that fact still haunted her. "I went to see Mr. Harrison the day after Jenny's birthday. He was very interested in the information I had to offer. When I told him about Jenny, he offered me more money than I expected. It was enough for both of us to live in France during her treatment, to pay the doctors and to come home."

"You told Harrison, but you didn't tell me?" Marcus's body stiffened with outrage and his grip tightened almost painfully on her arms.

"You weren't interested in my personal life," she reminded him.

He could cut the outrage act and at least deal with reality.

He spun her around to face him. "I was sleeping with you. How much more personal could we have gotten?"

She sucked in a breath, memories of that personal relationship tormenting her. "Do you remember the first time we had sex?"

She was careful not to call it making love. She didn't allow self-delusion anymore.

His hands moved caressingly up her arms while his eyes locked with hers. "How could I forget?"

"You told me then not to expect a future, not to expect a commitment. You said it was just sex, would be great sex, but it wasn't love. You don't believe in love."

"You took that to mean I didn't want to know anything about you except what you were like in bed?" He sounded incredulous.

"What else was I supposed to think?" But hope as insidious as ants at a picnic climbed up her insides.

He released her and pivoted toward the lookout, his big body taut with nameless tension. "I don't know, Ronnie. I was sleeping with you, touching you in ways no other man had ever done; you tell me."

"But not ways you'd never touched another woman." Women much more beautiful than she was, much more fun by Marcus's standards.

His hands curled into fists, but he didn't say anything.

She couldn't leave it at that. "You never said I was different. You didn't tell me you wanted more."

His hand moved in a dismissive gesture. "It doesn't matter now, does it?"

She found herself reaching out to him, her own hand extended in supplication, but she didn't touch him. She let her arm fall to her side.

"Probably not, but for what it is worth, I loved you."

The words couldn't mean anything now. Too much had happened. She'd made choices he still didn't know about, but she had to say them. To speak the truth of her feelings just once.

He shook his head, the blond strands glistening in the artificial lights from the street behind them. "You didn't trust me. You sold out CIS. You left me and you betrayed your own honor rather than come to me for help."

She couldn't tell if pain or condemnation darkened his voice. Could she have misunderstood eighteen months ago? Had he started caring for her? Would he have helped her? Would he have wanted the baby, been willing to share the burden of Jenny's illness?

The questions were pointless because whatever he had been willing to do eighteen months ago, this was now.

Tears pricked her eyes, but she didn't let them fall. She knew if she started crying, she wouldn't be able to stop.

It just didn't matter anymore. Nothing could undo what she had done. If he had cared once, he didn't care any longer. He'd said it. She had betrayed him and her own honor rather than trust him enough to ask for help.

Even now she wondered what exactly he could

have done if she'd gone to him. She had needed more than a shoulder to cry on to save her sister's life. Not that he appeared to appreciate that.

Bile rose in her throat when she thought about how he would react to the knowledge that he had a son she hadn't bothered to tell him existed.

Chapter Seven

Marcus slanted a glance at Ronnie's silent silhouette.

She had said very little since making her revelations about what had prompted her actions eighteen months before and nothing at all since getting into the car for the return trip to her apartment. It was as if she'd answered his questions and now she had nothing else to say to him.

Didn't she realize that her answers had only prompted a whole host of other questions?

To be fair, he hadn't said much either. Finding out about her parents' deaths and her sister's illness had completely gutted him.

Why hadn't she told him?

She hadn't trusted him worth a damn. Okay, so he'd made it clear that he wasn't a commitment-centered man, but did that mean she had to hide *everything* from him? Hadn't she realized that every man had his Armageddon? The spinsterish little automaton that used to be CIS's secretary had been his.

She had touched him in a way no other woman ever had, but she didn't realize that.

His desire for her had never abated, not over the brief months of their affair, not during the long months since. He'd been thinking in terms of a future and she had been thinking about how to save her sister's life—without his help.

Where did that leave them now? And what about the corporate espionage happening at Kline Technology?

"You told me before that your sister was okay now. Is that the truth?"

His voice seemed to echo in the silent car, but she eventually answered. "She's fine, physically."

"What does that mean?"

Ronnie's head turned to look out the window at the black-shadowed landscape. "It means her body is healthy again, but she has a lot of catching up to do. She spent her sophomore year in and out of hospitals and her junior year undergoing radical chemotherapy. She's home-schooled since finishing the treatment in order to catch up with her peers and let her hair grow again. She wants to attend her senior year at a regular high school and go on to college after that."

He heard frustration in Ronnie's voice.

"Is that a bad plan?"

Maybe she resented her sister going to college when she'd had to drop out of school herself. He remembered wondering why she'd done it and now he knew. Even Ronnie's formidable will could not maintain a full-time class load with her sister in and out of the hospital.

Her attention swung back to him and he could feel frustration and bitterness rolling off her in waves.

"It's a great plan. It's a wonderful plan, but it's also an impossible plan. She wants to go to high school with her old friends back in Portland. My job is here. She wants to go to a university, but I don't even know how I can afford community college tuition. And she's so darn understanding about it all. She doesn't complain when I can't buy her designer clothes like the other kids her age are wearing. She's . . ."

Her voice trailed off and he thought he heard a suspicious sniff.

"Are you crying?" Stupid question.

"Why would I be crying?" She sounded defiant, like he'd offended her by asking.

Hell. He probably had.

He reached out and laid his hand on her thigh, offering the only sort of comfort he knew how to give. "I'm sorry, baby."

The words were inadequate, but he didn't know what else to say. He was still a little stunned that she'd shared so much of herself with him *now* when before she had hidden her whole life from him. He suspected she would bitterly regret her candor tomorrow. From what she had said, she'd become almost fanatically private since her parents' deaths.

She'd also said that she had loved him.

Hell.

He didn't know about love, but he had been

thinking about commitment eighteen months ago. He'd even toyed with the idea of asking her to move in with him. She was right. He hadn't said anything. Somehow, he'd thought she'd known. His need for her had been obvious enough, but apparently she'd attributed that to lust and nothing more.

She'd said it had been more for her, but had it? If she had *loved* him, wouldn't she have trusted him with her secrets? Wouldn't she have come to him for help rather than abandon him and destroy their relationship?

She let out a pent-up breath. "Thanks, but don't worry about me. I'll figure it out. I always do."

Did figuring it out include selling corporate secrets to Kline's competitors?

Right now, with her scent filling his car's small space and her body so close he could reach out and touch it, Marcus couldn't make himself care. All through dinner and then later, when she'd made her explanations, his body had buzzed with an ever-present desire. He wasn't proud of it, but he couldn't deny its existence either.

He should be elated. His investigation looked close to being over, but at the moment, all he could do was feel. Her pain. Her frustration. And his desire.

It pulsed through him like an African drumbeat. He pulled the Jag into a parking space connected to her apartment complex. Switching off the engine, he turned to her. He didn't say anything because there wasn't anything to say. He wanted her so bad it was as if the last eighteen months had never happened. He needed to touch her and feel her responding beneath him.

She unclipped her seat belt but didn't open her car door right away. Did she feel the desire shimmering between them? Could she sense how much he needed to taste her again?

"Are you going to tell Mr. Kline about what happened at CIS?" Her words lashed against him and the tumble of his own emotions.

Damn it. He didn't want to deal with that right now. He didn't want to think about his investigation, or the responsibility to his client. He'd work something out, something that would protect Ronnie and still allow him to fulfill his obligation to Kline. He didn't know what, but he'd think of something.

"Don't worry about that."

Her head snapped around to face him. "How can you say that? By now, you must know how important my job is to me. I can't afford to be let go."

"You aren't alone this time."

He couldn't promise her that she'd keep her job. He didn't see how that would be possible if she'd been up to her old tricks, but he would help her. He wouldn't let her face the future alone again.

She laughed. "Yeah. Right. Just tell me what you're going to do about my past."

He shook his head. He couldn't think about Kline Technology, not when his mind and senses were filled with her. He laid his hand on her thigh again, feeling the tension of her muscles through the fabric of her skirt. He brushed his hand down her leg, gently caressing until it settled on her knee, clad only in the silky fabric of her stockings.

Oh, man. Did she still wear stockings? He re-

membered the first time he'd seen her prissy little
white garter belt. It wasn't from Victoria's Secret,
that's for sure, but it had turned him on and inside out.

"*Marcus.*"

He heard the sharp tone of her voice but ignored it. He had to taste her. Right now.

Not giving her a chance to argue, he bent his
head and swiftly took her mouth. She'd opened it
mid-rant and her parted lips felt like a desert oasis
to his thirsty soul. She tried to turn her head away,
but he followed her lips, seeking the response that
used to keep him awake long after she'd left his
bed to go home.

Her hands fisted in his shirt. Maybe to push him
away, but she ended up pulling him closer and he
let her. Grabbing her hip with one hand and a fist-
ful of her silky brown hair with another, he deep-
ened the kiss until their tongues were mating with
more than teasing intensity.

She moaned low in her throat, just like she used
to do, and he was lost. If he didn't touch her, feel
the incredible silken smoothness of her skin within
the next thirty seconds his body would explode from
the frustration. He yanked at her sweater, shoving
it aside with adolescent enthusiasm, and he couldn't
make himself slow down. Gone were his usual seduction techniques, his ability to take things slow.

His incredible lack of finesse was worth it when
his fingers encountered the naked skin of her torso.
His entire body shuddered at the impact of having
his hands on her again after eighteen months of
wanting.

She stilled and he felt like he had that first time,

like she was waiting in both agony and anticipation to see how he would touch her. Just like then, he did not want to disappoint her.

Letting his fingertips gently trail across her rib cage, he also changed the tone of their kiss. Where he'd been starving for a taste of her, he now melded his lips to hers with the intent to soothe.

He wanted her to want him as much as he wanted her. He didn't want her to fear their intimacy and he meant to be intimate with her—very intimate.

He pulled his mouth a centimeter from hers. "Touch me, baby, please touch me."

Her eyes flew open and he read panic in them. He almost swore but bit back the word in time. He didn't want to spook her. He wanted to love her. He kissed her again, letting his lips communicate silently with hers. She tried to pull back into the seat, to withdraw from him, but he wouldn't let her. Didn't she realize he couldn't let her?

He flicked his tongue along the seam of her lips, teasing her, coaxing her to open her sweet and tender mouth to more of his kisses. She groaned and her lips parted slightly. It was enough.

He entered her mouth with the intention of crashing the last of her defenses and allowed his hand to stray to her breast with the same objective. He cupped her through the thin cotton of her bra and felt her sensitive nipple stab into his palm.

"Oh, yeah. Baby, you make me so hot." He was melting and so was she.

All the tension had drained from her and he could taste her surrender in their kiss. Her shallow breath rasped the skin of his cheek. She pressed the pouting little mound of her breast into his hand and ran her own hand along his thigh, coming perilously close to his throbbing sex.

Unable to help himself, he shifted a little until her fingertips were brushing against him intimately. He moaned and moved again, wanting, needing a more complete contact, and ran into the gearshift.

They couldn't make love for the first time in almost two years in a car park. He pulled away, pleased by the look of raw sensuality on her face.

"Invite me up," he demanded.

"Yes." Then her eyes seemed to focus and a horrified expression replaced the passionate daze in her eyes. "I mean no. That's impossible."

"Why the hell is it impossible?" Did she have a boyfriend after all? Then he remembered Jenny. Of course, her sister would be home now. "Damn. I forgot about your sister. Come back to my place."

She shook her head, her eyes wild. "No. I won't do that."

He could feel his desire and passion coalescing into raging frustration.

"Why the hell not?" He asked again, this time in a near shout.

"I told Jenny I would be home by nine."

The blinking light on his dash clock told him it was already a quarter till. "You can call her from my place and tell her you are going to be late."

He turned and rebuckled his seat belt before placing his hand on the ignition key, intending to start the car.

"No." Her voice didn't waver in the least bit.

He gripped the steering wheel so tightly his hands felt molded to the leather grips. "You want me as much as I want you." He'd seen the evidence. He'd *felt* her need. She couldn't convince him otherwise.

She looked haunted. "Yes."

"Then why are you saying no?" he asked from between gritted teeth, his frustration morphing into anger.

Her eyes narrowed and her mouth set in a mutinous line. "Maybe I can't stomach the thought of going to bed with a man who's blackmailing me into it."

With that she flung open her door and rushed from the car, running from it and him as if the hounds of hell were on her heels.

Cursing viciously, he slammed his fist into the steering wheel. An agonizing drive home and a long, cold shower were all he had to look forward to for the rest of the night, and he had no one else but himself to blame.

With an angry twist of his fingers, the Jag came to life and peeled off with a squeal of tires.

The sound of Marcus's less-than-cool exit from the parking lot echoed in Veronica's head as she stood outside her apartment door, trying to bring her rampant emotions under control. Her hands shook as she dug into her purse for her keys.

She would have let him make love to her right there in the front seat of his car. She'd been that far gone from his kisses. It was worse than before.

At least then she'd been conscious of their surroundings. Marcus had often kissed and caressed her in semipublic places, but she'd always broken it off before it could get embarrassing. Not so now.

Instead of their time apart subduing her ability to withstand the intense attraction she felt for him, it had seemingly increased it. She sucked in a trembling breath and let it out again. If he hadn't demanded an invitation into her apartment, she would still be out there, kissing him and most likely half naked by now.

Only the reminder of their son had had the ability to cool her body's response to Marcus enough to get her out of that car. Even then, she'd been so very tempted to take him up on his offer to take her back to his place.

She'd wanted to. More than she wanted to admit.

Why *hadn't* she just called his bluff then? It had been the perfect opportunity.

Yeah. Right. The point was to get him to admit he didn't mean his threat by agreeing to meet his terms and having him reject her. From the way he'd been close to losing control in the car, that wasn't going to happen. He wanted her. The thought shocked her.

His desire when they had kissed had definitely been genuine. He'd been as desperate as she.

What if he *wasn't* bluffing about taking her to bed or telling Kline? Had she just signed her own pink slip by refusing to return to his apartment with him?

She couldn't accept that. Marcus just was not that slimy kind of toad. He could be selfish. He could be arrogant, impossibly certain of his own appeal to the opposite sex, and with reason. But he wasn't a blackmailer. Something else had to be going on. Something she didn't understand.

Okay. He wanted her. He truly wanted her. And that had to be about as palatable to him as a plateful of metal shavings. He wouldn't like wanting her, not when he considered her a thief and a liar. She'd explained her actions, but she could tell that he hadn't accepted the explanation. He did not understand why she had not come to him.

How could she explain something she did not understand herself? She'd been desperate, both with the feeling of helplessness in the face of her sister's illness and with shock at her own pregnancy. She'd regretted her choices so many times over the intervening months, but she couldn't change them.

Maybe the blackmail was his way of getting into her bed and keeping his own pride intact. Maybe the idea of a real relationship, even one of just the sexual variety, with her was so unacceptable that he had to make it something cheap and emotionless to deal with it. She shook off the depressing thoughts and unlocked her door.

She'd clearly misread Marcus's feelings a year and a half ago. He had been shocked that she hadn't shared her worries with him. What made her think she would be any better at comprehending his thoughts and motivations now?

"How did it go?" Curled up in one corner of the couch, Jenny looked up from her book.

Veronica laid her purse on the table by the door. "Fine."

She couldn't very well tell her sister that Marcus was trying to blackmail her into bed or that she'd tried to justify inexplicable actions from a lifetime ago. It may have only been eighteen months, but in some ways it felt like forever since the time with Marcus.

"Where did you guys go?"

She walked into the kitchen and poured herself a glass of water. "That fish place down by the water."

"The one with the cute waiter?"

Coming back into the living room, she sat at the other end of the couch from Jenny and picked up the afghan she'd started for Aaron's bed when he got bigger. It was the same vibrant blue of his and his father's eyes.

"Yes. He was there tonight. He kept bringing things to the table. He probably hoped I'd say something about you."

Jenny laughed, her expression wry. "Oh, definitely. The guy must have a thing for girls with hardly any hair and emaciated bodies."

Veronica dropped the ball of yarn she'd been unwinding to crochet.

Scooting across the sofa, she wrapped an arm around Jenny's shoulders. "Emaciated bodies are all the rage now, don't you know? Not that yours is all that skinny anymore. And your hair is gorgeous."

By looking at Jenny now, with her short brown curls framing her pixieish face, it would be impossible to guess that only a year ago she'd been completely bald. True, the curls weren't all that long, but she really did look great. "Sweetheart, you are beautiful."

Jenny laid her head against Veronica's shoulder. "You're my sister. You love me and you'd tell me I was gorgeous if I looked like a troll." Then she laughed. "But don't you dare stop saying it."

Veronica hugged her tight and then moved away, knowing that a little sisterly sympathy went a long way with her independent younger sibling.

Picking up her crochet project again, she said, "The mirror should tell you the same thing."

Jenny shrugged. "Tell me more about your date with Marcus. Did you tell him about Aaron?"

She tensed and missed a stitch.

Unraveling and starting the row over, she blew out a breath. "It wasn't a date."

"Hmmm. Did you go to dinner with him?"

"You know I did."

"Did you pay for your own meal?"

"No."

"Was the purpose of this nondate to discuss Kline Tech's expansion plans?" Jenny asked, her expression daring Veronica to lie and say that it had been.

"No."

"Sounds like a date to me. I suppose you're going to try to tell me he didn't kiss you goodnight either."

Veronica felt her cheeks heating and cursed the pale complexion that was such a contrast to her dark hair and gray eyes. "No, I'm not going to say that."

Jenny gasped. "He did try. Did you let him?"

The temptation to lie almost overwhelmed her, but she'd had all she could take of betraying her conscience eighteen months ago. "Yes."

She didn't elaborate. Jenny didn't need to know that it had gone beyond a casual kiss to something incendiary. Concentrating on crocheting the blue cotton yarn into something recognizable, she tried to ignore the palpable look that Jenny gave her.

"You let that creep kiss you?" She heard her own earlier disbelief in Jenny's voice and something else. Concern.

Pulling a length of yarn from the skein, she said, "He's not a creep and it didn't mean anything."

"Like it didn't mean anything when he got you pregnant?"

The words acted like explosives against her conscience, forcing her to acknowledge that she had made another huge miscalculation in not telling Marcus about their child. "I think maybe it did mean something." Then.

"What are you saying? Did he say he was upset that you took off for parts unknown? Did he miss you?" Her sister had swung from teenage cynicism to romantic melodrama at the speed of light.

What could Veronica say? He'd obviously missed her body, but he wouldn't let himself miss a spy.

She decided to focus on the past, rather than the present. "I never told him about Mom and Dad, or you and well . . . He acted like he was hurt by the omission, like he would have wanted to know and thought I hadn't trusted him enough to say anything."

"Did you?"

"Obviously not." She hadn't thought he was interested, but that was just a symptom of the lack of trust she'd had for him and the relationship they'd shared.

She'd gotten so accustomed to relying on herself that she hadn't considered sharing her burden with a man who saw her as nothing more than a current bed partner. But perhaps she *had* meant more than that to Marcus. Then again, she'd seen him break off more promising relationships than theirs. She couldn't have been wrong.

"I thought I had cause. He doesn't see it that

way. It hardly matters now. It's all water under the bridge."

"Except that bridge has a baby right in the middle of it."

"Yes." A baby she loved.

A baby she needed.

A baby she might very well lose if Marcus discovered his existence.

Chapter Eight

Marcus was lying in bed, awake and frustrated, when the phone rang.

Instinctively, he reached for it, but then he let his hand drop. It was probably Ronnie wanting to know what he intended to tell Kline about her past.

He didn't have an answer for her and it did not have a thing to do with her refusing to come home with him.

The answering service picked up the call and the ringing stopped. A few seconds later, his mobile phone started buzzing. Irritated, he threw back the covers and got out of bed.

He grabbed the small flip phone up from the top of the dresser and opened it. "Hello?"

"Marcus?"

The shock of hearing his mother's voice when he had been expecting Ronnie's left him momentarily speechless.

"Marcus! Are you there?"

"Yes, I'm here. What can I do for you, Mom?"

"Your father's had a heart attack. He's in the hospital. . . ." Her voice trailed off into a sob while Marcus's fingers tightened on the phone.

"How serious is it?" He felt concern for his mother's emotional distress, but curiously numb to his father's illness.

"I-I n-need you to c-come!" she said, without answering his question.

"I'll be there in an hour."

"Th-thank y-you. . . ." She was still crying when she cut the connection.

He got dressed quickly and was on the road in a matter of minutes. There was only one major hospital in the town of his youth and he went directly to it, knowing without a doubt that his mother would not have left as long as Mark was still a patient.

Sure enough, she was in the waiting room when Marcus arrived. She looked up when he walked in and a smile of gratitude crossed her features.

He crossed the room and pulled her into a hard hug. "Are you okay?"

She patted his back and nodded. "They said it was mild. They're still running tests, but it doesn't look like any permanent damage was done."

"I'm glad." And he was. He hated seeing his mother hurt and he didn't wish Mark any ill. He simply had nothing to give the man who had pretended he did not exist until his thirteenth year.

She pulled back and ran her fingers through blond hair that looked as natural as his own, a habit they both shared when they were agitated. "He's already making noises about getting discharged. I want him to stay the night, but he says that as soon as they're done running tests, he wants to leave."

Typical.

She sighed and sat down, patting the seat beside her, which Marcus took without saying anything.

"I was hoping you'd talk to him." She bit her lip. "I need to know he's in the clear. I'll be a nervous wreck if he goes home without even a single day of observation."

Of course she would. She cared about Mark Danvers more than her own pride.

"He's not likely to listen to me."

His mother's still beautiful face settled into a frown. "You are determined not to try with him aren't you? It's been almost twenty years; can't you forgive him?"

He didn't want to have this discussion with her, not right now. She was upset already and he didn't want to make it worse, but he couldn't give her what she wanted. He could not heal the bond his father had broken between the two of them. He didn't even begin to know how.

When he looked at the other man, he saw someone who had maintained two lives, hurting everyone involved for the sake of his own need. He saw a man whose convictions had dismissed the possibility of divorce, but had allowed him to maintain an adulterous relationship for over a decade. Some convictions.

Marcus loved his mother and he tolerated Mark, but he could never truly respect him.

"I'll talk to him," he said, in an effort to avoid the confrontation.

His mother smiled, her relief palpable. "Thank

you. Your brother and sister are on their way, but they have to fly in and who knows when they'll arrive."

He found it interesting that his siblings had experienced much less difficulty adjusting to his mother's role in their lives than he'd had dealing with the marriage between his parents. Probably because they were grown and had moved away from home by the time their mother died and his had taken her place.

Besides, his mother was a loving, generous-hearted woman whom it would be very difficult to dislike. She did not fit anyone's perception of the word *mistress*.

He found his father sitting up in the hospital bed when he entered the room. The older man looked as if nothing had happened at all, his dynamic presence apparent even though he was wearing the ridiculous standard hospital gown that usually washed out others.

"So, your mother called you. I'd hoped she would."

"She needed someone to be with her."

"Yes." Mark's eyes were the same color as Marcus's, but that was the only physical characteristic they had in common. "I worried her."

"You need to take better care of yourself." The words just came out.

He'd meant them to imply his mother would be lost without Mark, but his father seemed pleased by his apparent concern for his health.

"I will. More exercise, less fatty foods and less stress appears to be my dictum."

"Mom wants you to stay the night for observation."

Mark's face set in familiar stubborn lines. "She's a woman. She worries too much, but I'm going home. I'm fine now."

"She won't be if you insist on going."

Mark opened his mouth to speak and Marcus put up his hand.

"I know you care about her. I'm just asking you to show it this once."

Mark's mouth snapped shut.

"You're not the only person affected by your decision, and I think you should take that into account when you make it."

"You don't think I do that much, do you?" Mark asked, his voice surprisingly subdued.

"No, but there's a first time for everything." He wasn't accusing his dad, just stating a fact.

"If you think it's that important to her, I'll stay."

"Good."

His mother entered the room and was thrilled to find out Marcus had convinced his father to stay the night under observation. She wanted to stay with him and Marcus offered to go to the house to be there when his siblings arrived.

He ended up staying all the next day and returning to Seattle after his father had been discharged from the hospital. His half sister had offered to stay a few days and Marcus had felt no guilt leaving his parents in her capable hands.

Veronica put down the phone in frustration.

Marcus wasn't in his cubicle, he hadn't answered the phone at his temporary apartment and Mr. Kline's PA refused to give out any information on his whereabouts.

She needed to get the blackmail stuff out of the way once and for all so she could tell Marcus about Aaron, but he seemed intent on thwarting her. If worried thoughts were deadly, Veronica would be in the county morgue by now. She needed to know what Marcus was going to do about her past.

When she went home that night, she was short-tempered and snapped at Jenny, broke one of Aaron's toys trying to fix it and went to bed in one of the worst moods she'd been in since coming home from France.

Marcus settled into his chair, taking a sip of the bitter coffee he'd just poured from the employee pot located in the small alcove at the end of his and Ronnie's row of cubicles. He grimaced.

She hadn't made the coffee; that was for sure. Ronnie made coffee like she did everything else—extremely well.

He used to tease her and say that the coffee beans were afraid of malfunctioning when such a terrifyingly efficient person had hold of them. She laughed at the time, but now he wondered if that comment, like many others, had hurt her and contributed to her reason for not trusting him even though he'd been her lover.

He'd often joked about her robot-like efficiency. He'd been completely blind and insensitive to the fact that a woman, particularly a woman as passionate as Ronnie, might not like being referred to that way. *Was* it his fault that she believed he hadn't been interested in knowing anything more about her than how she responded in bed?

He wasn't sure it mattered. Facts were facts. She hadn't trusted him and he couldn't change that. But he wouldn't settle for the same misinterpretation of his motives now. And just as soon as he figured out what they were himself, he'd let her know.

He could no longer pretend he was only interested in solving the case, or even working Ronnie out of his system. His body and his heart wanted her back in his life. He had to decide whether he'd let his mind listen to them, whether he could take a risk on a woman who had already betrayed him once.

Even if her reasons for doing so had been pretty damn potent.

Pushing the thoughts away, he focused on the task at hand and morosely considered the stack of employee personnel files on his desk. He had requested copies of the files on all employees with access to the information that had been leaked over the past six months and he had a list of fifteen suspects, eight in design, six in marketing and one in corporate administration.

Veronica Richards was one of them.

The sound of her gentle voice answering a phone call broke into his thoughts.

With her cubicle only a few feet away from his own, the sensation was not a new one. He couldn't understand the words, but the soft tones of her voice were unmistakable and acted as a reminder of what she'd refused to give him after their date on Monday night. Herself.

Although he was more sexually frustrated than any other time in his life, he was glad she had said no. He couldn't afford to forget his responsibility to his client again and being around her made him do that.

She'd tried to talk to him after he returned from his trip, but he had put her off. He needed time. Time for his investigation and time to digest everything he had learned on Monday night.

No matter how he stacked it, he wasn't willing to accuse Ronnie of the espionage without solid proof, thus the pile of files for him to go through. He couldn't rip her life apart without just cause. He could only hope if he found it, he would have the moral strength to do right by his client.

He wasn't sure anymore and that scared him.

He had to face the fact that he still wanted her to be innocent.

He wanted to believe that she wouldn't betray her loyalty again in order to deal with her current financial problems. The feelings rocketing through him didn't make sense and they filled him with self-disgust, but he would do everything in his power to protect her until he had no choice to do otherwise.

That level of weakness toward a woman who had not only betrayed him, but had trusted her cohort in crime with more truth than her lover frustrated him more than his unrelieved sexual desire.

Cursing under his breath, he pulled the top file toward him and opened it; Ronnie's was on the bottom. He'd told himself that was because he already knew the pertinent facts of her life and work history. He knew she had a past that included corporate spying and selling secrets for money, but she'd also had a sister on the verge of dying.

Taking notes on the possible avenues for investigation in the file on another marketing admin, he was interrupted by the gentle tenor of Ronnie's voice.

"Jack wanted me to tell you that he'll meet you at the restaurant for lunch at twelve-thirty. He's running a little behind."

His head snapped up and he met cool gray eyes. She looked like a woman in complete control, like she'd never come anywhere near letting him ravish her unresisting body in the front seat of his Jag.

He casually shut the unmarked file. "Thanks."

She nodded but didn't turn to leave.

"Was there something else you wanted?"

Her eyes narrowed at his impatient tone.

He couldn't help it. Even knowing that it was impossible, he wanted to yank her down onto the desk and do wicked things to her body. The fantasy had been tormenting him all week and the last thing he needed was to have her actually standing inside his cubicle. Not that she'd come all the way in. She was very careful to maintain her distance in the doorway.

She took a deep breath, pressing her small, firm breasts against the black silk of her severe blouse. "Yes, there is something else."

He unstuck his gaze from the gentle swell revealed by the thin fabric and lifted it to her face. "What?"

She warily stepped into the cubicle. "There's something extremely important I need to tell you, but I don't feel comfortable doing it here." Her voice was barely above a whisper, but firm.

Was she going to admit to the espionage? Had she decided to trust him now, after everything,

with her secrets? The thought was as crazy as jumping out of a plane without a parachute. No way.

Then what? Was she going to agree to sleep with
him in order to ensure his silence? The thought
made him distinctly nauseous. Not only would it
be further evidence of her guilt, but the idea that
she would come to his bed as the result of blackmail infuriated him.

"Whatever it is, it will have to wait. I'm busy for
the rest of the week and over the weekend."

"But—"

"Look, I know you think you need to talk to me,
but I can't make the time right now. Maybe next
week." He turned as if to dismiss her and was completely unprepared for her next action.

She grabbed his arm with a grip of steel and
yanked him back to face her. The maneuver probably wouldn't have worked if he hadn't been sitting in an office chair that swiveled, but he was and
it did. His body came around with the chair and he
found his gaze level with the chest he'd been eye-
ing earlier. It heaved in and out with her agitation.

"You listen to me, you arrogant toad. I need to
talk to you and I'm not waiting until it's convenient. I didn't sleep at all last night working up the
courage and the least you can do is listen."

Somehow being called a toad in such a refined,
sweetly sensual voice just didn't carry the sting he
was sure she meant it to. She was one sexy woman
when she was angry.

He bit back the smile that wanted to let loose at
the thought. She might be small, but she looked
ready to throttle him, and he didn't want to push
her over the edge because it was taking all the self-

control he possessed not to just pull the spitting kitten into his lap and silence her in the most fundamental way possible.

"Listen, baby, I know what you're going to say and I just don't want to hear it right now. I've got more important things on my plate at this point in time and a client to satisfy. Your little confidences are going to have to wait."

He knew he sounded like the arrogant toad she had claimed him to be, but right now he didn't care. He would say anything, do anything to get her tempting body out of his cubicle, including making her mad enough to leave.

Her glare was hot enough to scorch his socks. "Fine. Let me know when you *do* have the time."

Her voice dripped with sarcasm that she wouldn't have been capable of eighteen months ago.

"Will do. Now, if you don't mind." He indicated the doorway with a tilt of his head.

She released his arm with quick precision and turned to go. "Don't forget your lunch date with Jack. He hates to be left waiting."

The reminder that she knew the other man so well did nothing to improve Marcus's mood. "Could you get me a map to the restaurant, Ronnie? I still don't know the area all that well."

He was lying. He knew exactly where he was going and he had no doubt she was aware of it, but he wanted to needle her, to make her suffer just a little of what he was going through.

She nodded jerkily but didn't say anything as she left.

* * *

Veronica pulled up the map and directions on the Internet and sent the file to Marcus's inter-office e-mail account. Calling him a toad had been an insult to all amphibians everywhere. He was worse than a toad. He had the emotional under-standing of a rock. She clenched her hands on the edge of her keyboard.

Strike that. Even a rock would be more sensitive than Marcus Danvers. She'd finally worked herself up to telling him about Aaron and he wouldn't lis-ten.

So why didn't you make him listen, a voice taunted in her head and she ground her teeth. Why *hadn't* she forced the issue? Why had she let him send her out of his office like a wayward student being dis-missed by the principal?

Because no matter how she'd convinced herself that he deserved to know, that she could not in all honor remain silent, she was relieved at the reprieve. She literally shook with fright at the thought of telling him about Aaron before she knew whether or not Marcus planned to make good his blackmail threat.

Would he try to take her son from her? Somehow, she could no longer convince herself that he wouldn't care that he had a son, not after the way he'd waxed poetic over Alex and Isabel's baby at dinner on Monday night. He'd been almost in-decently enthusiastic over his role as an adopted uncle. How would he react to learning he was a fa-ther?

For some men, being an uncle was about the level of commitment they could deal with, but she had the surprising conviction that for Marcus the thought of being a father would be a joyous one.

Turning to glare in the direction of his cubicle, she reminded herself none of that in any way diminished the man's total lack of sensitivity or courtesy. He was still a toad . . . a cement toad, she amended in deference to the amphibians.

"That's a pretty serious expression. Are you trying to cut through the wall with your supersonic sight?"

Startled, Veronica turned her head to see Sandy standing in her doorway. "What?"

The blonde stepped into the cubicle. "I've got to admit, it's a pretty creative way to put a window in, but I don't think it works for anybody but Superman."

"Superman has X-ray vision, not laser vision. That's one of the X-Men, I think." Not that she knew for sure. Aaron was too little for Saturday morning cartoons and Jenny hadn't watched them in years. "And I'm not trying to glare a hole in the wall."

"You could have fooled me," Sandy replied, with a small laugh. "Somebody's got you really miffed. I don't think I've ever seen you with quite that expression. You're usually so cool."

The perfect little robot, Veronica thought, with disgust. Did robots go berserk and hit their ex-lovers over the head with office supplies like she was tempted to do? A heavy stapler should do the trick, or maybe even one of the department's laptop computers. Something solid.

Sandy's laughter turned to wry consideration. "Now you look like you're contemplating your next Godiva chocolate fix. What is going on behind that normally emotionless façade?"

Veronica spun around in her chair and clicked on her e-mail for something to do. If Sandy thought she wasn't busy, the blonde could easily stand around shooting the breeze for thirty minutes or more.

"I'm far from emotionless," she felt driven to say.

"I can see that. My mother used to say still waters run deep. She was talking about my dad. He was a silent man, but now I see the same applies to quiet, efficient women."

Veronica stifled a groan. She really did not want to be psychoanalyzed by Sandy.

"I'm sure your mother's wisdom is more aptly applied to her husband than me. Was there something you wanted?"

Darn. She was sounding as rude as Marcus.

She frowned and turned to face Sandy. "Not that you aren't welcome to stop by to chat. It's just that I'm kind of busy this morning."

It wasn't a lie. She was always busy. Her department didn't really have enough admins to keep up with the workload, but she usually thrived on the pressure that created.

Sandy's smile made her usually beautiful face positively glow. "Don't worry about it, hon. I can tell you're a little stressed right now. Do you want to share?"

"Not really," she replied, with complete honesty.

Sandy's smile morphed into a husky laugh. "Well, I guess you can't get more straightforward than that." Her expression became cunningly thoughtful. "It doesn't have anything to do with the new guy on the block does it?"

Veronica could feel her flesh heat and she

averted her head, swinging back to face her computer screen. Her e-mail inbox held no inspiration.

"Why would you say that?"

Sandy did her usual perusal of Veronica's cubicle, stopping to read the calendar on one wall. "You've obviously known him before. Do you know something the rest of us don't? Like maybe he's looking at more than expansion. . . ."

Sandy had let her voice trail off meaningfully.

Veronica scanned an urgent e-mail, saw it was something she could easily deal with and refocused on her visitor. "Like what?"

For the life of her, she couldn't think of what the other woman was hinting at.

"Like encouraging Mr. Kline to consider a reorganization."

"Why would Marcus do that?"

"Several high-tech companies have done that lately and they've used the opportunity to let go of dead wood."

"But what would Marcus have to do with it? He's not a reorganization specialist. His expertise lies in growing and diversifying companies."

And making spinster-virgins pant for him. He'd certainly had her panting eighteen months ago and then again on Monday night, though she was no longer a virgin and wasn't sure a single mother could be considered a spinster. If he hadn't asked to come up to the apartment, she would have given him her body without another thought, because he was particularly good at that—making her head empty of its every thought.

Sandy shrugged, pulling Veronica's attention

from her increasingly lascivious thoughts back to her friend. "I was just making an educated guess as to why you looked ready to murder somebody when I came in."

"It was nothing."

Nothing that she would willingly discuss with the gorgeous blonde. Sandy was her friend, but the habit of keeping her emotions and thoughts to herself was too well ingrained to make confidences of the sort Sandy was encouraging possible.

"Ronnie, did you get that map for me?" Marcus asked from the doorway.

Shooting to her feet because she felt at a distinct disadvantage with him towering over her, she frowned. "I sent it via interoffice mail a while ago." And had hoped not to see him again today, she implied with a cool look.

"Hi, Marcus. I haven't seen you around for a couple of days." Sandy batted her lusciously made-up lashes at him and Veronica had a sudden, overwhelming urge to be sick.

"I had a family emergency."

So, that's where he'd been.

Finding out that he hadn't been avoiding Veronica for the sole purpose of tormenting her put a slightly more benevolent light on his actions, but only slightly.

Sandy's face took on an expression of deep sympathy. "Oh, I hope everything's okay."

"It's fine." But he didn't look fine.

He looked like the last thing he wanted to discuss was his visit with his family.

Veronica frowned in thought. It had been the same when they were dating. She now realized that a part of why she had been so sure Marcus hadn't wanted to know the intimate details of her life was that he'd been so reticent to share his own.

He turned to her. "The map?"

"As I said—" she started to say, but he interrupted with what could pass for an apologetic smile.

"Could you just print it off for me? There's something wrong with my printer drivers and I don't have time to play with them now."

"Sure."

She turned to do just that as Sandy stepped closer to Marcus, eating up his personal space.

"I could look at your printer drivers for you. I'm a wiz with that kind of thing. It's hard not to be, working for a computer manufacturer."

Veronica's muscles tensed as she waited for Marcus's answer to Sandy's clearly flirtatious offer.

"No thanks. It's not a big deal and I'll have plenty of time to look into it when I get back from lunch." He gave Veronica a killer smile. "And until I get it fixed, I can always borrow Ronnie's machine to print off of."

She gritted her teeth at his casual assumption that he could just use her machine and that he had all the time in the world to fiddle with his stupid computer, but no time to talk with her about a matter of grave importance.

"You can always borrow mine too. My office isn't as close as Veronica's, but it's available if she's busy," Sandy purred.

She might as well have said *she* was available. That's clearly what she meant.

Veronica fairly ripped the map from her printer's output tray. She really liked Sandy, but right now

Veronica could cheerfully have strangled her friend. She handed the map to Marcus without a word. He took it and smiled again, this time his eyes telling her he knew she was jealous and he thought it was amusing.

Somehow, she managed to repress the impulse to kick him in the shin and wipe that smug smirk right off his too handsome features. She turned away instead.

"What's the map for?" Sandy asked, all innocence.

"I'm having lunch with Jack today at a restaurant I've never been to. I thought it was best to have directions. I don't like being late."

Veronica heard the sound of paper rustling and then Sandy's voice. "Oh, I know where that's at. I could show you if you like. I've got some errands to run at lunchtime and I can pick up lunch and take care of them at the shopping mall nearby and then you can bring me back when you're done with Jack."

A sudden tension headache seized Veronica along with an absolutely insane impulse. She wanted to jump up and shout that *she* would show Marcus the stupid restaurant.

She didn't. She forced herself to remain silent as she waited once again for Marcus's reaction to the other woman's flirtatious sally.

She couldn't continue to stare at her computer, though. She turned her head slightly, to read Marcus's expression. He looked thoughtful. He couldn't possibly be interested in the blonde. Not after trying to seduce *her* so thoroughly on Monday night.

Marcus smiled at Sandy. "Thanks. I'd appreciate

it. The drive will give you and me a chance to get to know each other better and I can pick your brain about Kline Tech's future as you see it."

Sandy's eyes sparkled. "Let me just get my purse. I'll meet you in the front lobby in ten minutes."

Marcus agreed and walked out of the cubicle without another word or a backward glance.

Chapter Nine

Veronica stared at the empty doorway to her cubicle for several minutes before abstractedly placing her hand over her heart.

Yes, it was still beating. Funny, it felt like it had been ripped out.

Should it still be beating?

He'd taken the bait.

Marcus had gone to lunch with Sandy. Okay, so technically he was eating with Jack, but she didn't put it past her gorgeous friend to somehow finagle an invitation to horn in on that as well. Marcus, who had kissed *her* senseless and reminded *her* body of its insatiable craving for his, had taken the blonde with him, had said he wanted to get to know her better.

Did he mean that in the most Biblical sense? Was he tired of pursuing his former lover already and looking for an easier conquest?

Sandy was certainly more his normal type. In

fact, she could have been a stand-in for several of the women he had dated when Veronica worked with him at CIS before he'd fixed his interest on her. Had he grown bored with the idea of sleeping with a little brown wren, when he could have a beautiful cockatoo?

Feeling the hot rush of tears pricking at the back of her eyes, she took a deep breath and counted to ten.

She'd survived losing her parents. She'd survived Jenny's illness and giving birth to a son on her own. She'd survived losing Marcus. She would not give in to tears now at the prospect that her ex-lover was as fickle as a stallion at a stud farm.

Taking a deep breath, she turned back to her computer. Forcing her tumultuous thoughts on work, she downloaded the department's e-mail for the current project.

It wasn't uncommon for an admin to have clearance to check all e-mail for a project team. She was careful not to erase the messages off the server so the original recipients could still download their e-mail, but by reading the messages, she stayed on top of the project and was able to make sure all relevant schedules were in alignment.

Jack had balked at giving her clearance, as he usually did, but had ended up giving his approval—again, as he usually did. He had a thing about security.

She started skimming messages and clicked on one that had a blind sender and recipient. Odd. It seemed like excessive security to hide both, even on sensitive material related to a new product's launch. It took her two passes over the e-mail before she realized why it had been sent the way it had.

It said: Information received, but need exact date of product launch. Terms negotiable.

If it hadn't said "terms negotiable" she would not have wondered at the request. However, those two words implied something very different from one department making a request of another. The truth was, with the sender hidden, she had no way of knowing whether the e-mail had been sent interoffice or from the outside. She had a strong hunch it had been from an outside source—whoever was buying the corporate spy's information.

There really was a corporate spy at Kline Tech and that person was a member of the marketing department.

She couldn't ignore this piece of evidence. Not after both Sandy's and Marcus's comments about how much sensitive information had been leaked over the last few months.

Taking a deep breath, she tried to get a grip on her emotions. It wasn't working. She felt hot all over and clammy at the same time. Her stomach roiled and her cubicle walls seemed to close in around her. She was literally sick with fear.

Someone in the marketing department was selling corporate secrets, and if that information came out, she would be the first suspect. At least she would be after Marcus found out. He'd have no choice but to tell Mr. Kline about her past. His personal integrity would not allow him to keep the information to himself, even if she had slept with him.

Oh, Lord. It was more a prayer than a curse, a desperate plea for mercy and clemency for her past sins.

Marcus would never believe that she wasn't guilty, and because of that, neither would Mr. Kline. Her whole life was going to crash around her ears and she wasn't the only one who would pay the price.

She'd managed to give Jenny a chance at life, but what kind of life? The sister of a criminal? And Aaron? What child wanted to grow up knowing his mother had sold corporate secrets in a moment of weakness and desperation and had lost her job less than two years later for the same crime?

Her innocence would not matter. The weakness wouldn't matter nor would the desperation when her son wanted to look at her with respect and all he felt was disgust, or worse, pity.

Both Jenny and Aaron deserved so much better than that and she had no way of giving it to them. She could not give them a pristine past. She could not give them a secure future. Would this one act come back to haunt her forever?

She contemplated a future of lost jobs and moving from place to place, trying to hide from events that could never be erased. Right now, the only people who knew the horror in her past were Alex and Marcus. Once Marcus told Mr. Kline, that would change. Gossip would carry her misdeeds throughout the high-tech community and perhaps beyond.

Too many engineers moved from one company to another across the country for her to move away and be secure in the secrecy of her past.

She shook as she printed off the message and then moved it into a subdirectory for more study later.

She had to tell Mr. Kline about the e-mail. She supposed she should go to Jack first, but she instinctively felt that in cases like this, the fewer people who knew the better. Besides, if Mr. Kline decided to fire her, she could always hope he would refrain from telling anyone why. He couldn't prosecute. Not without proof, and there couldn't be any proof, because she hadn't done it.

Her stomach twisted in a tighter knot and she clicked into the subdirectory where she'd just moved the devastating e-mail. She had to delete it. If, for any reason, it was found on her machine, she would look even more guilty. She clicked on it, hit shift delete, then clicked "okay" when the computer prompt asked her if she wanted to permanently remove the message from her hard drive.

She folded the printed message into a small square and shoved it into her purse.

She had to have something to show Mr. Kline when she told him. She picked up the phone and dialed his secretary's number before she could lose her nerve. If she let herself think about it, she wouldn't tell him at all. Just look how she'd behaved about Aaron with Marcus. He'd been back in her life for a week and she still hadn't told him he had a son.

The professional tones of Mr. Kline's personal assistant came over the line. "Allison here."

"Allison, this is Veronica Richards in marketing. I'd like to speak to Mr. Kline, if I might."

"I'm sorry. Mr. Kline flew out of town for a meeting with IBM this morning. He won't be back until Monday."

"Could you . . . could you put me on his calendar for Monday, then?"

"Is this urgent, Ms. Richards? Mr. Kline is often very busy the first day back from a business trip."

But he had an open-door policy, for which Veronica was presently very grateful. She had no desire to explain to Allison what she needed to discuss with Mr. Kline.

"I can wait until Tuesday, if that's more convenient."

"Are you sure it isn't something you can discuss with your immediate supervisor?" Veronica had always sensed Allison wasn't as comfortable with her boss's open-door policy as he was, and now she had proof.

"Yes, I'm sure. What time on Tuesday is best for Mr. Kline?" she asked, with as much professional assertiveness as she could muster with her insides feeling like taffy that someone was twisting into shape.

Allison named a time and Veronica thanked her before hanging up. Five days of thinking about the revelations she would have to tell Mr. Kline lay ahead of her in seemingly unending torment.

Closing the file on Kevin Collins, an engineer on the design team, Marcus stood and stretched. He'd been working his way through the suspect files since returning from his late lunch two hours ago. Clasping his hands above his head he twisted from side to side, working the tension out of the well-developed muscles of his shoulders and back.

He could really use a swim right now. The apartment complex Kline had set him up in had an indoor pool on the basement level. He'd have to make use of it as soon as he got home that night. Inactivity didn't sit well with him.

He briefly fantasized about talking Ronnie into

joining him but gave up the thoughts as beyond
his imagination. He'd give a month's salary to see
her in a swimsuit but doubted he ever would. She
had some sort of aversion to water. He wondered
now if it had something to do with her parents
dying in a boating accident.

Letting his hands fall to his sides, his attention
reverted to the closed file in the center of his desk.
Kevin Collins. The engineer had worked at four
different high-tech firms in the last five years. He'd
had sufficient opportunity to make contacts for
selling corporate secrets, not to mention live the
classic lifestyle of a spy—making quick and dirty
deals and then moving on. To cast him under suspicion further, he had an address in a pretty up-
scale neighborhood of Seattle considering he was
a single man living on an engineer's salary.

Marcus now had three piles in his suspect list.
The employee files he hadn't worked through yet,
the ones that showed almost no promise and the
smallest stack—those that had discrepancies he
planned to look into further. He moved the Collins
file to that pile.

Restless, he went for another cup of bitter coffee from the employee pot. It was worse than the
last one and he ended up wincing and tossing it
after only one sip.

Ambling back toward his cubicle, he gave in to
the urge to peek in on Ronnie.

He'd decided to avoid her for the time being,
but what his mind had decided hadn't made an
appreciable impact on his body, and his body was
stopped dead center in the opening to her office,
his eyes locked on her.

He savored the ability to simply watch her before she became aware of his presence. It was so much more satisfying than staring at the one picture he had of her, a shot taken in a restaurant on one of their dates. He'd tried to throw the thing away no less than three times, before finally giving up and leaving it on the stand by his bed.

He'd told himself it would be a constant reminder never to let a woman make such a blasted fool of him again. It was a reminder of something all right, but not necessarily that.

Right now his personal torment was working on some sort of report, her focus split between the computer screen in front of her and a thickly bound document lying to the left of her monitor on the desk. With small, birdlike movements, she would turn to look at the papers for several seconds before her hands would let loose in a flurry of typing.

Watching her fingers move with such quick precision brought back almost painful memories of the way they used to move across his flesh. She had very talented fingers. She had gone from virginal hesitation to wanton willingness in her touching their first week together as lovers.

He expelled a frustrated breath as his body responded to the memories with very current need.

She must have heard him because she tensed and whipped around in her chair to stare up at him with wary eyes.

"*Marcus.*" Lines of strain bracketed her mouth and her eyes looked haunted.

He frowned at her reaction. "Stop looking at me like that. I'm not exactly Jack the Ripper looking for his next victim."

Her eyes widened and then her mouth firmed into that prissy line that drove him straight up the wall. "No, he murdered his victims. Your game is blackmail, not that I intend to be a victim."

His jaw clenched. She knew just how to get to him.

"I'm not interested in blackmail," he bit out.

She didn't look impressed with his assurance. "Right."

He closed the distance between them until he was close enough to see the rainwater shades in her gray eyes.

"Right. When you come to my bed again, Ronnie, it's going to be because you can't damn well stay away, not because I've blackmailed you into it."

He spoke quietly, having no desire to share the intimacies of his relationship with Ronnie with the occupants of nearby cubicles.

Her face set with a mulish expression he recognized well from the early days of their dating. "I'm not coming back to your bed voluntarily or otherwise, Marcus Danvers, so you can just get that idea right out of your head."

To his knowledge, she'd never worked in a library, but she had the perfect intonation and prissy outlook to fit the caricature of an old-fashioned librarian. And right now, more than anything, including common sense, he just wanted to wipe that smug look of certainty right off her tiny features.

He leaned down and gripped the armrests on either side of her office chair. She leaned back against the black upholstery, but he just moved in closer until their faces were centimeters apart.

"You will, baby, you will, but I repeat, it won't be under the duress of blackmail. I won't give you that face-saving out. You'll have to admit you want me."

Man, he wanted to kiss her. Her tantalizing lips were so close and yet he knew this was the last place he could give in to his craving for her. She deserved better than to have her coworkers gossiping behind her back about the relationship between her and the new consultant. Steeling his resolve, he released the arms of her chair and moved away.

She swallowed, her mouth working and then amazingly, relief flickered briefly in her eyes.

"So, our past stays just between us," she said, ignoring his assertions about making love.

He tensed, wishing he could promise her that, but knowing he couldn't. Not if she was guilty of corporate espionage.

"I won't say anything as long as there's no reason to do so," he said, by way of a compromise.

She drew herself up stiffly in the chair and asked in an almost whisper, "What would constitute a reason to do so?"

"If I thought you were back to your old tricks."

"One fall from grace in a moment of desperation does not constitute old tricks, Marcus." Her voice was taut, her expression frozen but for the pain in her eyes.

He shrugged, wanting to look a lot more casual than he felt. "Then you have nothing to worry about."

He really wanted to believe that. He'd come to her cubicle feeling better than he had in days now that he had a solid suspect not named Veronica Richards. Her actions since his arrival could be explained if she was nervous about his messing up her barely together life by dredging up past mistakes.

Or she could be feeling guilty about present sins and scared to death of being caught.

She sucked her lower lip into her mouth and nibbled on it. "What if you *thought* I was guilty of doing the same thing again, but I wasn't? What if it looked like I was?"

He felt as if all the air had suddenly been sucked out of his near vicinity.

"The same thing?" he croaked, realizing cool and casual had just gone out the window. "You mean corporate espionage?"

She jerked in reaction to the words, her face going pale. "Yes. That's . . . that's what I mean."

It took all of his experience as a corporate investigator to maintain an impassive expression when all he wanted to do was shake her and demand a reason for her questions. A reason he could live with.

"I'd make sure I was right before I said anything."

Hell, wasn't that what he was doing, what he'd been doing since their first shock-to-his-toes encounter? He couldn't help feeling like a fool, though, wondering if he was just wasting his time and Kline's money. Because she sure acted like a woman racked with guilt and fear of being caught.

He turned away, deeply regretting the impulse to come and talk to her. He'd felt so good, damn it.

She grabbed the fabric of his shirt. "Wait."

He spun around to face her, bothered by the desperate tone of her voice. "What?"

She had stood up and faced him with tense expectancy. "What would you do to make sure I was guilty? You're not exactly a corporate investigator."

Her words were so ironic he couldn't suppress a wry smile. "Then I guess I'd just have to go with my instincts in gathering information."

Her hands clenched at her sides.

"So, hypothetically speaking, if there was a corporate spy here at Kline Tech, what would your instincts tell you to do in order to figure out who it is?" she pressed, depressing the bejeebes out of him.

Did she know he was an investigator? Was this all an elaborate plot to find out his method of ferreting out the guilty party?

He frowned down at her. "I'm not interested in answering hypothetical questions."

He sounded mean and curt and wasn't surprised when she took a hasty step backward.

She nodded jerkily. "Of course. I was just curious, is all."

Not likely.

"Did you have a good lunch with Jack?" she asked, in an obvious bid to change the subject.

"It was informative." The other man had been subtle in his desire to know what direction Kline planned to go with expansion, and Marcus had deftly parried his questions while digging for his own information.

He'd learned that Jack thought Kline Technology should take a much more aggressive stance in the market and diversification. That hadn't surprised him. What *had* surprised him was the information that Ronnie *never* dated.

Jack had made the comment that he thought she was too wrapped up in her role as a single parent. Marcus hadn't thought to apply that term to a woman who had gained custody of her teenage sister after the death of their parents, but he realized now that it was apt. Her role as a single parent hadn't stopped her dating him, he thought with satisfaction.

But it had torn their relationship apart when she betrayed their company to come up with the money she needed to take her sister to Europe for medical treatment.

Ronnie smoothed an invisible wrinkle from her skirt, drawing his attention to the shapely legs beneath. "Good. I'm sure you enjoyed the drive there and back with Sandy. She can be very entertaining."

The blonde had been more than entertaining; she'd been transparent. "She wants to know what Kline Tech's future holds. I told her I wasn't a crystal ball."

Ronnie reclaimed her chair and positioned herself in front of the computer monitor again. "I'm sure that's not *all* she wanted."

No. Sandy had been interested in him, too. *She*'d made that clear enough. *She* wouldn't make any sweeping statements about never darkening the door of his bedroom. And suddenly the fact that the brassy blonde wanted him and Ronnie didn't just made him mad. He'd been *celibate* and all she could talk about was how she was *never* going to bed with him again.

"I don't think she'd bring me to an aching erection and leave me hanging, if that's what you're implying."

One second Ronnie had been sitting, impossibly straight in her office chair, and the next she was five feet, four inches of wounded and raging femininity in his face. "You're so crude! You *know* why I left the other night. I wasn't willing to sell my body for your silence. And it didn't take that long for you to forget about me, did it? Not with you flirting like Casanova with Sandy and *getting to know her better* this afternoon."

Just as quickly as his fury had come, it melted away. "You were jealous."

He'd suspected as much when Sandy had been coming on to him earlier, but pure male satisfaction filled him as Ronnie confirmed it.

She glared. "I was *not* jealous. What you do with your blond bimbos is *none* of my concern."

He couldn't resist needling her. "I thought Sandy was your friend."

Ronnie looked disconcerted, her face tinged pink with shame. "She is."

"Do you call all your friends bimbos, or just the ones who are interested in your ex-lover?"

"I didn't mean it like that," she said, through gritted teeth. "Sandy's a very nice person."

"She's also stunningly attractive."

He was totally unprepared for the moisture that filled Ronnie's eyes or the way her lower lip quivered. She pivoted, giving him a view of her back.

"Yes, she is," she said, her voice stifled.

To hell with one-upmanship. He couldn't stand to see her cry.

He laid his hands on her shoulders and pulled her back toward him until their bodies touched. "I *am* an insensitive pig. I'm sorry, baby."

"Toad. Not a real one either. A cement toad and I don't know why you're sorry for speaking the truth. Sandy is gorgeous." Her voice broke on the last word and she tried to pull away from him.

He tightened his grip on her shoulders. "The only woman I want right now is you. Sandy could just as well be a piece of pretty furniture for as much as she stirs my libido."

Ronnie sniffed. "It doesn't matter."

The urge to shake her returned. It damn well did matter. It mattered so much that he'd been celibate for eighteen long months. It mattered so much that his Ronnie, indomitable of will and as dry-eyed as the Sahara in the face of life's most upsetting trials, was crying.

"Oh, it matters all right."

She tried to pull away again, but he held tight and turned her to face him. She refused to look at him while straining against the circle of his arms.

"Don't be difficult," he admonished her.

She stopped struggling and dropped her forehead against the bright cotton covering his chest. "I'm not trying to be difficult. I'm just trying to be reasonable. Getting involved with you again would not be reasonable."

He agreed. Going to bed with Ronnie would be criminally stupid, but every day that went by only increased his need and he didn't know how much longer he would be able to withstand the temptation. Particularly when he knew she wanted him too. He could feel it in her trembling body as she stood in the circle of his arms.

"Come to my place for dinner tomorrow night."

She shook her head against his chest but said nothing.

"Please, baby."

Why was he begging her? Shouldn't it be the other way around? She was the one who left him.

"I thought you said you wouldn't have any time for me until next week."

"I was being stupid." He had believed that he could resist her. That thought had used less than a full brain cell to develop.

She hiccupped a small laugh at that. "Yes, you were."

"So, you'll come?"

"I don't think it's a good idea."

"But you'll come." He made it a statement, hoping she would agree. "I'll grill some steaks."

"Just dinner."

He wrapped his arms around her, pulling her closer, and said nothing. He couldn't promise anything that prosaic. He might have two years ago. Two years ago he had been willing to do or say just about anything to seduce her into his bed. He wasn't playing those kinds of games anymore. If she came to him, she had to know what she was agreeing to.

She pushed away from him and this time he let her.

Giving him a gimlet stare, she said, "I'm not going to have sex with you."

"That's okay." He didn't intend to have sex either. He wanted to make love and Veronica Richards was the only woman with whom he'd ever made that distinction.

Chapter Ten

Veronica stood knock-kneed with tension outside Marcus's temporary apartment.

Temporary.

He was only in Seattle for a consulting assignment. Then he would be gone. If she allowed herself to get involved with him again, she'd go through the same devastating withdrawal she'd had to suffer the last time. She didn't think she could survive that kind of pain again.

Dinner. It was just dinner, she reminded herself.

She'd told Marcus she didn't intend to have sex with him and he'd agreed. She had nothing to worry about. He'd also said that he wasn't interested in blackmailing her into bed. So, she was safe. Totally and completely safe . . . wasn't she?

Lifting her hand, she pressed the doorbell.

The door swung open almost immediately and Marcus stood framed in its portal. He wore his customary Hawaiian shirt, this one in shades of blue, but instead of the Dockers he wore to the office, his legs were encased in faded blue denim. Very sexy, very tight denim.

Sucking in a breath, she thrust the chocolate torte she'd prepared the night before toward him. "I brought dessert."

Smiling lazily, Marcus took the blue-and-white plastic cake carrier from her hands. "Thanks."

He moved back so she could precede him into the apartment. His spicy male scent, made up of equal parts Polo aftershave and Marcus, surrounded her as she was forced to pass by with only a few inches to spare between their bodies. The assault on her sense of smell carried a lot of memories. She couldn't help the brief weakening at her knees as she recalled the way that scent changed to an earthier fragrance after they made love. This was *not* what she should be thinking about.

He closed the door and dangled the cake carrier from one finger by its handle. "It looks delicious, honey. Is it that sinfully chocolate thing you made the one and only night I had dinner in your apartment?"

With a sense of sickening clarity, she realized it was. Why had she made *that* dessert, of all desserts? She could have made something, anything, else. She would have liked to lie and say she didn't remember, but she no longer took even minimal liberties with her sense of honor.

"Yes."

His smile was knowing, his expression smug.

She managed not to grit her teeth with an effort of will. Striving for an air of cool she did not feel, she removed her lightweight denim jacket and laid it casually over the back of a white leather over-stuffed chair. She'd gone for relaxed informality in her attire and wore a pair of well-worn jeans and a pink Henley shirt tucked in. She figured she couldn't have gotten any less sexually suggestive in her attire.

Turning around to face Marcus, she had to wonder if he agreed. His eyes burned with latent male hunger as he intently studied her. What had he found to stir such blatant sexual desire in her androgynous clothing? For the space of an entire minute, she could not move or break her gaze away from his.

Then he spoke. "*Ronnie.*"

Just that one word, but so full of desire that she leaned against the back of the sofa for support.

"Dinner, Marcus. You promised." She couldn't help the breathless sound of her voice, but she didn't let that bother her.

She thought she was doing pretty good remaining upright and capable of any speech at all under such intense male scrutiny.

He closed his eyes and took a deep shuddering breath before exhaling just as slowly. "Dinner. Right."

Opening his eyes again, he turned toward a hall-way that must have led to the kitchen. "The grill's warmed up and it won't take any time at all to cook the steaks."

"Great." She exhaled a sigh of intense relief at his apparent willingness to stick to their bargain, because she didn't think she had the strength to do so on her own. "I'll fix the salad."

He led her into a bright, well-appointed kitchen

about twice the size of her own. She sighed. She'd give a lot to have a kitchen this big to experiment with her baking in, but she'd gone for other considerations when renting her current apartment. Things like price and the number of bedrooms.

Jenny deserved space that she could call her own after spending so many months in the invasive atmosphere of hospitals. Even though it had meant renting an older apartment with smaller, shared living areas, Veronica had readily signed a lease on the three-bedroom unit in the mostly residential neighborhood.

Marcus pulled a glass bowl with plastic wrap over the top from the fridge. "The salad's done."

Looking at the table in the adjoining dining alcove, Veronica noticed that the table had already been set as well. "Is there anything I can do?"

"Keep me company while I grill the meat." He opened the sliding door to a small balcony and stepped out.

She followed, wishing she'd left her coat on. The brisk spring air made her shiver, even through the thick cotton of her shirt, and she was made uncomfortably aware of the sheer fabric of her bra. She stepped closer to the barbecue for warmth, hoping her tightening nipples would not be too noticeable.

She crossed her arms over her chest protectively. "It's chilly out here."

He turned his deep blue gaze on her and smiled. "I can keep you warm, honey. You just have to say the word."

She stepped back hastily from the barbecue and him. "I'll get my jacket."

His laughter trailed after her as she fled into the house. She thought she heard him call her a coward but wasn't sure and she wasn't about to go back right that minute and ask. Stopping to don her jacket in the ultramodern living room, she tried to get hold of her seesawing emotions. One minute she felt absolutely certain that the last place she would ever find herself would be in Marcus's bed and the next she wanted to grab him by the hand and drag him there.

Coming back out onto the balcony a minute later, she found her sexual nemesis lounging casually against the half wall. Blue sky and water in the distance made an impressive, but nerve-racking backdrop for his intimidating height.

Her stomach lurched and her heart sped up. She wanted to grab him by the front of his brightly colored shirt and yank him away from the wall.

"Marcus, get away from there. What if the wall doesn't hold?"

His eyes widened with amusement. "I'm sure the building was put together with the prospect of inhabitants leaning against the railing a time or two."

Her hands curled into fists at her sides. Feeling really foolish, she averted her gaze from him. "Yes, of course."

She knew he was right. Her unreasonable fear of heights had always embarrassed her; she didn't understand why she had this fear. When her parents were alive, her dad, who walked exposed steel girders ten stories high, would tease her about it. As she'd gotten older, she'd learned to control her reaction for the most part.

But she still overreacted to the sight of a loved one anywhere near a cliff edge, or a glassed-in wall on an elevator. She'd had to grit her teeth and pray her way through every jump her sister took off the high dive when Jenny had been involved in swimming competition before her disease had put an end to all sports activities.

Marcus pushed away from the balcony wall and came toward her, stopping less than a foot away.

Reaching out, he tugged her face toward him with a blunt finger angled against her chin. "You're frightened of water. You're nervous about heights. You're terrified of me. Is there anything you aren't afraid of?"

She opened her mouth to speak, but one look into his mesmerizing blue eyes and she couldn't remember the question. "Wh-what?"

He smiled, his eyes going the color of the Caribbean Sea just before sunset. "Never mind. It's not important."

He started lowering his head. His lips were centimeters from her own when his earlier words came back to her.

In a desperate attempt to head off his kiss, she blurted, "I'm not afraid of water and I'm not terrified of you."

She was terrified of what he made her feel, but she wasn't about to admit that salient fact.

He stopped his descent but didn't pull back. "You would never go swimming with me."

"I didn't want you to see me in a swimsuit."

He laughed incredulously, the warm breath from his mouth fanning her lips. "I saw you in a lot less."

And she'd seen him the same way. Images of Marcus wearing nothing but his sexy smile took her breath right out of her chest. "That was after you asked me to go swimming."

He seemed to take that in. "I see. So, is there any chance I could convince you to share the pool on the basement level with me in the near future?"

Too tempted for comfort, she blurted out, "No!"

"Why?" His husky voice warmed her nerve endings just like a caress.

"I don't want to see *you* in a suit," she admitted rawly. She didn't think she could handle it.

"You said you weren't afraid of me."

"I'm not, but I'm also not stupid."

"So you admit the sight of my nearly naked body would be a major turn-on for you." His eyes challenged her while his scent and warmth tantalized her.

She refused to answer and remained stubbornly mute. He darn well knew what the sight of his body did to her. She'd heard that women were not visual creatures, that the sight of a naked man was not supposed to be all that enticing, that what went on in their heads and hearts was far more important.

Well, all she knew was that the sight of Marcus without his shirt on had always sparked unbelievably hot fantasies, and the less he wore, the hotter those fantasies got.

She'd once admitted as much to him, expecting him to laugh. Instead he'd told her that she was the most incredibly special lover he'd ever had. Even memories of that sentiment brought heated moisture to the back of her eyes.

He gently pulled her glasses off her face, making her feel doubly vulnerable to his gaze. Stepping back, he laid them on the table by the grill and then returned to invade her personal space. Space that crackled with her need for him.

"You're going to see me in a whole lot less," he promised before letting his mouth finish its initial descent and lock onto hers.

And the world spun away as her entire universe shrank to encompass the taste of his lips and the feel of his body so close to hers. How had she ever thought she could refuse this? She needed Marcus like she needed the air she breathed, and for the past eighteen months, she had lived as if starved for life-giving oxygen. If she hadn't had Jenny and Aaron relying on her, she wouldn't have made it.

Monday night in his car had been the first time in over a year that she had felt anything resembling whole.

How could she withstand the temptation to feel alive and complete again after living the life of a ghost for so many months?

She parted her lips without thought and he took immediate advantage of her willingness to deepen the kiss. He explored her mouth with erotic savagery, the hunger so blatant in his gaze earlier now transmitted to his devastatingly talented mouth. She melted under the onslaught, allowing her body to press against his. Feeling the hard press of his masculinity against her stomach, she marveled at the rapidity and obvious firmness of his erection.

Trailing her fingers around his back, she slipped her hands under his shirt and explored the heated satin of his skin with starved intensity. His muscles bulged in rigidity as he shuddered under her exploration. She slid her questing fingers lower until she reached the waistband of his jeans. Without stopping to think, she continued until she had worked her hands under the denim. He wasn't wearing his usual snug knit boxers. She smiled a secret smile as she cupped the muscular curves of his butt and he groaned low in his throat.

She didn't know where this boldness had come from. She'd lived the life of a single parent uninterested in sex for almost two years.

She had ignored every male invitation and come-on, not that there had been that many. But the ones that had come had all been treated with the same level of cool dismissal. She just wasn't interested in making another mistake, she'd told herself. And now she had to face the truth.

She'd been waiting for Marcus.

Her body's response to him was too intense, too instantaneous for her to dismiss that truth. She had wanted him with shattering intensity eighteen months ago and she wanted him now. She pulled Marcus's body closer to hers and he spread his legs to encompass her. She lowered one hand until the tip of her fingers could reach the beginning of the soft flesh of his scrotum.

Pressing gently in a move she'd read about in a woman's magazine regarding the male "G" spot, during one of her sojourns in the hospital waiting area, she felt his entire body go rigid, and then he moaned in the most amazingly primitive way. She would have smiled at the success of her foray, but her lips were too busy melding with Marcus's.

The kiss, which had already been incendiary,

went to molten lava in the space of a second. His lips ate at hers while his tongue explored the interior of her mouth with devastating efficiency.

Pulling back from the kiss for only a moment, he mumbled something irritably about her height. Then he locked one hand in her hair and his other forearm under her bottom and lifted her until their mouths could cling without him having to bend very much while aligning her intimately with him. She was forced to release her grip on his backside and abandon her exploration of the newly discovered erotic zone.

Unwilling to give up contact with his skin, she dug her fingers possessively into the hair-roughened hard plains of his chest. Desperately needing more and not willing to remove her mouth from his to ask for it, she pressed the juncture of her thighs against his hardness and squirmed for better contact. Moaning raggedly, he took two steps forward and she felt the cool glass of the sliding doors against her back.

It seemed the most natural thing in the world to spread her legs and then lift them until she had locked her ankles behind his buttocks. Oh, Heavens, it felt good. Better than good. It felt mind-blowing.

He thrust his hips against her as if he were inside her and she experienced the most sensually frustrating pleasure imaginable. The two layers of denim felt like instruments of torture that prevented the kind of intimacy she desperately craved, skin to skin.

She wanted him inside her.

Breaking her mouth away from his, she gulped in necessary oxygen. "*Please, Marcus.*"

She didn't know what she was begging for, whether she wanted him to stop the insidious torment of that kiss or tear both their clothes off and finish the erotic game he had started.

He didn't respond but bent his head to kiss the tender underside of her jaw while he removed his hand from her hair in order to tug at her top. He got it untucked with a couple of strong yanks. He didn't put his hand under the nibbly cotton but pushed it up to expose the revealing fabric of her bra to his gaze. With an expert flick of his wrist, the front clasp came undone and the slight fullness of her breasts quivered in all their bare glory.

He touched each one reverently with the tip of his forefinger. "You're so beautiful."

She whimpered.

"They're fuller than I remember. How could I have forgotten?" He sounded dazed.

"You didn't." The words were out before she thought better of them.

How could she explain the fuller curves of her breasts, a side effect of breast feeding Aaron for the first six months of his life, without telling Marcus the truth?

"You've gained weight, too." He drew a line down the exposed flesh of her stomach. "I like it."

She said nothing. She'd been a size six before pregnancy and a size eight after. Her hips had filled out, she had a slight curve on her tummy and her breasts had grown a cup size, which still hadn't given her the figure of a centerfold by any stretch of the imagination.

He circled her nipples with that same enticing finger and the already tight buds pebbled and swelled in a plea for more direct attention. She ached for that attention so much, she moaned with the pain of it.

"This is the same. You're still so responsive, you take my breath away." He lowered his head and gave her aching flesh what it wanted. His mouth.

Oh, my goodness. He was wrong. She was more responsive. Way more responsive. Nipples that had ached constantly during pregnancy now responded to the slight sucking motion of his mouth with overwhelming intensity. Sensation shot from her breasts to her femininity with startling power and she cried out. He increased the suction of his lips and she writhed against him in a mindless frenzy of unfulfilled desire.

Using his hand, he plucked and played with her other nipple to overpowering effect. Unbelievably she felt the inner clenching that signified imminent orgasm. "Please, Marcus, harder! Don't stop. Please . . ."

Her voice ceased working as he obeyed and increased the pressure on her rock-hard nipples. And then she exploded, her legs tightening around him until her thighs hurt from the strain. Her head banged back against the glass door, her nails digging into his chest, and a primal scream exploded from between her passionately parted lips.

Marcus went rigid against her, but he didn't stop the ministrations to her sensitized flesh and the inner contractions went on and on until, finally, she went limp.

"Please, no more," she begged.

He kissed each breast softly, and tenderly laved her nipples with his tongue before raising his head.

His stunned gaze met hers. "How?" he asked.

Having no answer for him, she let her head drop forward and buried her face in the crook of his shoulder. She kissed the salty skin of his neck and then let her mouth rest against him. She could feel his body still rigid with sexual tension, but right then, she couldn't make one move to help him alleviate it.

Not that she didn't want to, but she was too drained by the response of her body.

He didn't push it, seemingly content to stand there holding her all night. His hand caressed the back of her head and he kissed her temple. The kiss was soft, gentle and wholly without expectation. A great swell of love for the man she'd wrapped her body around rolled over her. She was too overwhelmed by what she'd just experienced in his arms to deny the feeling, so she tucked it away for examination later.

Slowly, the reality of their surroundings penetrated her passion-exhausted brain. She could smell the steaks cooking. She hoped Marcus had thought to set the grill far above the hot briquettes because neither of them had thought of their dinner for quite a while.

The sound of traffic from six stories below reminded her that she had just screamed out her sexual release for all of west Seattle to hear and hot embarrassment climbed up her neck and into her cheeks. Oh, Heavens. She burrowed more tightly against Marcus, hiding her nakedness against his body.

His grip on her tightened and he kissed the exposed skin of her cheek. "Let me love you, Ronnie."

The words were as seductive as his tone. He had always referred to their intimacy as sex. Her body experienced a resurgence of desire at that simple four-letter word. *Love.*

Could he possibly have realized he loved her after losing her? It seemed very unlikely. How could a man love a woman who had betrayed her own honor and him in the process?

"The steaks," she forced herself to remind him.

"Forget about them."

"When they turn to charcoal themselves and motivate a neighbor to call the fire department, you'll remember them quickly enough."

"How can you worry about the damn steaks after what just happened? Can't you feel how much I need you?" He thrust his hardened manhood against her and she shuddered.

If he had sounded angry, or demanding, she might have been able to withstand him, but he asked the question in a voice of genuine bewilderment underlaced with very real masculine need.

And he'd said that darned "L" word.

He'd asked her to let him love her and she didn't know how she could refuse. She'd tried to stop loving Marcus. She really had, but had known it was a lost cause during her pregnancy.

How could she eradicate love for the father when she had the child to remind her of all that she missed and desired? And how could she refuse his urgent need to love her body when her own desire matched his?

Finding release hadn't brought her fulfillment. Only the sensation of Marcus's body filling hers could do that. She wrapped her arms around him, hugging him to her as if he were threatening to leave rather than begging her to stay.

Kissing his throat again, she inhaled his scent and then kissed the underside of his chin for good measure.

"I don't care about the steaks. I don't even particularly care that I've just had a significant sexual encounter with you on the balcony of your apartment in full view of God, birds and neighbors with binoculars. Take me to bed, Marcus. *Please.*"

Chapter Eleven

Marcus stiffened at Ronnie's words. *She'd agreed.* She wanted him. His hardened flesh throbbed at the thought, while his mind wrapped around her assurance that she wasn't even going to let the fact she'd just screamed her pleasure out for God, birds and neighbors with binoculars to hear bother her.

Eighteen months ago, the knowledge that she had been so wild in a potentially public setting would have sent her into hysterics.

Unwilling to risk her thinking about it some more and changing her mind, he kept her wrapped around him and carried her inside, his long-legged stride eating up the distance to his bedroom. He laid her on the bed and came down on top of her, putting his weight on his arms so he didn't crush her. With her shirt all bunched up above her pretty little breasts and her hair in disarray, she looked wanton and wild.

And he wanted her.

His sex continued to pulse with the need to be inside her. He wasn't even sure he'd be able to unzip his jeans without doing bodily damage to his masculinity.

"I need to be inside you, baby. I need it so bad."

"Yes." She rocked under him, just one sexy little wiggle, but he felt like exploding.

An animal-like growl crawled up his throat and exploded from between his teeth clenched with sexual tension.

If he didn't get hold of himself, he was going to take her with all the finesse of a teenager looking for his first score. He needed a breather, just sixty seconds not connected to her body in which to pull himself together. He hesitated.

If he took time away from her and left her alone, she might change her mind about letting him make love to her.

She gazed up at him with that unfocused look that indicated she was under the influence of her passion rather than her brain.

Hell.

He didn't have a choice.

He levered himself off her. "I'm going to go rescue the steaks."

Her eyes widened and her lips parted on what might have been a protest, but he shook his head in denial of her speaking.

He backed out of the room, forcing his limbs to take him in the opposite direction from the one they wanted to go—toward the bed. "I'll be right back."

Then he spun on his heel and practically sprinted into the kitchen.

Walking through the brightly lit room, he went back out onto the balcony and pulled in several deep breaths of the chilly evening air before he removed the steaks from the grill. They were more cooked than he usually liked, but not unsalvageable. When he reentered the kitchen, he decided to torture himself by putting away the salad and other food for dinner.

His body had not appreciably relaxed, but he wanted to give Ronnie time to collect herself. To decide if *she* was ready to let him make love to her.

Since the first time they made love, she'd had no self-control where he was concerned.

He'd liked that. He'd liked it a lot, but he wasn't going to use it. Not this time. This time he was playing for a future and he wasn't going to risk her walking away again without saying good-bye. If she let him make love to her, she was going to know what she was doing and he wouldn't let her leave him again afterward.

With every passing minute, he became more convinced that he would return to his bedroom to find Ronnie dressed and put back together. Or gone. No, not gone. Her glasses were on the table on the balcony. She couldn't drive without them. He went back outside to retrieve them.

Then, taking a deep breath, he walked slowly back toward the bedroom, the uncomfortably tight fit in the front of his jeans a reminder that though his thoughts were pure, his body was weak as hell.

The bedside lamp was off, but enough light filtered in from the hall to illuminate his bed and the completely naked woman waiting in the middle of it.

He stopped dead in the center of the room.

"You took long enough to eat your steak. Don't tell me you slaked your hunger?" She'd clearly meant it as a joke, but she sounded nervous. On edge.

Had he taken too long and hurt her feelings? He'd just wanted to give her time to make up her own mind.

"Never." He'd always be hungry for her.

He'd learned that lesson very, very well.

She smiled, her lips tilted in almost feline anticipation. "Then what are you waiting for?"

"You used to be shy." His voice came out gravelly, rather than teasing, as he'd intended.

She shrugged even as her skin took on a faintly pink hue, and the pouting swell of her breasts rose and fell in a fascinating movement.

"Blame yourself. I'm only this way with you."

He tore his shirt off and then carefully worked the zipper down on his jeans. "I only want you this way with me."

The thought of her naked in any other man's arms made him see red. Speaking of . . . "Where the hell did you learn that little move you used on me outside?"

She'd never done it before and the prospect that she'd learned it with someone else gutted him.

Her blush intensified, her natural shyness returning. "*Cosmo.*"

More relieved than he wanted to admit, he pushed his jeans down his thighs, freeing his penis. It bobbed up to full attention and he almost laughed at the look of undisguised longing burning in Ronnie's eyes. Toeing off his shoes and socks, he finished removing his jeans and then stood completely naked, letting her look her fill.

She loved to look at his naked body. He could remember times before when he'd woken up from a satiated doze to find her kneeling next to him on the bed, just staring.

"Seen enough?" he asked.

"Never," she said, repeating his earlier answer.

He walked toward the bed, feeling like a predator ready to move in on its prey.

He wanted this woman under him and he wanted it yesterday. "You're going to feel so good."

She shuddered and a needy sound escaped her lips while her legs parted in a blatant invitation as old as time. He was really, really glad she'd already climaxed on the balcony because he didn't think he'd last more than a few thrusts after eighteen months of celibacy and the highly erotic foreplay that had brought about her shocking orgasm.

He'd never seen a woman climax from having her breasts stimulated before. True, he'd been rubbing himself against her, but how much sensation could she have received through two layers of denim and her panties?

"What are you thinking?" she asked, her voice sounding croaky.

"How sexy you are. That I probably won't last worth a damn." He would not have admitted that weakness to any other woman.

She bit her lip, her legs shifting, but not closing. "I thought you might not like what you see. I've changed."

He nodded, moving toward the bed, toward her,

stopping when his shins hit against the end of the mattress. "I told you I liked it. Even more now that I can see everything."

She had the sweetest curve on her tummy and her hips were fuller. He didn't understand it. His mother had always lost weight when she was stressed, but Ronnie had filled out some even though the last eighteen months had to have been hell with her sister in the hospital and trying to start a new life here in Seattle.

Regardless, he really did like her new look. He wanted to feel every inch of her lusher body, getting to know each new curve completely and putting his brand on her with his hands and his mouth.

But not right now. Right now, all he could think about was getting inside her.

The basic mating act.

He came down on top of her and shuddered at the impact of her warm, welcoming nakedness against his skin. It felt so good that he wasn't sure he'd even make it inside her. She moved restlessly under him, spreading her thighs wide to make a place for him there. He felt the tip of his penis against the entrance to her femininity. The soft, wet warmth beckoned him and he wanted to surge inside in one strong thrust.

He stopped himself just in time and asked the question that needed asking. "Birth control? Do I need to protect you?"

He wasn't going to get into a discussion about safe sex, not when he'd spent the last eighteen months celibate and had the distinct impression she had too.

Her breath caught and she tipped her pelvis toward him. "Yes. I didn't think. Do you have something?"

He reveled in this further proof that she hadn't been sexually active since she'd left him. She'd gone off the Pill and hadn't had any reason to go back on. He reached across her, his sex brushing against the silken smoothness of her stomach, and yanked open the drawer of the nightstand.

He grabbed a small foil packet and handed it to her. "You do it." His hands weren't steady enough.

She arched up toward him, letting her body caress his excited flesh while she concentrated on opening the condom and pulling it from the wrapper.

"Okay," she said when she had it open.

He lifted up until he was kneeling above her and she gently rolled the condom in place.

His head fell back at the touch and he groaned. "Aw, honey. That feels so good. It's been so long. Too damn long."

"How long?"

His head snapped back up at the question and he met her eyes, her gaze wary. She was scared of his answer. He could see it in her eyes.

He smiled with as much reassurance as he could muster with his flesh ready to explode. "Eighteen long, lonely months, baby."

She gasped in shock, but he wasn't up to discussing his celibacy at the moment. Moving his body back over her, he took her just the way he'd been longing to do, with one smooth thrust. She gasped again and he tensed.

"Did I hurt you?" It cost a lot just to ask the question.

"No. It's just a little tight, that's all. You're a big man, Marcus."

He would have laughed at that boost to his masculine ego, but he didn't have the breath. He lowered his mouth and took hungry possession of her lips while he thrust his body into hers in one pounding drive after another. When she came again, her body contracting boa constrictor fashion around him, he exploded inside her with mind-blowing intensity. Then, he collapsed on top of her, his muscles no longer able to bear the weight of his body.

He vaguely thought he was probably crushing her, but she didn't seem to mind. Not if the stranglehold she had around his neck was any indication.

Tears ran wet and warm down her temples and into her hair, as Veronica lay crushed under Marcus's welcome weight. Common sense made a bid to reassert itself and tell her what a stupid thing she had just done, but her emotions and her body weren't listening. They felt sated for the first time in so long that she didn't want to think what she'd just experienced could have been anything less than the best choice she could have made.

He lifted his head and wiped at his own cheek, then touched her temple. The light from the doorway cast his face in shadow and she could not read its expression.

"You said I didn't hurt you." His voice washed over her with masculine concern.

She shook her head against the pillow, unable to speak at first. She blinked, stemming the flow of tears. "You didn't."

"Then why are you crying?"

"I missed you." The words were bald, but the truth.

She had spent eighteen months away from him, and not one day of that had gone by that she hadn't physically ached for his presence.

"You left me." He didn't sound accusatory. He didn't even sound angry. He sounded bewildered. "Why?"

"I didn't think I had a choice."

"You didn't trust me."

"I didn't know you." How could you trust a man you didn't know, particularly a man who had told you that all he had to give you was sex?

He shifted and she could feel his still semierect flesh move inside of her. "How can you say that? You knew me more intimately than any woman ever had."

She stared at him, bemused. Did he truly believe that? "Marcus, I don't even know your parents' names, if they are alive or dead, if you have siblings. You hide all the intimate details of yourself behind your atrocious sense of humor and overwhelming sensuality."

A sensuality that had given her the courage to strip naked and wait for him in bed although he'd taken long enough "saving the steaks" that she would have been excused for believing he'd had second thoughts.

He kissed the corner of her mouth and moved his hips again, and the semi state of his erection altered to a much more solid reality. She murmured in protest when he withdrew from her body, but the sound died in her throat when he opened the nightstand drawer again and went about changing condoms with swift efficiency.

He came back to her, pushing her thighs apart to enter her once again, this time inch by leisurely inch.

He smiled with sensual promise into her eyes. "My mother's name is Sharon and my father's name is Lionel Marcus Danvers the fourth."

She sucked in her breath and ground her hips in a circular motion against him. "Tell me later. . . ."

Then she was lost once again in the whirlwind that always carried her away when he touched her. His thrusts were agonizingly slow and overwhelmingly deep. He kissed and caressed her until she panted with her need for fulfillment and then he gave it to her in a series of hard, body-jarring thrusts until her mind splintered and her body convulsed in wave after wave of sensual release.

She dozed after that. She didn't know how long, but when she woke up, the bedside lamp was on. Marcus sat next to where she lay on the bed, wearing a pair of black knit boxers and nothing else. She scooted into a sitting position, dragging the sheet with her, so that it covered her chest.

He helped by pulling the pillows into place behind her to support her back and then smiled and winked, giving the sheet a significant look. "Good idea. If you don't keep yourself covered, I think we'll miss dinner again."

He picked up a tray from the nightstand and put it between them on the bed. Dinner. The smell of grilled steak and the tangy odor of Italian dressing made her stomach rumble with hunger pangs.

His brow rose mockingly. "Worked up an appetite, did you?"

She blushed and nodded just before he fed her a bite of her salad. Dressing clung to her lips and she flicked her tongue out to lick it off. His eyes dilated with remembered desire and she felt warmth unfurl inside her.

It didn't matter how many times they made love; she would always want more. Her love and need for this man were insatiable. She would have pushed aside the dinner if the experience of being fed weren't so enjoyable in its own right.

She was chewing a bite of well-done steak when he said, "I have a half brother and a half sister, neither of whom are particularly fond of me."

Swallowing hastily, she asked, "What?"

Still disoriented from sleep and the drugging desire he sparked in her, she didn't understand what he was telling her at first and then it clicked. His family. "What are their names?"

"Lionel Marcus Danvers the fifth and Patricia."

"Your brother must be older than you."

"Yes, by several years."

"And your sister?" She still couldn't quite grasp that he was telling her about his family.

He'd always been so closemouthed on the subject, acting as if talking about his family ties was tantamount to sharing state secrets.

"She's older as well."

"So, you're the baby. Is that why they don't like you? Did your parents spoil you rotten?" She smiled when she asked the question, reaching out to caress the line of his jaw.

His eyes did not reflect her gentle amusement. "No."

She waited for him to elaborate, but he didn't. He seemed to be waiting for her to ask him more questions, so she did. "Isn't it awfully confusing to have so many males in your family with similar names? I mean, I assume your father goes by Lionel. What do they call your brother? Junior?"

He did laugh at that, a deep, rich chuckle. "Lionel would have a fit if anyone called him by such an undignified title."

"*Lionel?*"

"My father is called Mark."

So, his mother, clearly the second wife because his siblings were only half relations, had claimed a place on the family tree for Marcus by giving him his father's middle name. "I still think it must get confusing."

"Since I'm rarely there, it isn't a problem."

"You told Sandy that you had been home to see them recently. Some kind of family emergency," she probed.

"Mark had a heart attack. My mother needed my support."

"Mark?" Now she was confused. She thought *Mark* was his dad.

"My father."

"You call your father by his first name?"

"Actually, I address him as little as possible."

Dinner forgotten, she stared at the stark lines of his face. "But why?"

He didn't answer and after several seconds of complete silence, she convinced herself he wasn't going to.

She turned her head away, hurt and yet not surprised. "None of my business. I know. A casual bed partner doesn't rate discussion of the intricate relationships within your family."

Marcus grabbed her shoulders. "You're more than a casual bed partner, damn it. You always were."

"Is that why you told me not to get sex and love confused the first time we were together?"

She couldn't fathom why he wanted to rewrite their history, maybe to make their separation all her fault, but she wasn't having it. She carried enough guilt without taking responsibility for their lack of true intimacy as well.

"That's all it was—at first."

She knew that. She really *knew* that, but it still hurt to hear him say it.

"But everything changed. I started wanting you to spend the night, but you never would. I was thinking about asking you to move in with me and then you left. Without saying good-bye."

The pain and confusion in his voice so closely matched her own, and she turned her head to meet his gaze. His eyes were dark with emotion and fixed on her in almost desperate intensity.

"I'm sorry I didn't say good-bye."

"I'm sorrier you left."

"I explained why I had to go."

He nodded. "Now, I guess it's my turn to explain, huh?"

"Only if you want to."

"My mother was Mark's mistress for fifteen years. They'd been together a little over a year when she got pregnant. I think she believed he would leave his society wife and make their relationship permanent. It didn't happen that way. He moved her to another small town nearby and provided for us financially, but he refused to divorce his wife. He didn't believe in divorce and then there was the social stigma attached to it as well. He wasn't willing to put his other two children through it."

She felt her insides tighten in response to the pain Marcus must have experienced as a child and the bitterness she could still hear in his voice. "Did he ever come to see you?"

"Twice a week."

Then she remembered him saying that his mother had been his father's mistress for fifteen years. "They had an affair for *fifteen* years?"

She couldn't fathom something like that. It sounded so sordid, so pointless. She wondered if living it had felt the same way for Marcus.

"Yes," he said, in answer to her question. "When I was little, I didn't understand why my dad only lived with us two evenings a week. Why he never stayed over. My mom left him once, when I was about five. I remember begging her to take us back to my daddy and how she cried."

"She took you back?"

"Yes. She left again when I was ten. By then, I understood that I wasn't legitimate, that my dad belonged to a couple of other kids first."

"She went back again?" Veronica was trying to understand.

"Mark hired a private investigator to find us. He showed up one day and took us back. I didn't want to go. In my new school, I wasn't somebody's bastard son; I was just me. Mom had moved us to

Seattle and things were different. No one cared about our past."

"But your parents are married now."

"Mark's wife died when I was twelve. He waited a year for decency's sake after her death and then he married my mom. My older brother and sister were already away at college. He thought the three of us could play happy family."

"It didn't work?" But then, how could it?

A man with Marcus's immense sense of compassion would despise the man who had hurt his mother so much and his pride would be unwilling to forgive the stigma of being the slighted son, the one who only had his father two nights a week.

"No."

Cold dread poured through her at the prospect of telling Marcus about his own son. After hearing his parents' background, she didn't think he was going to take too well to discovering that she had given birth to his son without the benefit of marriage or even telling him about it.

She took a deep breath. "Marcus, there's something I need to tell you."

Chapter Twelve

Marcus felt every muscle in his body tense at Ronnie's words. She'd told him she had something she needed to tell him yesterday morning, but he had refused to listen.

Out of fear.

He might as well admit it. He didn't want to know she was guilty of selling company secrets again. And he couldn't fool himself anymore into believing her confidences had anything to do with his attempt to blackmail her into his bed.

They'd dealt with that.

But now, he realized he'd rather hear the truth and get it over with. Somehow he had to protect her from the consequences of her actions. He didn't know how he would succeed completely, but he had a suspicion that if they took it straight to Kline and she confessed her guilt, the older man would be reasonable.

Particularly if Ronnie told him about what she'd

been through with Jenny since their parents' deaths. It would take a rock to remain condemning in the face of the choices she'd had.

He moved the tray with dinner onto the floor and then met her gaze squarely. She looked wary, but determined.

He bit back a sigh. Hell. He wanted to build a future with a woman who sold her loyalty to the highest bidder. It didn't make him feel like the brightest spark at the bonfire.

"Okay, Ronnie. Let's hear it." If his voice sounded resigned and slightly bitter, he could be excused.

She jerked back, her gaze veiling, her mouth thinning.

She took a deep breath and let her eyes focus somewhere to the left of his shoulder. "This isn't easy. I'm not sure where to begin or how to say it."

"The truth would be nice, though I realize that might be a tough one for you." He hadn't meant to let his bitterness spill over into his speech.

He felt like cursing at the way her face drained of color.

"Yes. Well, it's not really a matter of having lied to you *per se.* It's more a matter of not having told you something. Something pretty important."

Her rambling explanation wasn't making him feel any more charitable. He had damn well figured out that part. It wasn't as if he'd come right out and asked her if she was guilty of espionage again. No. She hadn't lied. To him.

"Spit it out," he ordered, his voice harsh.

He just wanted this part over so they could start picking up the pieces.

She swung her gaze back to him and glared.

"You don't have to be so impatient. This isn't easy for me."

He glared right back, doubly irritated because her look of censure was turning him on for some inexplicable reason—maybe just the male chromosome's natural inclination to solve a dispute between him and his woman with physical pleasure and intimacy. It was a primitive response and he'd heard women didn't think it worked. He wasn't so sure. He was more than willing to give it a try . . . after she told him the truth.

He waited, trying to be patient, feeling more frustrated as every second of silence ticked by, and he came close to blurting out the truth for her, just to get it over with.

"Marcus, I—"

The phone rang. Shrill and unwelcome. She stopped speaking.

He frowned. "Ignore it. Finish what you were saying."

She shook her head. "No. Please. I gave Jenny your number in case she needed anything."

Unwilling understanding of her concern for her once very ill sister warred with his irritation at the interruption. "I doubt very sincerely your sister is going to call."

The phone rang a third time.

Ronnie's eyes turned pleading. "Please, Marcus."

He picked up the white receiver from beside the bed, his movements jerky with tension. "Marcus here."

"Hello, Mr. Danvers. This is Jenny Richards. Is my sister still there?"

Looking at the naked woman who seemed to be

shrinking against the pillows propped behind her, he sighed incredulously. "Yes."

He shoved the phone toward Ronnie. "Your sister."

Her eyes widened in panic for a fleeting second before she masked her expression. "Jen?"

Her sister said something.

"No. It's all right. Don't worry about it. He doesn't mind." She shot Marcus another pleading glance and he took the hint.

Picking up the dinner tray, he left the room.

Veronica felt a twinge of shame at the relief she felt at both the interruption of the phone and Marcus's willingness to leave the room. He wouldn't have had to go anywhere if she'd told him about Aaron immediately upon arrival, as she'd planned. She would have been able to speak freely in front of him, but somehow the words simply would not come. She didn't know an easy way to tell her ex-lover that they had a child together.

Strike that. She moved under the sheet, the feel of the soft percale against her naked body reminding her that she could no longer call Marcus her *ex* anything. She didn't know *what* to call him, though. Were they lovers again? Did they have a relationship now? Had he meant it when he had spoken of a future on Monday night and was that future still possible?

"Veronica? Are you there?" Jenny's insistent voice brought her abruptly back to reality.

"Yes, of course, Jen. Did you think I'd hung up on you?"

"I didn't know what to think," Jenny replied, her voice chatty and teasing. "I've been blabbing on about Aaron for the past few minutes and you haven't even bothered to say uh-huh, or anything. Is there something going on there I should know about?"

Mother worry raced through Veronica like a shot of adrenaline and she ignored Jenny's teasing to focus on the words that had sent her heart into overdrive. "Is he okay? Did something happen to Aaron?"

"No, he's fine, but he's teething. Like I said a minute ago."

"I must have missed that."

Jenny laughed. "I guess you did. What's going on with you and Marcus? You sound really out of it."

Veronica caught sight of her clothes strewn across the bottom of the bed and Marcus's on the floor. No way was she going to tell her kid sister that she'd leapt back into Marcus's bed with all the enthusiasm of a chocoholic greeting Hersheyland, Pennsylvania. "I'm not out of it. I was just thinking about something else there for a minute."

"Something tall, blond and, according to you, oh so sexy?"

"Jenny!"

"You're so easy to tease. You know that, Veronica?"

Marcus used to say the same thing. He'd laughed because she took life so seriously and he'd found it embarrassingly easy to draw a reaction from her. And yet there had been a time, before her parents had died, when people actually thought she had a sense of humor. She grimaced.

"I guess you haven't told him about Aaron yet, huh?"

She scooted into the pillows against her back, as if she could hide from her own cowardice. "Uh . . . no." First, she hadn't had the words and then he'd literally swept her off her feet with passion. She was still reeling from the aftereffects, not to mention the emotional dilemma created by learning what she had about his past.

"Maybe you should just invite the guy over. He can meet Aaron and put two and two together, since you seem to have such a hard time getting four to come out of your mouth." Jenny's tone clearly indicated she was kidding.

But Veronica's emotionally battered brain latched on to the idea with the force of a hurricane wind off the coast of Florida. *Why not?* Why not *introduce* Marcus to his son rather than try to muster her courage to *say* something? She didn't know how to tell the blond giant that they'd made a child together, especially after his revelations about his own background.

At one time, she had believed the hardest problem she faced in telling Marcus about their child was his desire to avoid commitment. Now she feared his reaction based on an entirely different set of concerns.

Would Marcus hate her when he realized she'd exposed his son to the same illegitimacy at birth that had so devastated him? Would he think she'd deliberately withheld the knowledge of his son in order to hurt him? She hadn't, but he didn't see the past through the same set of memories as she did.

She had thought he wouldn't be personally affected by her disappearance. He acted like the personal aspect of her betrayal was the most devastating.

By inviting him over, she would short-circuit her own ability to cave in to her fears. The truth would be obvious as soon as he saw their baby. Aaron looked so much like Marcus and Marcus knew he had been her only lover. His agile brain would have no problem putting two and two together and coming up with a solid four, the four she *had* found impossible to utter.

"Veronica, you've gone silent again."

"I was just thinking that you're brilliant."

"Uh . . . thanks. But what makes me so smart all of a sudden?"

"You've always been smart, but right now I'm impressed with your insight. Showing Aaron to Marcus will be a lot easier than telling him about our son."

"I was just kidding!"

"I know, but it's a really good idea. I wish I'd thought of it before."

"But, Veronica—"

She wouldn't let Jenny finish. "No buts. I can't seem to make the words come out of my mouth. I've never considered myself a coward before, but I'm starting to wonder if there isn't a streak of yellow a mile wide running down my spine. If I invite him over, there won't be any choice but to tell him. Don't you see?"

Jenny's silence vibrated across the phone line.

"Jen?"

"Yeah, I see." She sighed and then laughed. "Maybe you're right. Besides, when he sees how lovable Aaron is, he won't be able to stay mad."

Veronica hadn't thought of that, but she had a sneaking suspicion that her sister was right and an equally disturbing thought that her subconscious had already grasped that truth when she'd latched so firmly onto the idea.

"Just don't bring him by tonight. Aaron's teething and you know how cranky he gets around strangers when he's in pain or tired."

And teething, her son was both. He slept little during that time, always ran a mild fever and, by the way he gummed anything within reach, suffered a lot of discomfort. In fact, the teething symptoms could last up to two solid days.

"Okay. I'll invite him over for dinner on Monday night."

"Sounds good. Do you want me to make myself scarce that night? I can go to the library."

Veronica thought about it. "That would probably be best. I think Marcus would appreciate privacy for his first meeting with Aaron."

He would also probably appreciate advance warning, but he couldn't have everything.

"Okay. Anyway, are you going to stop on the way home and get some teething ointment for Aaron?"

"Sure. Are we out?"

"That's why I called."

She could hear the smile in Jenny's voice.

"Oh." She smiled herself. "Will do, then." She took a peek at the clock. It was already close to nine. "I'll be home in about forty-five minutes."

"Don't rush. We aren't out of the teething ointment, but we're low."

"Thanks, hon. You're really a blessing to me, you know that?"

"Right. I'm sure taking care of a sick teenager is just how you wanted to spend what should have been your college years. That doesn't make me any kind of blessing that I can see." Jenny tried to laugh, but to Veronica's discerning, sisterly ear it came out strangled.

The words and the sentiment they represented shocked her, so much so that she clutched the phone in stunned silence for a full five seconds before breaking into impassioned speech.

"Don't ever say that again! I mean it. When we lost Mom and Dad, you were all I had left. Taking care of you, being there for you when you were sick . . . that was an honor and I won't let you think otherwise. You *are* a blessing to me. You've helped me so much with Aaron. I don't know what I would have done without you."

"*Oh, Veronica.*"

When Marcus came back into the bedroom, Ronnie was just hanging up the phone. "I have to leave."

No way. "You said you had something important to tell me."

Her expression turned pained. "I do." She waved her hand in a vague gesture. "It's just that I realized it would be a lot easier if you came to my house and I told you there."

He stared at her in silence, waiting for her to elaborate.

"I mean sometimes a picture really is worth a thousand words," she said, adding another layer of obscurity to the problem at hand.

"A *picture?*" he asked, feeling helpless in the face of her meandering thoughts.

What kind of picture could she have at her house that would make telling him about her activities as a corporate spy easier?

"Well, not really a picture, but a visual aid. You understand what I mean, don't you?" she asked, pleating the sheet with her fingers. "Remember, in school when the trigonometry teacher would drone on about those really confusing theorems and they didn't make any sense until he started drawing on the chalkboard?"

"I found trig theory pretty straightforward," he admitted, before he realized that he had let himself be pulled into the bizarre discussion rather than press for resolution to their real problem, her confession.

Her face fell and she bunched the pleated fabric of the sheet in her fists. "Oh. Well, *pretend* you didn't understand. Now, do you see what I mean?"

"No."

Her fisted hands moved restlessly against the mattress, causing the sheet to pull dangerously low and expose the upper curves of her small but delectable and *very* sensitive breasts. Primitive man's resolution to domestic harmony was looking better and better.

She met his gaze, completely oblivious to the precarious state of her covering. "Look. It's like one of Alex's matrices. You know those little box things he does to keep track of information for a client?"

"I don't need you to explain Alex's information-gathering methods to me. He's my partner." The reminder shouldn't have been necessary, but then this whole conversation seemed bizarre.

Rosy tints slashed across her cheekbones. "Right. Well, the point I'm trying to make is that those little boxes help him to put the relevant information into perspective."

His ever-practical, always logical former office automaton was babbling like an airhead. The knowledge shook him.

"What you're saying is that whatever it is you need to tell me will be easier to tell if you have a visual aid available at your apartment?"

The concept boggled. Did she plan to show him proof of her perfidy toward Kline Technology? If so, he was clueless as to what it could be.

She was nodding vigorously in response to his question. "Yes, that's just what I mean."

He bit back a sigh. "Honey, you don't need any visual aids to tell me what needs to be said. If you've got trouble at work, just tell me what it is and I'll help you fix it."

She stared at him, her face pulling into a frowning mask, her eyes filling with confusion. "I don't have trouble at work. This hasn't got anything to do with Kline Technology. Where did you get that idea? I love my job. At least most days."

The silence stretched and he realized she was expecting an answer to her question.

"I don't know. I just assumed it had something to do with work," he said lamely.

She pursed her lips and then her eyes widened in apparent understanding. "*Oh.* Because I brought it up at work to begin with?"

"That and the fact that some things you said

when I was visiting your cubicle yesterday got me thinking." There, that should help her open up, make her realize he wasn't as in the dark as she assumed he was.

"What I want to tell you has absolutely nothing to do with my job, Kline Technology or the state of the business world in general."

His mouth gaped and he felt like a fish that had been landed in some kid's net after spending the whole season avoiding the lures of more practiced fishermen.

What in the hell did she need to tell him, then? "You're making me crazy, honey. Do you know that?"

She chewed on her bottom lip. "I don't mean to."

He closed his eyes and counted to ten, then opened them. "I believe you."

"Listen, Marcus, this would be a lot easier for me if you'd just come to my apartment for dinner. I swear it will all be clearer then."

One fact stopped him from pushing for more information regardless of the lack of "visual aids" currently at hand. Her confession had nothing to do with work. If she *was* Kline's corporate spy, she wasn't ready to admit that yet to Marcus.

And maybe, just maybe, she wasn't the spy after all.

Regardless, his poor baby looked stressed to the max and her pretty gray eyes were full of pleading. The woman needed the relaxation therapy of sex. She did not need him to grill her into some disjointed confession he probably wouldn't understand in her current mood anyway.

He felt himself smiling. A man did what a man had to do for the woman in his life.

She took his smile as agreement and returned it. "So, you'll come to dinner, then?"

"Yes." He let his gaze wander down her body, feeling a definite reaction in his lower extremities to her now almost completely bared breasts. The sheet had born the brunt of her nerves. "Would tomorrow night work for you?"

No matter what it was she wanted to tell him, he didn't want to wait forever to hear it.

"Um, actually, I'm going to be tied up pretty much all weekend. How about Monday?"

He frowned. "What have you got going this weekend?"

It would be ridiculous to even consider that she might have a date after the way she'd given herself to him, but that didn't allay the sharp spurt of jealousy that pierced him.

She shrugged and one pouting nipple played peekaboo with his libido. "Domestic stuff."

That didn't sound like a hot date, but Jack had been right. She did take her role as a single parent seriously. Hell, if he'd had a younger sister that had gone through what Jenny had, he would too.

"I've got a dinner meeting with Kline on Monday." He was supposed to give his client a status report on his investigation when Kline got back from his business trip. "I could come over afterward, but it might be late."

Disappointment and relief both swirled in Ronnie's for once completely revealing eyes. "Oh, late wouldn't be good. What about Tuesday night?"

"I'll come straight over after work."

"Um . . . could we make it six-thirty? I want a chance to put stuff together."

He assumed she meant dinner. "Yeah, sure. Whatever."

His interest in their current conversation dwindled in proportion to the amount of skin revealed by Ronnie's nervous movements with the sheet.

"You said you had to go?" he asked.

She nodded again, this time more slowly, but made no move to leave the bed. Her gaze roamed over his bare chest and then lower, her expression slightly dazed.

He slipped off the knit boxers that had begun to tent over his growing erection. "Do you have time for a shower before you leave?"

She swallowed and then licked her lips, her focus entirely on his male sex. He loved the effect his naked body had on her. "Sh-shower?"

"I thought you might want to go home smelling like something other than me."

Her head flew up and she seemed to notice all at once where his gaze had strayed.

She made a small sound of distress in her throat while tugging the sheet back up, but her expression had turned smoky with desire. "Yes."

That was one of the things that fascinated him about her—the contradiction between her shyness and her passion.

"We could take one together. It would save time."

"How?" She cocked her head to one side and considered him. "You don't have to shower before I leave." His practical Ronnie had returned with a vengeance.

He grinned. "But I do need to touch you. If we shower together, I can take care of that and get you clean all in one fell swoop. What do you say?"

Her mouth opened, but nothing came out.

"It wouldn't be the first time," he cajoled.

Erotic memories of showers shared eighteen months before arced between them as he waited for her answer, uncertainty adding zing to his already reactivated libido. The thing he loved best about the physical relationship between them was how she always managed to surprise him. Something she adored one minute made her shy the next, and then she'd shock him with an earthy sensuality that literally sent him to the moon and back.

What would it be this time? Would she refuse to take a shower with him, would she agree or would she expect him to convince her of the *wisdom* of his plan?

Anything was possible with his Ronnie.

Letting the sheet drop, she stood from the bed.

"I'm always a fan of efficiency," she finally said, her voice husky and sweet, her cheeks bright pink with shy embarrassment even as she so clearly offered herself to him.

He swept her up into his arms and carried her into the bathroom.

Chapter Thirteen

As Marcus lowered her to her feet in the small shower stall, Veronica could not focus on anything but the overwhelming experience of sharing such a small space with him. They'd showered together before, many times. However, the shower in his Portland condo was oversized and had a molded seat in one corner of the enclosure. While decadent and sexy, it had lacked the tight fit that forced physical connection with such devastating effectiveness.

Marcus's body towered not six inches in front of her while he adjusted the water to a comfortable temperature. Then, as he turned to face her, his hip brushed her stomach and his arm rubbed against her breast. Her breath hitched and he smiled.

"Let me wash you, baby."

She nodded, mute with desire. It would have taken a natural disaster for her to say no to his invitation. Not only had Jenny told her not to hurry, but the fear that this would be her last opportunity to share her body so completely with the man she loved spurred her.

Once he learned how she had hidden their baby from him, he might very well hate her.

As his soapy hands began an erotic glide over her shoulders and down her arms, even that devastating thought melted away in a haze of pure pleasure. He made a production of washing her hands, massaging her palms with his thumbs until her body thrummed in response to the unexpectedly torturing caress. Though no sexual response to him should surprise her anymore.

Hadn't she learned that where he was concerned, her entire body was an erogenous zone?

"You're such an incredible lover," she admitted, helpless to keep the words locked inside, where they belonged. The man didn't need an ego boost in this department.

"It isn't me, baby. You're so responsive. I can't go wrong." He replenished the lather on his hands and moved to her back, forcing her body into contact with his.

His already swollen sex pressed against her and she groaned, letting her head fall forward to rest on the muscled wall of his chest. "Yeah, right, like all those other women have nothing to do with you knowing just how to arouse me."

She didn't know where that had come from. Even thinking about the scores of gorgeous women who had drifted through his life hurt. So, she had done her level best not to. Why was she bringing them up now?

She didn't want to ruin this moment with misplaced feelings of envy for women who had nothing to do with Marcus's current life. She'd always managed to keep her jealousy under lock and key before. Never letting him know how much it bothered her that he was so experienced while she was such a novice in lovemaking, she had flat out refused to acknowledge the fear that she somehow wouldn't measure up to the lovers of his past.

Marcus's hands stopped moving on her back and he brought one around to force her chin up so that her gaze met his. She blinked at the blue fury she found there.

"When I'm with you, no other woman exists for me. I don't try things out on you that worked on someone else's body. Got that?" The anger blazing in his eyes spilled into his voice as well.

She tried to nod again, but his hold on her chin was too firm. "I . . . yes."

His mouth was a grim line. "No other woman has ever haunted me the way you did when you left. I haven't wanted anyone else in the whole damn time you were gone and if you think that makes me happy, you're a fool. You left me without looking back, still, I wanted you and only you. Don't ever mistake what we have between us for the meaningless relationships in my past. There's no comparison."

His words slammed into her with the force of a battering ram, but instead of leaving her feeling bruised, they caused the most amazing sense of elation. *There hadn't been anyone else.* There really hadn't been. She *knew* it and that knowledge burned through her like a fire blazing out of control.

She opened her mouth to speak, but his lips

slammed down on hers and his tongue invaded her mouth with marauding hunger. Steam from the hot shower surrounded them, but it didn't feel nearly as heated as her body. Running her hands up his chest, she felt him shudder before she gripped his shoulders and pressed herself more fully against him.

She wanted him. She wanted him right now. She didn't want to wait. Not one single second, but she couldn't tell him so. Not with his tongue plundering her mouth and his lips sealed to hers with the force of superglue. So she tried to show him by pulling herself up his body and rocking her pelvis against his erection. He rocked back, forcing her body against the wall of the shower, but he didn't complete the connection.

She moaned. She writhed and she kissed him back. Kissed him with all the passion she'd been storing up for eighteen months, just as if she hadn't already found completion in his arms three times that night. She spread her legs, making it as obvious as possible that she was ready.

He growled and did the impossible, deepening a kiss that already felt hot enough to set her mouth ablaze . . . along with the rest of her body. One strong, masculine, soapy hand came down and gripped her bottom, pulling her up and forward until the tip of his penis pressed against her sweet spot. Her body jerked and she cried out against his lips.

He used his male flesh to tease her sensitive nub until she thought she'd scream with the frustration of it.

She didn't know how, but her hands were now

locked in his hair and she yanked back on his head, dragging her lips from his. "*Now,* Marcus. I want you inside me, *now!*"

Pushing the words out past a throat constricted with the force of her passion hadn't been easy, and she didn't appreciate the fact that they appeared to have absolutely no effect on him. He continued the torturous teasing and added to it by covering one breast, slick with warm water, with his free hand. He squeezed and she felt like she'd just been jolted by a maverick electric current.

"*Marcus.*" She wanted to kill him . . . after he made love to her.

He played with her nipple and squeezed her bottom, increasing the sensation of his hardness rubbing against her vulnerability. "Yeah, baby?"

"*Please.* I want you inside." She couldn't make it any clearer than that.

She grabbed his head and brought his mouth back down to hers for another soul-stirring kiss. He lifted her the small increment necessary to poise his erection at the opening of her feminine flesh. She brought her legs up and clasped her ankles behind him, just above his gorgeous bottom. Then, she pressed down, taking the magnificent width and length of her lover into her in one strong downward thrust.

It felt so good, so right, that tears leaked out of her tightly closed eyes to mingle with the water cascading over them from the shower. She went still and so did he, their mouths and their bodies connected, but unmoving. She wanted to stay this way forever, locked together with him, secure in the knowledge that for at least this moment in time he belonged one hundred percent completely to her.

Then he moved. Just one long, slow thrust. She wanted more of the same, more of those long, slow thrusts that pressed him deeply into her body and connected them in a way that she had never been connected to another person.

She almost blurted out her love for him right then, but her last shred of sanity saved her and she said his name instead. "*Marcus* . . ."

He cursed and her eyes flew open.

His face wore the expression of a man facing the rack. "I forgot the condom."

Her inner muscles clenched around him and he moved within her, just the tiniest bit, but enough to let her know that her body was on the very verge of going cataclysmically over the edge. She wanted to tell him not to worry about it.

Desperately.

But memories of nine months as a single, pregnant woman pushed entirely different words from her tight throat. "Get it."

He nodded and pulled away from her, a low rumble of displeasure rolling out of him as their bodies separated.

He set her on her feet and she sagged against the wall, unsure if he'd find her standing when he returned. Her legs felt like she'd just done a two-hour thigh workout. Pushing open the glass door to the shower stall, he stepped dripping into the bathroom and walked through to the bedroom without bothering to shut the door or grab a towel. He was back seconds later, an already open foil packet in his hand.

He didn't wait for her to put it on him but took care of donning the condom with more speed than a NASCAR driver, his beautiful mouth set in grim lines of extreme desire. His eyes had turned such a deep shade of blue that they looked almost black and his cheekbones were scored with color. He grabbed her without preamble and lifted her high against the wall before driving into her with satisfying urgency.

They both groaned as her body once again molded itself to him. She locked her legs around him again, this time holding him even more tightly, feeling almost afraid that something else would end their time together before their souls had completely meshed.

"Oh, man, baby. I wanted this to last." His words had barely registered in her desire-fogged brain when he began thrusting with all the power of his six-foot, two-inch frame while holding tight to her hips to ensure deep penetration.

She didn't bother to answer. She couldn't have if she'd wanted to. It took all her concentration just to breathe as the ultimate pleasure began to take hold of her. She didn't know how long he pounded into her receptive flesh before the world exploded around her and in her head, but when it was over, he was shouting something and pulsing inside of her so strongly that she could feel his climax to the core of her being.

"I love you, Marcus. I love you so much."

She'd been biting back the words since practically the first day they'd met, but they exploded out of her in the aftermath of their lovemaking with volcanic force.

He stilled and then held her so tight, she felt like her ribs might crack. "I'm glad, baby. So damn glad."

So it wasn't a vow of undying affection, but it wasn't the reaction of a man running from strong emotion and possible commitment either. All in all, she found herself smiling as she buried her face in his neck.

"Me too," she whispered against his slick, warm skin.

Monday morning, Veronica slid into her office chair at five minutes to eight—ten minutes later than she normally arrived for work. Adjusting her glasses, she resisted rubbing tired eyes. Aaron had been up off and on all night long with his teething. The poor little bunny had had not one, but two teeth come in at once and to her way of thinking, his misery had more than doubled. He'd been irritable, restless and whiny.

She was more than a little relieved that Marcus had plans that night. Hopefully by the next day, she would have gotten sufficient sleep to face the challenge of introducing him to their son.

Though she couldn't even pretend to herself that she didn't want to see him, that she didn't miss him. Only every second of every day. It had been bad enough when he'd first come to Seattle and the hot kisses they'd shared in his car hadn't helped. But all her defenses had crashed and burned on Friday night as they made love.

She could only pray that he would understand what had motivated her to leave him in ignorance about her pregnancy eighteen months ago and then about the birth of their son eight months later— because she couldn't imagine the future without him.

She flipped on her computer and then turned to check her voice mail while it was booting up. She wrote several quick notes to herself in response to the expected messages left on Friday after she'd gone home. She also listened to a rambling message left on Saturday by one of the design team engineers. She couldn't figure out exactly what he was asking her and made a quick note to herself to call him. About to hang up, she was forestalled by the digitized voice telling her that she had three messages that morning.

She gave in to the urge to rub her temples. Monday morning crises were not her favorite things. And *crisis* was the first thought that came to her mind when she discovered that three people had needed to talk to her before she'd even made it into her cubicle that morning.

The first message began to play. Jack had called at seven-thirty, looking for her. He didn't sound stressed, though, and left no specific request. She frowned over that oddity. Was he looking for a date again?

She had hoped that Marcus's embarrassing little comment that day in the cafeteria had at least had the effect of ridding her of Jack's overt interest. Then, again, remembering the way her boss had referred to her as Ronnie simply to get male one-upmanship with Marcus, she sighed. Obviously the more challenging, the better, as far as Jack was concerned.

Sandy had also left a message. This one was both specific and annoying.

The blonde wanted to know if Veronica knew if Marcus was attached and, if not, did she have Marcus's telephone number at his temporary apartment? Sandy lived with the belief that as an admin, Veronica had access to the answers to the universe.

Was Marcus attached? She wanted to believe he was—to her. He'd made it clear he wanted only her right now, but he wasn't happy about that fact and she couldn't blame him. It couldn't be very soothing to his male ego to want a woman who had not only sold company secrets, but also abandoned him in the process.

So what should she tell Sandy? *I love the guy and you'll stay away if you know what's good for you?*

Somehow that message seemed just a little melodramatic. Which did not mean she felt no temptation to send it in an all-caps e-mail to her friend. Maybe if she ignored the message, Sandy would look elsewhere for her information. Maybe she would even go straight to the source and Marcus could tell her he wasn't interested. Then, again, maybe he wouldn't.

The third message started playing. She smiled, her heart picking up its beat. It was from Marcus.

"Hey, babe. I was just checking to see if you were in yet. I missed you this weekend. Maybe next time, we can do your domestic stuff together."

She hit the button to repeat the message three times before finally hanging up without deleting it. That sounded like a man committed to one woman. At least now she knew what to say to Sandy if she did indeed decide to call the blonde back.

She could only hope that circumstances would not drastically change after she dropped her bombshell on Marcus the following night.

Dialing Jack's extension, she simultaneously clicked her e-mail to download messages from the weekend. She got Jack's voice mail and left a brief message saying she was returning his call before hanging up. Then she turned her attention to the e-mail. Making a quick scan of the new project team's e-mails, she noticed that the message implicating espionage had been removed from the server. All of the messages she'd downloaded had recognizable senders and recipients. *Thank you, Lord.*

She skimmed them, looking for required action on her part before deleting all but two off her system.

"Hi, sweetheart. Busy?" Marcus's voice had her spinning around in her chair to face him.

He stood in the opening to her cubicle, looking sexier than any man had a right to look in a garish red Hawaiian shirt and khaki-colored Dockers.

She felt her mouth curve into a smile. "Hi, yourself."

"Did you get my message?"

She nodded.

"And?"

"And what?"

"Next time can we do the domestic bit together?"

The prospect of sharing Aaron with his dad suffused her with a warm glow. "I'd like that very much."

His smile spread that glow into the tiniest recesses of her heart. "Great."

He looked over her shoulder and his body went stiff. "Isn't that e-mail addressed to someone else?"

She turned back to her machine, momentarily at a loss as to what he could be talking about, and then she noticed that she'd left the technical marketing engineer's message on-screen because it was something she had to coordinate with the design team's admin regarding schedules.

She refocused on Marcus, feeling lighthearted enough to tease him. "Yes, but you're not supposed to be reading my e-mail over my shoulder."

It was a matter of common courtesy and company security. Of course, by rights, she should have blanked her screen when she heard his voice, but she trusted Marcus.

He shrugged. "You know me. I'm always looking."

She felt another silly smile overcome her good sense. "I know. You're an information monger. It's what makes you and Alex so good at what you do."

His frown surprised her. "I'm beginning to wish I wasn't so good at my job."

"Why?"

"So what *are* you doing with someone else's e-mail?"

Typical Marcus to ignore her question to ask one of his own.

She didn't see any reason not to answer, however. "It's pretty common for admins to be given access to a team's e-mail in order to keep track of schedules and project details. It's kind of like having your mom listening to your messages and writing stuff down on the calendar for you."

"I wouldn't want my mom hearing some of my

messages." His sinfully sexy voice had gone low and seductive.

She laughed out loud, surprising herself. "I can imagine. Some of these messages aren't appropriate for moms either. I try not to read anything personal."

Then her lighthearted mood vanished as she remembered what she'd unwittingly read last week. Maybe she should talk to Marcus about it before she went to Mr. Kline. She chewed on her lip, weighing the pros and cons, and in the end decided she should trust him enough to at least ask his advice, unlike last time.

Only she didn't feel comfortable doing it in her cubicle, or anywhere else at Kline Tech for that matter.

"Do you have plans for lunch today?"

He'd been studying her and she wondered what he was thinking. He looked so serious and almost sad.

His expression turned regretful. "I'm having lunch with Sandy and then—"

She didn't let him get any further. "You're having lunch with *Sandy*, after *Friday night*?"

She tried to keep her voice down but knew it sounded shrill. She felt shrill. She felt shredded. How could he be thinking about dating her blond friend after Friday, after what he'd just said this morning? She spun away from him, not wanting him to see the distress on her face, not wanting to see the cool distance on his.

His hand brushed the hair up from the nape of her neck and then she felt soft lips pressed to the sensitive spot just below her ear. "It's not a date, sweetheart. It's work. You know what I do. Don't read anything more into it than that. You're the only woman I want right now."

That *right now* sounded ominous, and instead of feeling comforted like she was sure he meant her to be, she felt a cold stone form in the pit of her stomach.

"And if that changes tomorrow? What then?"

She'd never asked those kinds of questions of him before. She'd played their relationship by his rules, but that had left her miserable and desperate. She needed more now. She needed to know if he was hedging his bets, or if he was committed to a real relationship—one that included the prospect of a future.

He forced her chair around until she faced him.

He was squatting in front of her, his gorgeous blue gaze eye level with her own. "It hasn't changed in eighteen months; I sincerely doubt it's going to change tomorrow."

At the reminder that he hadn't had anyone else in all that time, she relaxed a little. "I guess not."

"I know not. If there had been any way to eradicate you from my heart, I would have when you left."

She didn't like hearing that and glared at him.

He shook his head, his expression exasperated. "What do you want me to say? That I enjoyed pining for a woman who left me without a backward glance?"

She reached up and touched the firmness of his jaw. "It wasn't like that."

He closed his eyes and turned until his mouth met the palm of her hand. He placed a soft kiss right in the center and then opened his eyes again. Remembered pain warred with an unnamed emotion in his blue gaze and she wanted to comfort him, but didn't know how.

"I understand a lot better, now that you've told me about Jenny, but I'm still having a hard time accepting that you didn't tell me about her to begin with. I don't know what the future holds for us, honey, but I do know that I don't want to face it without you anymore."

She felt a lump form in her throat at his words. "I would have given anything to hear you talk like this before."

He grimaced. "Yeah, I guess I held my feelings pretty close to my chest."

She wanted to ask him what those feelings had been, but this wasn't the time or the place. She could hear her coworkers going about their business, and any second she and Marcus could be interrupted by someone needing to speak to her. The thought of another employee catching her in such an intimate position with him had her scooting her chair back. He seemed to know what she was thinking and understood because he stood up and stepped away as well.

"I'm sorry about lunch today, honey."

She nodded. "Me too."

"What about tomorrow?"

"But we're having dinner together tomorrow night." And she would have already spoken to Mr. Kline.

"Is there any reason why I can't see you more than once in a day?" he asked.

She took a deep breath and let it out, feeling the

familiar elation that this incredible man wanted to spend time with her—ordinary, practical Veronica. "No. No reason."

At least she'd be able to tell him about the corporate spy then and maybe get his advice on whatever Mr. Kline said in her meeting with him.

Marcus was smiling again. "Good. I'd better get going. I've got a status report to write before I see Kline tonight."

She smiled back. "Then, you'd better get to it."

He nodded and turned to go, stopping in the cubicle entrance. Looking at her over his shoulder, he said, "I wish we were getting together tonight. Friday made me hungry."

Her entire body just melted. "Me too," she whispered.

His eyes dilated with desire. "Tonight . . ." He let his voice trail off, the suggestion hanging in the air between them.

She wanted to say yes so badly she had to bite her tongue in order to keep herself from blurting it out. She couldn't. It wouldn't be fair to leave Jenny with Aaron again after the teething episode.

"You said you didn't know how late you would be," she reminded Marcus.

He swore, low and under his breath. His jaw set. He didn't like to be thwarted sexually.

"What about tomorrow? Will you come back to my place after dinner?"

She thought about what she would be telling him over dinner and her stomach knotted. "If you still want me to."

His eyes narrowed at her words. "Oh, I'll want

you to. Just don't be surprised if I have my own plans for dessert."

She hoped with all her heart that those plans would not change once he learned her secret.

Chapter Fourteen

"You put Allison on your list of suspects?" Kline sounded shocked.

"As your PA, she's had access to all the information leaked by the perpetrator." Marcus hadn't bothered to sit down for this short update meeting with Kline Tech's owner.

He planned to give very little information, but recognized that if he gave nothing, George Kline would grow restive. And restive clients caused problems.

Kline slammed his desk, his expression ferocious. In fact, he looked like Marcus would look if someone were threatening Ronnie.

"She's not your corporate spy."

Marcus shrugged. "She doesn't exhibit the behavior pattern of one, but that could be camouflage."

He knew better than anyone else how capable a supposedly loyal secretary was of hiding her actions and her motives.

"Let me see the rest of your list."

George Kline was not happy and Marcus frowned. "Fine, but I don't want you mentioning the investigation to Allison."

Kline stood up behind his desk. "It's my investigation."

"No, it's mine and if you want me working for you, I call the shots."

The older man nodded. "It's not an issue. I didn't think she needed to know when I brought you in and I don't plan to tell her you suspect her of betraying me."

Marcus was almost positive that Kline had a thing going with his PA. He hoped for the older man's sake that Allison was innocent.

That kind of betrayal hurt and he didn't wish it on anyone.

Eighteen months after the fact, he was just beginning to get his emotions back together and it was because he had Ronnie in his life again. And she wanted to be there.

That made up for a lot.

Veronica waited in a chair near Allison's desk, her palms sweaty and her heart beating at what felt like twice its normal speed. She'd arrived fifteen minutes early for her appointment with Mr. Kline and Allison had informed her that he would be late. She'd been sitting in the barely padded gray chair for half an hour.

The sleek lines of modern furniture in the waiting room would inform any visitor to Kline Technology of its evident place in the world of hi tech, but she had to wonder if the small sofa kitty-corner to her chair and a black melamine table was any more comfortable than her seat. It was entirely too easy to imagine herself sitting on a hard wooden bench outside the principal's office.

Taking a shallow breath and letting it out again, she reminded herself that Mr. Kline had not requested this meeting—she had. *And it was the right thing to do.*

"Mr. Kline can see you now." Allison didn't smile, nor did she sound particularly friendly.

In fact, she reminded Veronica very much of herself when she'd worked for CIS. Did the supremely efficient administrative assistant have her own reasons for imitating an automaton, as Veronica had? If so, she wondered if there was a Marcus on Allison's horizon ready to smash through the other woman's unemotional façade.

Veronica stood up, smoothing down her gray slacks and adjusting the short matching jacket she wore over a white silk shell. She didn't normally wear suits to the office, preferring simple skirts and blouses, the wren look.

However, today, she'd needed a bolster to her confidence, so she'd dressed up a little. Considering the stylish apparel of his administrative assistant, who always managed to look like an automaton who just happened to dress in Paris business fashions, she doubted Mr. Kline would be impressed.

Allison opened the office door and ushered her inside. "Miss Richards to see you, sir."

Mr. Kline looked up, an expression of amiable interest in his eyes. "Thank you, Allison."

The other woman clearly took that as a sign to

depart because she did so, closing the office door behind her.

"Thank you for your patience in waiting for me, Veronica. Now, what can I do for you?" he asked, while waiving her to a black leather sofa near the huge window overlooking the Seattle skyline.

It looked a lot more comfortable than the furniture in the waiting area and added the rich smell of leather to Mr. Kline's office. Sitting down, she forced herself to stop clutching her purse as if someone would grab it and steal the implicating e-mail. She set the small black carryall beside her.

Not knowing where to start, she waited in silence for him to take a seat in one of the matching chairs at either end of the sofa.

Instead, he walked over to a cubbyhole in the wall behind his desk. "Would you like a cup of coffee?"

"Yes, thank you." She didn't really want any, but agreeing put off the moment of truth just that much longer.

A moment that would have been much less stressful if she didn't have her own past to contend with.

He poured two mugs decorated with Kline Tech's logo and handed her one. "Cream or sugar?"

She shook her head, taking in the surprisingly tempting aroma of the dark liquid. "Black is fine."

He sat down and waited, as if he had all the time in the world, as if he wasn't the president of a multi-million-dollar business that needed his constant attention.

She took a sip of her coffee, letting the smooth hickory flavor wash over her taste buds as she considered what to say, and then set the mug down on the glass table in front of her. Its pedestal had been designed in the form of a hunting panther. Her startled eyes took in the animal's grace and obvious menace before she turned her gaze back to the owner of her company.

Somehow that table seemed to symbolize her predicament. She felt as if in doing the right thing, she was putting herself in the path of a hungry and possibly deadly predator. "I've discovered something I feel you need to be aware of."

"Yes?" He didn't lean forward or go tense, and yet she got the distinct impression that he'd just gone from casual to subtly alert.

She unclasped her purse and withdrew the folded e-mail from inside. After unfolding it and taking unnecessary care to smooth it, she handed the paper to him. "I think someone in the marketing department may be selling corporate secrets."

He raised his brows in question but took the proffered e-mail and read it without saying a word.

"You'll notice both the sender and the recipient are blocked." She didn't know if he had, or not, but wanted to point it out to him.

He didn't reply and the longer the silence stretched, the more foolish she felt. She was making a mountain out of a molehill. The e-mail probably meant nothing, but she'd read something into it because of her past and the comments both Sandy and Marcus had made last week.

Where had she gotten the idea that the obscurely worded message had sinister undertones?

She felt her face heat with embarrassment and tried to think of something to extricate herself from the situation. How could she backpedal without sounding like a complete idiot, while also convincing Mr. Kline that she wasn't prone to dangerous bouts of melodrama?

She took too big a sip of coffee, her mind whirling, and had to breathe in through her open mouth to cool her burning tongue.

Mr. Kline looked up from the e-mail. "Are you okay?"

Hot with embarrassment, she mumbled, "Yes."

He went back to the e-mail and she felt as if she were reading it with him, so well did she know the message.

She'd read it so many times, she knew it by heart. As the exact words played once again through her brain, she rejected her earlier misgivings. She couldn't help thinking she was right. She had to convince Mr. Kline that the threat was real. She had to.

She didn't ask herself why she felt so strongly about it. She didn't need to. It felt as if Providence had put this information in her way so that she could, in some way, make up for her betrayal of CIS by alerting Mr. Kline to the reality of a similar situation at his company.

She pulled in a deep breath and tried speaking again. "I thought that combined with the number of information leaks we've had over the past few months, that message was too suspect to ignore."

He laid the paper down on the glass table, right over the panther's head. "Yes."

She couldn't hide her relief that he apparently believed her. "I'm so glad you see it the same way."

His eyes, which had been warm and benevolent

when she arrived in his office, had narrowed and darkened to resemble the predatory gaze of the panther under the glass. "How did you come by this e-mail?"

She swallowed, her mouth having gone suddenly dry. "I-I'm the admin for the new product team."

He tipped his mug of coffee to his lips, all the while his disturbingly intense gaze rested on her. "And?"

"And . . ." She inhaled and sent up a quick prayer for guidance.

She felt as if her mind had stopped working and along with it, her mouth. Did he already suspect her, even without knowledge of her past? Or had Marcus told him? She rejected that idea as ridiculous. He would not betray her that way.

"And as the admin for the team, I have access to all their e-mail. When I download mine, theirs comes in as well. I delete most of it, but sometimes I need to act on things in the messages. You know, a schedule change or if I have access to information I know a team member will need because of what's being said." She realized she was rambling and cut the flow of words.

His gray hair shone metallic in the spring sunlight coming in through the huge window behind her as he bent his head and studied the e-mail further. "So, you have no way of knowing who this e-mail was intended for?"

"No, sir. I don't."

"I see that it was written last week. I have to assume it's already been picked up and deleted from the server." His head had lifted and that intent gaze once again pinned her.

"Yes, it was gone when I checked my e-mail this morning."

"I also assume you kept a copy of this on your machine. We may be able to trail to the source yet." Satisfaction radiated in his voice.

So tense her neck ached from the strain, she confessed, "Actually, no. I, um . . . I deleted it."

He stared at her, total disbelief written on his face. "*You did what?*"

She didn't want to say it again, but she had no choice. "I deleted it."

He took a visible rein on his temper. "Do you mean you deleted it to your delete file or off of your machine completely?"

"Off my machine completely." She looked down at her coffee, not wanting to see his reaction to her words.

Silence met her statement. She waited for him to ask her why she'd done such a stupid thing, but he didn't.

Instead, he stood. "I think it's time we called Marcus in on this."

Her head lifted of its own volition. "Marcus?"

Did he mean her Marcus? His investment information consultant from CIS?

Mr. Kline didn't halt on his path to his desk. "Yes. He'll be very interested in this development."

Why would Marcus be interested in the possibility of a corporate spy working in the marketing department? She felt as if she were missing an important piece in the puzzle.

She'd come to Mr. Kline to tell him her concerns. He'd listened. He'd believed her and now he was calling Marcus. Why not internal security? Why not Allison?

She listened with fractured attention while he spoke tersely to Marcus, telling him about her discovery. From his side of the conversation, she gathered that Marcus was on his way up to Mr. Kline's office. That fact stymied her. She just could not make the connection here.

Why Marcus?

After ringing off with Marcus, Mr. Kline punched another number on his phone pad. He said Allison's name, but Veronica could not focus on the rest of the conversation.

Her mind was too occupied by the one fact that made no sense. Mr. Kline had called Marcus . . . before anyone else. Allison came into the office, carrying a notepad. She proceeded to pull two chairs that matched the ones in the waiting room into place across from the sofa and glass table. She then sat down in one of them, saying nothing to Veronica.

A minute later, the head of internal security, Ben Warren, came into the office. He said something in an undertone to Mr. Kline, who was still on the phone, and then came across the room to sit next to Allison. He smiled at Veronica and she forced herself to respond in kind, though a sense of unreality was beginning to take hold.

Seconds later, Marcus arrived. Mr. Kline hung up his phone and conferred in whispers with Marcus, glancing Veronica's way several times before both men came to join the group by the window.

She felt like an animal on display at a zoo, the way they kept looking at her. Did they expect her to stand up and do tricks? What was going on now? As more questions popped up in her mind, like numbers on an old-fashioned cash register, she tried to ignore the unease skittering along her spine and her feeling that Marcus had told Mr. Kline about her past wasn't such a silly fear after all.

Ignoring the empty chair across from the one Mr. Kline returned to, Marcus sat down on the couch next to her. Veronica gave him a sideways glance, but kept her body facing forward. She could not help wondering if he was here because he *had* told Mr. Kline about her past. Would he sit in accusation and condemnation of her now, asserting that she had something to do with the e-mail she'd shared with the company president?

The idea seemed too far-fetched to be believed, but then she realized she was not feeling or thinking in a particularly rational manner at the moment. Feeling guilty for doubting the man with whom she had so recently shared her body and part of her soul, she pushed the doubts away and focused on breathing in a normal, relaxed manner.

It wouldn't look good if she started hyperventilating for no apparent reason right there on Mr. Kline's designer leather sofa.

Marcus leaned across her and picked up the e-mail. She got a whiff of his aftershave and the clean, male scent she always associated with him. She wanted to reach out and touch him, take his hand and draw on his strength as her sense of unreality grew in proportion to the strangeness of the situation.

"Is this the message you found when you downloaded the team's e-mail last week?" he asked, turning his head so that his attention fixed firmly on her.

"Yes." She looked at him, trying to read something from his closed expression, but not succeeding.

She wished he'd smile at her, subtly brush her leg with his own, anything to reassure her that her fears were ungrounded.

"When did you receive this message?"

"Thursday." Why was *he* asking the questions? Why not Ben, *the head of internal security?*

He looked down at the paper and then back up at her. "The recipient and sender are blank. Do you have any way of telling who either might be?"

"No. I've already been over this with Mr. Kline."

Marcus shrugged. "Kline said you deleted the actual electronic message off of your system. Is that right?"

She nodded jerkily, her feeling of disorientation growing.

Looking around, she tried to gauge if the rest of the people in the room found Marcus's behavior as strange as she did. He was acting like a corporate investigator, not a consultant. Allison had her notepad flat on her lap and she'd clearly been taking notes, but there was a tension in her posture that hadn't been there before.

Mr. Kline looked expectant and Ben Warren looked both respectful and gravely interested.

Suspicion began to crawl up her spine like a black widow moving in for the kill.

She turned to Mr. Kline. "I don't understand. Why is *Marcus* asking me all these questions?"

Mr. Kline steepled his hands, resting his elbows on the armrests of his black leather chair. "Ben first came to me with his suspicion that someone was leaking important confidential information here at Kline Technology several weeks ago. We conferred and decided that bringing in outside consultation would be the best alternative."

Allison dropped her pen. She leaned over to pick it up, her movements jerky.

Ben nodded, his expression grave. "I did some research and Mr. Kline hired a firm with a reputation for getting answers in record time."

"CIS?" She could barely get the question out past the big lump of betrayal sticking in her throat.

Kline smiled lethally, his expression smug. "Yes. They're very discreet. Even you hadn't realized that they'd opened an investigative arm and you used to work for them."

As his words sank in, her feelings shattered like a plate glass window struck dead center by the *Mariners* pitcher's fastball. Marcus had been lying to her all along. He was investigating corporate espionage at her company, and suddenly every conversation they had had since his arrival in Seattle took on sinister overtones.

He'd been using her.

Her throat ached from the effort it took to hold in the curses she wanted to hurl at his head.

She'd learned to trust him.

The depth of that betrayal ripped her heart to bloody shreds as she sat there trying to appear calm.

He probably thought she was his chief suspect. And he'd made love to her. No, damn it, not love.

It had been sex. Sex to gain her trust.

The room swirled around her, but she remained upright by the sheer power of her will. She would not fall apart in front of her employer. She would not allow Marcus's betrayal to destroy her. She needed this job, now more than ever, and she wasn't going to screw it up by letting her emotions take over.

Schooling her face into an expressionless mask, she turned to Marcus. She had to appear cooperative. She couldn't risk him mistaking her desire to thwart his every endeavor as somehow indicating a false guilt on her behalf, but the last thing she wanted right now was to help the lying, conniving snake in any way.

She'd rather eat ground glass.

She couldn't quite make herself meet his eyes, but fixed her gaze on a point over his left shoulder. "Was there anything else you wanted to ask?"

His expression revealed nothing. "Why did you delete the e-mail, Ronnie?"

She couldn't prevaricate, not with the knowledge of her past simmering between them. So, she opted for honesty and hoped he would accept her explanation.

"I panicked. I thought if it was found on my machine, I would somehow be implicated."

Mr. Kline made a noise of irritation.

She flinched but kept her gaze steady in Marcus's direction.

"Why didn't you tell someone about it when you found it?"

Were all these questions leading her down a path to implicate herself?

She couldn't afford to let her mind go down that terrifying path. "I tried. I called Allison immediately and asked to see Mr. Kline, but he was out of town."

Marcus turned to Allison. "Did Miss Richards call you Thursday?"

Just having him ask the question drove home how completely Marcus didn't trust her word, and her already bleeding heart ached with a pain she could barely stand.

The other woman nodded. "She wanted an appointment with Mr. Kline, but I asked if she could wait until today. He's usually very busy his first day back from a trip and Miss Richards agreed quite easily to waiting."

Allison sat up straighter and smoothed her pad. Veronica wondered if anyone else realized the president's personal administrative assistant was nervous. Allison wasn't sure now she'd done the right thing in putting Veronica off, and she was trying to cover her backside by putting the blame back on her for the ease with which she let herself be put off.

Marcus nodded, but Allison wasn't looking at him. Her gaze was fixed on Mr. Kline, who glared at his assistant. "You could have asked what Veronica needed."

"I did try. She said she wanted to speak to you."

Even in the midst of her emotional devastation, Veronica admired the way the other woman refused to apologize or cringe in the face of her employer's rising temper.

Marcus unzipped the black case in which he kept his palm organizer and turned the small machine on. "Give me the names of the new product team."

She assumed he was speaking to her again and listed off the marketing team and the two design engineers for whom she got mail as well.

When she finished, she couldn't believe she had managed to speak to him in a normal tone of voice, when all she wanted to do was scream at him. How could he have used her that way? How could he have used her desire for him to further his investigation? It was sick.

She was sick, inside. She felt nauseous with the pain.

Marcus took notes with his stylus on the small screen.

He turned his head toward Mr. Kline. "Four of the employees Ronnie mentioned are on my list of suspects."

Mr. Kline's face had gone grim. "That narrows it down from the fifteen you mentioned in your status report yesterday."

"List of suspects?" She knew she sounded idiotic, but the reality of Marcus's investigation was sinking only slowly into her pain-fuzzed brain. He had a list of suspects fifteen people long? "Was I on the list?"

She regretted the question as soon as she asked it, but she couldn't help herself.

Mr. Kline looked pained. Marcus looked grim and she felt as if her face would crack from strain if she so much as moved a lip muscle.

She did anyway. "I was, wasn't I?"

This time she met Marcus's look dead on.

He nodded. He was trying to say something with his eyes, but she wasn't listening to messages of a personal nature from him any longer, no matter how they were presented.

"Yes, but as of today, you're off it."

Was she supposed to be glad about that? He had

just confirmed that she'd still been a suspect when he slept with her on Friday night.

"Why?" Was that shrill voice truly hers? "Maybe I'm the guilty one and I brought the e-mail to Mr. Kline's attention as a red herring."

Why was she going on in such a self-destructive way? If Marcus hadn't already started thinking along those lines, why was she leading him there?

Her emotions were getting the upper hand and she had to suppress them. There would be time to grieve later, time to hurl accusations at his head like bricks from the crumbling wall of her restraint. But not right now.

Right now she had to help him find the spy, thereby proving it wasn't her.

Ben made a soothing noise and she noticed him for the first time in several minutes.

His brown eyes twinkled at her as if she'd just told a very good joke. "Don't go talking that way. No one's going to believe a sweet little thing like you is guilty of selling off the company's secrets. Hell, anyone who knows what a rattletrap of a car you drive knows you don't have a secondary source of income."

Only someone *would* think she was guilty.

Marcus.

And he'd know he had justification for doubting her innocence. A year and a half ago, she'd done exactly what the security chief said she couldn't possibly be guilty of. She'd sold company secrets. She'd betrayed her position of confidentiality at CIS and Marcus was aware of that fact.

She'd had reasons for doing what she did though none of them had been related to wanting to be rich. Alex had wanted to destroy a company that employed hundreds of people, all for the sake of revenge. He wouldn't have been happy if he had succeeded and she wasn't at all sure his marriage would have survived. Not with his wife being the daughter of the man who owned the company.

And Veronica *had* needed money to save Jenny's life and start a new life for herself and her child. She'd gone about getting it in a way that still haunted her, but would Marcus understand that? Clearly not. Not if he'd been investigating her all along. All of the confidences she'd shared with him rose up to taunt her.

She'd told him about her parents, about Jenny, and still he'd doubted her. What did he think? That she would have sold company secrets again to pay Jenny's college tuition?

His silence since the other man's comments was telling.

Pain washed over her like a fever and she desperately needed to get out of that office before she lost it. "If you don't have any further questions, I'd like to go."

She went to stand, but Marcus laid his hand on her arm. It took every ounce of self-control she possessed not to yank it from his grasp. She remained seated, her expression one of cold disdain . . . she hoped. If the torment she felt were mirrored in her eyes, she would be mortified.

"Just one more thing."

She nodded, not trusting her voice to speak.

"Is it possible for me to get the same access you have to the team's e-mail?"

"Not without Jack's okay."

"He's on the list," Mr. Kline said.

Marcus frowned. "We can't go that way. I'll have to use your system for that angle on my investigation."

Have Marcus in her cubicle on a regular basis after the way he'd betrayed her? She couldn't bear it.

She swallowed past the constriction in her throat. "Fine. Anything else?"

She had to get out of the office. Now.

Marcus withdrew his hand from her arm. "Not right now. If I think of anything, we can go over it at lunch."

He thought she was still having lunch with him? With his ego, he probably thought she would still willingly go to bed with him too.

She wanted to tell him to go to hell. She wanted to stomp on his toe and grind the heel of her pump into the soft leather of his loafers. She wanted to pour her now cold coffee right over his arrogant blond head, but she did none of those things.

She stood and turned to go.

"Veronica," Mr. Kline said.

She stopped halfway to the door. "Yes?"

"Thank you for bringing the e-mail to my attention. Not every employee would willingly get involved in something like this."

She nodded jerkily and started walking again. Just ten more feet and she would be free, free of Marcus's presence and free of an audience when her emotions felt on the verge of exploding.

Those ten feet felt like ten miles, but finally she was out of the office. She sagged against Allison's desk.

How could she have been so stupid? So gullible? How could she have believed Marcus's smooth talk about a future? He was allergic to futures and deadly opposed to commitment.

Well, there was no way in the world or her place on it that she would be sharing lunch or anything else with Marcus Danvers—ever again.

Chapter Fifteen

Allison waited until Ben and Marcus had left George's office before speaking.

"You've had a company investigating a possible corporate spy here at Kline Technology?"

He looked up from his notes and his expression made it clear he was surprised she was still there.

Why wouldn't he be? She didn't linger in his presence during the day. It wasn't allowed. He expected her to suppress her emotions completely, to play the office robot, so no one would suspect the president of the company of fraternizing with his PA.

"I thought that was obvious."

"You didn't tell me."

"There was no need to have you involved."

"I'm your personal assistant."

"Yes, but you aren't my shadow. I'm capable of making a business decision or two without you." The sarcasm stung, but she ignored the pain.

She had grown accustomed to his brusque manner. He made up for it in the off hours. Or at least she'd told herself he did.

"Was I on the list?"

It was the question Veronica Richards had asked. The same emotional devastation she'd seen in the younger woman's eyes filled Allison at the possibility the answer would be yes.

"That's not important. In fact, this conversation is not a value add. If you're finished, I'd like to get back to work."

"Don't you dare use your business double-speak on me. Answer the damn question."

George laid his papers aside, with exaggerated precision. "Would you care to repeat that, Ms. Jennings?"

"Answer. The. Damn. Question."

His eyes opened wide in shock. He'd expected her to back down when he started his lord-of-all-he-surveyed imitation, but she didn't even care if she got fired right then.

Something far more important was at stake than her job.

Her heart.

"Yes, you were on the list."

"So, you chose not to tell me about the investigation. Because I was a suspect."

"You had access to all the information that was leaked," he said, which was neither affirmation nor a denial of her assertion.

"I had access to information that could have been far more damaging to your company and I didn't leak it."

"You didn't leak anything. The source has been

identified as coming from the marketing department."

The physical weight of disappointment pressed against her. "You didn't think that as your lover I deserved something more than to be kept in the dark?"

"You know I don't let my personal life affect my business decisions."

He was so arrogant, he should have been born royalty.

"I thought we had something special."

"I would prefer not to discuss this now."

She stared at him, her body aching from the emotions she was suppressing. "If I do want to discuss it?"

"I will remind you that you are my PA, not my wife. When we are in this building, my wishes reign supreme."

When didn't they?

She turned on her heel, intent on getting out of that room before she did something she would regret, like tell the arrogant SOB just what he could do with his job.

"Allison."

She stopped at the door.

"Are you going to be okay?"

She nodded her head in a jerky movement. "Yes."

"Good. I wasn't looking forward to calling in a temp. There's a lot of work to get through this afternoon."

And that told her. She might make him feel like a teenager, but sex was secondary to her role as his PA. And sex was all it was, she realized, in a blinding moment of clarity.

He'd never once taken her out on a date.

He'd never introduced her to his grown children or asked if he could meet hers.

The only personal part of their relationship was her role as his *personal* assistant.

And it was the only role she played in his life that really mattered to him. Unfortunately, it was a role she could not play any longer.

Marcus tracked Ronnie down in the supply room for the marketing department.

Although *room* was too strong a word for the enclosed space created out of one wall separator covered by open shelving and two very large metal storage cabinets. Located on the opposite side of the building from his and Ronnie's cubicles, it had been low on his list of places to look when he discovered she wasn't around when he went to pick her up for lunch.

Looking at the neat shelves, stacked with every sort of office supply imaginable and labeled for efficiency, he had no doubt that Ronnie was responsible for the room's upkeep and the ordering of supplies.

She had the tall metal door to one cabinet open and her head and upper body were hidden in its interior. All he could see was the delectable outline of her bottom and thighs in her neatly trimmed gray slacks.

He would have preferred a skirt cut about six inches above her knee, but the figure-flattering pants were the next best thing. She probably thought they were the perfect disguise for her sexy little body. She thought wrong.

"Weren't we supposed to meet at eleven-thirty for lunch?"

A muffled exclamation emanated from behind the door, and then Ronnie stumbled backward with all the natural grace of a drunk leaving a bar at closing time.

"*Marcus.*" She looked shocked to see him.

It wasn't like her to forget an appointment, but, then, the events of the morning no doubt upset her. He hadn't liked her obvious tension during the meeting in Kline's office, but he had no doubt fear that her past would be exposed had been its source.

She was probably worrying herself sick that he'd told Kline about her actions before leaving CIS.

He would set her mind to rest about that over lunch. And they could talk out some other stuff too, like the fact that he'd had to hide his real reason for being at Kline Technology from her.

She would understand. Ronnie was a sensible soul, and in all fairness, she couldn't blame him for suspecting her of the espionage. She had to admit the circumstances were pretty damning.

Besides, once he told her that he had never had any intention of letting her be hurt by it, she would understand that he'd done what he had to do for the job. It had almost torn him apart, but he hadn't had a choice. He had never felt as much relief in his life as he had felt when Kline called to tell him of Ronnie's discovery. He'd known deep in his gut right then that she was innocent.

"It's almost noon, honey. It wasn't easy to find you."

In fact, he'd had to search the entire floor before running her to earth in the supply room.

She drew herself erect, her expression a cool mask that made him nervous. "Maybe I didn't want to be found."

He didn't like hearing that. And he really didn't like the way she was looking at him, as if he were dog poop she'd discovered on the bottom of her sensible gray pumps.

"Why would you hide from me, baby?"

Her eyes narrowed, and for the space of one second, her expression was lethal enough to send him six feet under.

Then the cool mask fell in place again. "I am not your baby. I am not your honey. I am not your *anything*. Therefore, I would appreciate you not using meaningless and subsequently demeaning endearments to address me."

Meaningless? Demeaning? This was getting out of hand. The least she could do was find out if he'd told Kline about her past before getting all annoyed and making rash statements like she wasn't his *anything*.

"What the hell are you talking about?"

Her perfectly arched brows rose above the black frame of her glasses. "It's quite simple. You can stop your smarmy seduction techniques. I'll cooperate fully with you for the investigation. So, there is absolutely no need for you to sacrifice your body for the job."

She had moved backward until she stood as far away from him as the small space allowed, and it irritated the bejeebes out of him. She was acting like she couldn't stand to be near him, not to mention the fact that she was going on about his investigation as if they were in a secure environment—which they were not.

"I don't think talking about my job is a good idea right now," he said warningly, in a low voice. And then as the rest of her words registered completely, anger surged through him and his voice went up a couple of decibels. "*Smarmy seduction techniques?*"

Her soft lips compressed in a tight line and he wanted to kiss them until they were red and swollen, until she stopped using them to spout garbage like that.

Forcing his voice to a more even keel, he said, "I don't know what you're talking about, but I can pretty much guarantee we're not going to discuss it here."

No way was he going to get into an argument about the *sacrifice* of his body where one of her coworkers could overhear, and if she mentioned the investigation again, it might very well be compromised.

"We don't need to *discuss* it anywhere. As far as I'm concerned, the only relationship we have from this point forward is a professional one limited to the—"

He cut her off before she mentioned his real reason for being at Kline Tech again. "*Ronnie.*"

She looked cool enough to chill ice cream, but looks were deceiving because she wasn't using her head or a guard on her tongue. She was obviously a lot more upset than she wanted to let on. Once they talked, it was going to be okay, but he had to get her out of the building before she blew his cover.

Not giving her a chance to say something else incriminating or irritating, he grabbed her arm. "Come on. We're going to lunch."

She tried to tug her arm from his grip and he let her go in order to move his hand to her waist. Her already unyielding body went into iceberg mode and he swore under his breath.

Working things out between them after this morning's revelations wasn't going to be as easy as he'd thought. He could live with that, but they *would* work them out because there was no way in hell he was going to lose her again.

He dragged her by her cubicle to grab her purse and then led her out of the building, stopping on the way to check out with security. He practically had to shove her into the passenger seat of his Jag, but once she was inside she didn't make any idiotic attempts to jump right back out again. For that, he was grateful.

Chasing her across the parking lot could only lead to further complications.

They'd been driving for maybe five minutes when she asked in freezing tones, "Where are you taking me for lunch?"

"My place," he answered, without hesitation.

Rejection radiated from every pore of her stiffly held body. "Forget it."

He flicked his gaze over her before turning his attention back to the road. She stared straight out the windshield and refused to meet his gaze.

"We have several sensitive matters to discuss and that cannot be done in a public setting. It's either my place or yours," he added, hoping to soften her anger by giving her a choice.

Her hands clenched into fists against her thighs. "Why can't we talk in a park, or something?"

He switched on the windshield wipers as spring rain spattered the windshield. "Because this is the Northwest and there are only a handful of days out of the year on which a park would make a good setting for a discussion of any kind. Today isn't one of them."

He'd meant to insert a little humor into the tense atmosphere, but from her rigid profile, he gathered it hadn't worked.

"So, what's it to be?" he asked.

"Your place."

He took that to mean that as little as she wanted to return to his apartment, she wanted him in hers even less. Would she try to slam the door in his face tonight when he showed up for dinner as planned? He shrugged off the thought to focus on the present. It definitely had enough trouble of its own.

He pulled into a drive-through for a Mexican fast-food chain. "What do you want?"

She continued to gaze fixedly out the window, not giving an inch. "Nothing. I'm not hungry."

He ordered her a soft taco and a diet pop. He ordered himself a meal with a large root beer. He'd never acquired a taste for cola. He handed her the bag of food and drink tray before driving off. Once they reached his apartment complex, he took the food back and carried it up to his place.

She followed him, carefully maintaining her distance.

When they reached his apartment door, he couldn't help grinning at her with just a shade of wicked humor. "Could you grab my keys out of my pocket? My hands are full."

He'd meant to tease and she fell for it like a water balloon dropped out of a second-story window. Her eyes got all crinkly and her mouth pursed as if she'd just sucked a lemon wedge, showing she'd taken him seriously.

Alex was right, one day Marcus's sense of humor was going to get him in real trouble.

Grabbing the food, she snarled, "Get them yourself."

He sighed and did as she said, opening the door and stepping back only far enough to let her pass. "Ladies first."

He knew he was pushing her, but he'd learned eighteen months ago that if he gave her even a small breathing space, she'd use it to erect every emotional barrier known to man.

Still, she looked as if she wanted to kick him, and he had to bite back another grin. Even pissed, he loved teasing her. She was just such an easy target. Besides, anything was better than that automaton façade she'd been hiding behind again. She sidled through the small opening, managing to escape touching him. Barely.

She headed straight for the kitchen and plopped the bag and the drinks on the table when she got there. He came in behind her and set the food out.

She frowned at the taco he'd put in front of her as she sat rigidly in a metal-framed chair. "I said I wasn't hungry."

"So, don't eat it, but my mother would skin me alive if she found out I bought myself lunch and left my date to starve."

"I'm not your date," she grated, from between gritted teeth.

Her insistence on that score was starting to get to him. "Did we, or did we not have a lunch *date* for today?"

She ripped the paper off her straw with enough force to bend the plastic. "*Had* is the operative word. I broke it."

"You're here, aren't you?"

"To discuss your investigation, nothing else." She closed her lips over the plastic straw and took a drink of the diet cola, her expression full of furious disgust.

He'd never been jealous of a straw before and hoped never to be again, but right then that little piece of plastic tubing was a hell of a lot closer to Ronnie's lips than he was likely to get.

"Fine, let's discuss the investigation."

She stared at him in silence, clearly expecting him to open the conversation. He wasn't going to disappoint her.

"I didn't tell Kline about what happened at CIS and I have no plans to do so." He waited for her to smile at him again, to say she was glad.

Relief flickered in her eyes before she schooled her features into immobility again. "Why?"

Okay, he couldn't say he hadn't expected that question. His answer should please her. "As long as you aren't guilty, there's no reason for him to know."

She played with the edges of the wrapper around her soft taco, then fixed him with gray eyes filled with condemnation. "But you *were* planning to tell him if you *thought* I was guilty?"

He didn't like the direction their conversation was taking, but he wouldn't lie to her. "Yes."

Instead of telling him what a jerk he was to have had plans to hurt her like that and giving him a chance to explain his good intentions, her lashes dropped to veil her gaze.

"I see," was all she said.

"But you aren't guilty, so we don't have anything to worry about." He wanted to make that very clear.

He trusted her.

Her lashes came up and her gaze locked with his, her clear gray eyes mirroring naked disgust. "There is not and has never been any *we* about this. If you had decided I was guilty and told Mr. Kline about my past, *I* would have paid the price. So, don't you dare talk about *us* being worried about *anything*."

"You think I would have just thrown you to the wolves?" After Friday night? After the way he'd shared his soul with her, his past?

Anger and frustration washed through him as she nodded.

"Why not?" she asked. "You were hired to do a job. Discovering the woman who had betrayed you was guilty of the crime you'd been hired to investigate could only be a perk. Not only do I think you would have thrown me to the wolves, but I think you would have enjoyed it."

He felt like she'd landed a sucker punch to his gut. "You think I wanted some kind of revenge?"

"What else was that sordid scene here the other night about, if not revenge?"

She'd posed it as a question, but he had no

doubt that she thought she already knew the answer. She thought he'd made love to her to somehow get back at her for her actions eighteen months
ago. The fact that she could believe such a thing
after the way he'd opened up to her hurt and it fed
the anger already seething in him.

"That sordid scene, as you call it, had everything
to do with me wanting you and not a damn thing
to do with getting back at you for deserting me
eighteen months ago."

"Oh, really?" She managed to infuse those two
words with a wealth of sarcastic disbelief.

"Yes. Damn it, what we have together is too special to mix it up with ugly motives like revenge."
He couldn't accept that she truly doubted that.

She lounged back in her chair, her fingers playing idly against the table. "We had sex and there's
nothing special about sex. It happens all the time,
especially for you."

He wanted to strangle her, but more than that,
he wanted to make love to her and force her to
admit that it was more than sex, more than revenge, more than her present anger let her admit.

How could she sit there looking so relaxed after
saying something like that?

"If it happened all the time, why were we *both*
celibate for the past eighteen months?"

She shrugged. "Maybe your sex drive is flagging.
You *are* almost thirty."

He refused to react to that pointed slam against
his masculinity. Instead he demanded, "What's your
excuse?"

"I was celibate the first twenty-three years of my
life. Sex was the aberration, not the lack of it. I can

assure you it wasn't anything *special*—not the sex and not the abstinence after it."

He knew she was angry. He realized that she had some crazy ideas about why he'd made love to her, but the words still stung a raw path through his insides. She had the power to hurt him like no one else in his life, not even his mother.

And because of that, because his emotions were raw, he retreated. "Maybe we should go back to the original topic, Kline Tech's corporate spy. We can talk about our relationship when you're feeling more rational."

"We don't have a relationship to discuss."

He let that slide. What else could he do? If he pushed it and she remained adamant, he didn't think he could handle the pain that would result.

It felt way too much like the fear he'd experienced once before when he was eleven years old. And that time the fear had been justified.

He'd been at the park in his hometown when he realized his dad was in the crowd watching a baseball game.

By then he'd known he wasn't his father's legitimate son. He'd learned to live with the fact that his dad was never seen in public with him and his mom. Or he thought he had, but that summer day he had wanted to sit with his dad watching the ball game. So, he had summoned up his courage and climbed onto the bleachers, squeezing into a spot next to him.

Marcus knew his dad would be angered by his actions, but he'd decided he could face his dad's wrath. What he hadn't realized was that he'd exposed himself to something far worse. His dad had sat next to him through the remaining six innings and pretended not to know who he was. An eleven-year-old kid had sat there biting back tears and dying inside.

When his dad showed up the next night to visit him and his mom, Marcus had made sure he was out. His dad had told his mom what had happened.

She'd come to Marcus and tried to explain about a prominent man in the community not being able to risk public censure. About how divorce wasn't an option for his dad because of his religious beliefs. Stuff she'd said before. Stuff he'd believed and listened to, but Marcus had stopped believing. He never acknowledged his dad again.

Not the next time Mark came to visit and not two years later when his mom and Mark got married. He'd lived in Mark's house for five years, but he had remained distant from the family his mother and father had created with their marriage. He didn't belong and he never forgot that fact.

Marcus pushed the painful thoughts away. "I'll need to check your e-mail regularly to try to catch another one of those messages, but I'll be honest—I'm not holding out much hope."

"Why not?" She seemed a little surprised by his return to the investigation.

Had she wanted him to argue with her about their relationship? He wasn't going to play that kind of guessing game with himself. Seventeen years ago he'd tried to convince himself that his dad would be glad to sit with him. He'd been wrong.

"I'm assuming the fact you download the team's e-mail is not a big secret, so we have to go on the belief that your getting that particular message was a fluke."

She sat in silence for several seconds, unwrapping her taco and taking a bite in what appeared to be an automatic reaction to having food in front of her.

She finished chewing. "So you think our spy doesn't regularly communicate via e-mail?"

"Or he has a set time for sending messages, like in the middle of the night, when you wouldn't be likely to make a check on the team's e-mail. Our spy could be picking up his messages via remote access from home, or he could get into the office before you in the morning. You're a creature of habit and all he'd have to do is pick up his e-mail by seven-thirty to be certain you wouldn't see the message once it was cleaned up off the server."

He'd been musing out loud, trying to work out the logistics in his mind as he spoke, but it made sense.

Ronnie seemed to think so too because she nodded as she took another bite of the unwanted taco. He carefully controlled his urge to smile triumphantly. She did not need to miss any meals, in his opinion.

"So why bother checking my e-mail?"

"The spy screwed up once; he could always do it again."

"I guess. Marcus?"

He'd taken a bite of his own food. The spicy beef burned in a way he liked.

He swallowed. "Yeah?"

"You seem pretty convinced of my innocence, now."

"Yeah."

They ate in silence for several minutes.

"Why?" she asked, as she carefully folded the paper wrapper from her taco into a small square.

He wasn't sure. He had wanted her to be innocent all along. It had taken all his dedication to professionalism to keep her in the dark about his role as an investigator and not compromise his job at Kline Tech. He wasn't going to tell her that, though. She'd probably accuse him of lying. She was feeling pretty feisty right now.

Better to stick to the prosaic, then drift into the realm of emotion again. "You wouldn't have taken that e-mail to Kline if you were guilty."

"Maybe I just wanted to throw suspicion off of me."

And maybe her next job would be dancing naked on tabletops.

Even thinking about such a thing made him frown. "Not likely."

"Why not? It would make sense. I know you know my past. Maybe I was sure you wouldn't tell Mr. Kline about it if you thought I was innocent."

He didn't know why she was talking like this, but he had every intention of setting her straight. "First, you didn't know I was the corporate investigator. You would have had no reason to believe that Kline would share the information with me once you'd told him. Second, if you had been the spy, why try throwing the scent now? No one knows about the investigation but Kline, Warren and now Allison."

"And me."

"Yeah, you know, too. But, the point is, you didn't."

"Are you sure about that?"

He glared at her. "Yes, I'm sure. Why are you trying to convince me you're guilty?"

Her complexion went pasty. "I'm not. Damn. I just can't seem to keep my mouth shut, can I?"

She sounded really rattled and she'd sworn.

He reached out and grabbed her hand and squeezed it. He wanted to do more. He wanted to hold her, but he didn't think she was ready for that yet. Her gaze flew to his and he saw the vulnerability she'd tried to hide earlier.

"Don't worry, baby. I know you're innocent and you aren't going to convince me otherwise with a whole bunch of nonsense."

She shook her head as if to clear it and pulled her hand away from his. "You came to that conclusion five days too late."

Once again, he didn't like the sound of her words. "What do you mean? I know you're innocent now and that's all that matters."

She stood up. "You're wrong. You used my desire for you to gain my trust. You made love to me believing I was the spy you'd been hired to find. I'll never forget that. I can't. And I can't forgive it either."

Chapter Sixteen

Ronnie's personnel file open in front of him, Marcus sat at his desk two hours later, wondering where the hell the spitfire masquerading as an office automaton got off talking about forgiveness.

Eighteen months ago she'd betrayed his trust and deserted him without a backward glance. *And she'd done it carrying his child.*

A son.

His hands clenched so tightly that the muscles in his forearms ached in protest.

According to the file, their son was ten months old. The same age as Isabel and Alex's daughter. Gut-wrenching pain tugged at his insides. Ronnie had given birth to Aaron Marcus Richards in a French hospital without so much as a phone call telling him of his son's existence.

She'd dismissed Marcus from her life as easily as his father had dismissed his existence between visits.

Tidal wave in its proportions, the most overpowering sensation of rage he'd ever felt washed over him. Ronnie hadn't just dismissed him from her life; she'd excluded him from his son's life as well. His son had cut his first tooth without Marcus knowing a damn thing about it. He'd learned to roll over. He'd learned to crawl.

Marcus thought of all the things Alex's baby girl had done over the past ten months and alien moisture burned his eyes as he was forced to accept the fact that he'd lost all that with his own son. He'd seen his little adopted niece smile for the first time with a tooth. He'd seen her crawl across the floor to pounce on a stuffed red bear he'd bought her at Christmas. He'd watched her try to take her first step and fall flat on her diapered bottom.

He'd scooped her off the floor and offered comfort before Isabel could stop laughing long enough to leave her chair.

Had Aaron tried to walk yet? Did he cry when he was tired, or just fall asleep? Did he like applesauce, or did he spit it out like little Hope?

Marcus's eyes burned with moisture that just would not go away, no matter how many times he blinked. *He didn't even know what his son looked like.*

Ronnie had said she loved him on Friday night.

A bitter crack of laughter erupted from his throat and he wanted to slam his fist right through the fabric-covered cubicle wall. *Love.* Right.

Ronnie felt something for him, but he wouldn't call it love. Love encompassed trust. She had assumed he'd taken her to bed to earn hers. She had said so, not two hours ago. He bit back another laugh. *As if.* As if he was ever in danger of doing that.

She hadn't trusted him eighteen months ago, not enough to tell him about her desperation for Jenny, not enough to tell him about the child they'd created together, and she didn't trust him worth a damn now, either. She'd withheld her worries over the e-mail she had accidentally downloaded. She'd hidden knowledge of their son from him.

She *wanted* him. He gave her body pleasure. He'd awakened her to a new experience. Sex. She'd said it hadn't been anything special. He had wanted to think she was lying because she had been angry at the time, but now he knew the truth.

Lust. Now *there* was a word that fit her supposed feelings for him. Anchored in the physical, unrelated to the deeper emotions, lust was the beginning and the ending of what she felt. She had wanted to dress it up, pretend it was something more, something her prudish little mind could deal with, but if it had been he wouldn't be sitting in a borrowed office cubicle discovering the existence of his son for the first time from a personnel file.

He jumped upright, propelling his chair backward several feet. He slammed her file closed and shoved it in the locking cabinet above his computer monitor along with the files of the other Kline Technology employees who were no longer suspects. Grabbing the remaining four files, he tore out of his office.

He had to get away. He couldn't stand being able to hear the soft tones of her voice over the cubicle walls. He couldn't stand knowing she was only a few feet away not feeling the way he did. He didn't trust himself in the same building with her. He couldn't.

She'd hurt him, but that wasn't the worst of it. She'd hurt their son.

She had condemned Aaron to a childhood without a father who belonged to him—just as Marcus's own parents had done—and he couldn't stand it.

Bile rose in his throat and he picked up his pace until he was practically sprinting from the building.

Veronica's doorbell rang at six o'clock that evening. She put down the small plastic plane she'd been using to entertain Aaron. Standing up, she smoothed the oversized cotton shirt over her black denim leggings. She and her son were alone in the apartment. Jenny had gone to the library as planned. Veronica hadn't wanted to tell her sister about the day's events at Kline Tech. She hadn't wanted to upset the younger woman.

Nor had she wanted to share a pain that felt too personal even for a sisterly confidence.

She had been dreaming of futures and forever with Marcus when all he'd been doing was cementing his investigation, following up on a lead. Her.

Looking out through the peephole, she saw a bright blue Hawaiian shirt and her hand froze on its way to the doorknob. Her gaze skittered back to her son playing happily on the carpet and, then, against her volition, she fixed her eye on the peephole again.

She couldn't see his face. He was standing too close, but she had no doubt whatsoever who stood on the other side of the door. Marcus.

His fist pounded on the door. "Open up, Ronnie. I know you're home. Your car's in the lot."

Why was he here? Her thoughts flew erratically from one option to another.

She could pretend not to have heard him, but then he'd keep pounding on the door and most likely disturb a neighbor. She could whisk Aaron into the bedroom and try to get rid of Marcus before he realized a baby was in the apartment. She could pretend to be baby-sitting for a friend.

Or she could tell him the truth.

No matter what the present condition of her personal relationship with Marcus, she could not in all conscience continue to hide their child from him. She had planned to tell him tonight. Now fate had forced her hand and in one sense she wasn't sorry. She had never felt good about hiding the truth.

He pounded again, his voice booming through the door loudly enough to arrest Aaron in his play. "*Open the damn door, Ronnie!*"

Wiping her sweating palms down the front of her jeans, she did so before a concerned neighbor called the police to report a domestic disturbance. As she pulled the door toward her, she beheld Marcus as she had never seen him.

Other than the signature Hawaiian shirt, he could have been a different man. His hair stuck straight up, like he'd been running his hands through it, and his ready smile was conspicuously absent. In fact, his mobile mouth was set in the grimmest line she'd ever seen.

His eyes were bloodshot, as if he'd been out on an all-night drinking binge. Since she'd seen him only five hours earlier, she knew that wasn't the case. It almost looked as if he'd been crying, but the idea of Marcus giving in to such maudlin emotion was so unreal she dismissed it.

No way would their argument earlier have affected him so deeply. It just wasn't possible.

"I want to see my son." Gravelly with unmistakable pain, his voice arrested her.

Lightning fast, his words penetrated her thoughts. He *knew*.

And the knowledge was tearing him apart. Guilt warred with sorrow as mute, she slowly stepped back to allow Marcus entrance into the apartment.

His gaze zeroed in on Aaron immediately and unnatural stillness overcame his tall frame. "He's got blond hair."

The words sounded choked and she studied his face with fearful intensity. He looked savaged.

"Yes. He looks a lot like you," she practically whispered, for lack of anything better to say. "How did you find out?"

Had someone at Kline Tech said something? Sandy, maybe.

The look he gave her froze the marrow in her bones. "Certainly not from you. I read your personnel file."

"You did what?" She didn't mean it as an accusation. She simply didn't understand. When had he read her file? If he'd done so before, when he thought she was guilty, he wouldn't just now be showing up at her apartment.

Why would he read it now?

He turned his attention momentarily from Aaron to fix it on her and she wished he hadn't.

She'd never seen true hatred in Marcus's eyes before, not even when he'd first come to Seattle. She realized the emotion she'd seen then had been a pale reflection of the feelings seething in him now.

"I read your file. I had files on all the suspects, but I didn't want to read yours. I didn't want you to be the culprit, so I tried to focus my investigation in other places." The words sounded disjointed, as if Marcus's normally agile brain wasn't working at its full capacity.

His gaze slipped back to Aaron and settled there.

Their son sat on the carpet, gnawing on the end of a toy caboose, oblivious to his parents' intense emotions.

The import of what Marcus said penetrated. He hadn't wanted her to be guilty? He'd tried to find a more likely suspect?

"But you read it."

Why had he read the file if he trusted in her innocence?

Pain mixed with the loathing in his brilliant blue eyes as his attention reverted to her once again. "You said you couldn't forgive me today. You insisted I take you back to the office. I didn't know when you'd let me be close to you again. It was like some kind of compulsion. I read it as a way of being with you. Isn't that pathetic?"

The self-derision in his voice lacerated her. He sounded like he truly cared, like she'd really hurt him with her rejection at lunch. Just as she'd been hurt.

"N-no, not pathetic . . ." Her voice just trailed off because she didn't know what else to say.

He wasn't listening anyway.

He'd gone back to looking at Aaron. "Is he afraid of strangers?"

The question sent an arrow of guilt to pierce her heart. Marcus shouldn't be a stranger to his own son and it was all her fault.

She swallowed before speaking. "Not usually."

As Marcus moved farther into the room, closer to the baby, she prayed Aaron would react favorably.

Marcus hunkered down beside Aaron and reached out to touch the baby's soft blond hair with one tentative finger. "He's beautiful."

Her heart was breaking. "Yes."

"Does he walk yet?"

"No, but it isn't for lack of trying. I expect he'll be early. He has been on just about everything else. He got his first tooth when he was four months old and he already says *no, mama* and *jen-jen.*"

Aaron turned to study the blond giant beside him with open curiosity. He reached out one pudgy hand and touched a blue flower on Marcus's shirt; then he smiled and Veronica felt tears fill her eyes.

"Hi, buddy. I'm Daddy. You'll learn to say that too."

As Marcus introduced himself to their son, she had to suck in air to stop a sob from escaping. How could she ever have believed Marcus wouldn't want to know about his child?

"I'm sorry, Marcus." Tears thickened her voice.

He shook his head, as if dismissing her words. "Not now. I don't want to get into this in front of him."

"Yes. All right."

He sat down and picked up the plastic plane she'd been flying over Aaron's head earlier. Making the sound of a jet engine, he pretend flew it in front of Aaron's rapt gaze.

Landing the plane on Aaron's corduroy-covered legs, Marcus allowed the baby to grab the toy and shove it into his mouth.

"I should have waited to come over until I had myself completely under control, but I couldn't. I've already missed ten months. It probably sounds crazy, but I couldn't wait even another twenty-four hours."

She bit her lip until she tasted blood. "No, not crazy."

The next hour and a half flew by as Marcus and Aaron got acquainted. They played on the carpet, at one point Marcus lying down to let Aaron climb all over him and explore to his heart's content.

Veronica made dinner while Marcus held the baby on his hip and watched. After they had eaten a late meal and Marcus had fed Aaron, the baby almost falling asleep in his high chair, she decided it was time to put him to bed.

The last ninety minutes had exhausted Aaron and she felt limp as a wet dishrag herself. She'd been going through the emotional wringer since finding out about Marcus's role as a corporate investigator, and this evening had only added crushing remorse to the list of emotions vying for supremacy in her overburdened heart.

Every time the baby smiled at his daddy, every time Marcus's eyes misted over, she felt a burden of guilt that weighed with ten months' worth of memories she'd denied them both.

Surprisingly, Marcus didn't argue when she said it was time to put their son to bed.

He helped her dress Aaron in his jammies after changing the baby's diaper. As in every other aspect of his interaction with Aaron that evening, Marcus showed himself to be truly proficient with little people. He hadn't been exaggerating when he had said he was a stand-in uncle for Alex and Isabel's baby girl.

He laid their son in the crib and then stood with his hand on Aaron's back for several silent minutes while their child slipped into the oblivion of sleep.

Blinking back more stupid, useless tears, she led Marcus into the living room. "We need to talk."

He nodded but asked, "Where's your sister?"

"At the library. She's researching a paper. She should be home between eight-thirty and nine."

Thank the Lord Jenny had gone. Veronica could not imagine what the evening would have been like considering Marcus's antagonism toward her and Jenny's similar feelings toward him.

"That doesn't give us much time to talk."

She bit her lip and winced when she encountered the abrasion she'd caused earlier.

No it didn't, an hour, maybe an hour and a half. But then it wouldn't matter how much time she had, saying she was sorry would never be enough for keeping Marcus in the dark for the first ten months of his son's life.

"Do you want coffee?"

He sat down on one end of the sofa. "No."

She took her usual place, moving her bag of crochet to the floor. "I know it doesn't make up for not telling you about him, but I'm so very sorry."

Marcus's jaw hardened. "Why?"

She didn't pretend to misunderstand what he was asking. "I didn't think you'd want to know. I mean you had this thing against commitment and you'd made it clear we didn't have any kind of future. I just assumed you'd feel the same way about a baby."

He fixed her with disbelieving eyes and she blurted out the rest of the truth. "And I was afraid."

"Afraid of what?" he demanded, his tone raw.

He was only at the other end of the sofa, but she felt as if he was on the other side of an uncrossable abyss.

"That you would try to take him from me. I'd betrayed you, sold company secrets, and I knew you didn't love me. It's no excuse, but I wasn't thinking straight at the time. I was too distraught about Jenny to consider your rights as a father rationally when my whole world was falling apart."

His blue eyes chilled her. "Actually, I can understand your initial panic. You *weren't* thinking straight or you never would have sold out Alex, but I still don't understand why my son is ten months old and I had to find out about him from a personnel file."

A small measure of relief washed over her.

At least on this count, she wasn't completely guilty. "I planned to tell you about him tonight. That's what I was trying to tell you Friday."

"I thought . . ." his voice trailed off.

"You thought I was going to tell you I was guilty of espionage." She'd already worked that one out. "Well, surprise, surprise. I'm not."

"Finding out I had a son was a hell of a lot more surprising than discovering you were innocent." The slashing pain in his eyes made her regret her momentary lapse into sarcasm.

"I know. I'm sorry," she said again.

"Aaron was your idea of a *visual aid?*"

Grabbing the bag of crochet, she pulled out Aaron's blanket and started working on it. She needed something to keep her grounded. It also gave her an excuse to avoid his gaze.

"I know it's hard for you to understand. You're so blatant about everything, but I just didn't know how to tell you about him. I couldn't get the words out and even if I could have, I didn't know what they should be."

"Marcus, you have a ten-month-old son?" he suggested, with biting irony.

She focused on the bright blue yarn in her hands and took a deep breath and expelled it slowly. "Yes, well, as I said, you're blunt."

"Honest."

That had her looking up from the blanket in a hurry. "Oh? And what aspect of honesty covers pretending to be a corporate information consultant when you were in reality investigating me as a suspected espionage agent?"

His blue eyes blazed with fury. "That was my job and don't you dare pretend it stands on par with you denying my paternal rights for ten months of my son's life."

Her hands twisted in the yarn. "How can you sit there in such sanctimonious judgment? You were preparing to rip apart the life I've worked desperately hard to piece together for my son and sister.

You used my desire for you as a weapon against me and you sit there saying—"

She stopped speaking midsentence when he jumped off the couch to tower over her. "I'm sick and tired of you accusing me of using sex as a weapon with you. Do you remember me telling you I hadn't been with another woman since you left me?"

She had no choice but to nod in agreement. He had said that and she had believed him. She still did, which didn't say a lot for her intelligence level.

"Do you remember me telling you I wanted to make love? That I didn't just want sex with you? That I was looking for a future?"

His voice grated rawly against her nerves, and she gave a jerky nod of assent to each of his biting questions.

"I took you to my bed on Friday night because I wanted you. Because, God help me, I needed you."

"Marcus—"

His hand slashed the air. "No. I'm doing the talking now. You've accused me of using you when all I wanted to do was protect you. Even if you had been guilty, I had every intention of going to Kline on your behalf and begging for mercy to protect your reputation if I needed to. I understood the desperation and pressure you've felt since your parents' deaths. I wanted to help you, but you couldn't damn well trust me today any more than you did a year and a half ago."

His gaze burned down at her, his face taut with suppressed emotion. She could not discern in his current state even a shadow of the laid-back charmer she had always known.

"You lied to me," she said helplessly.

"I lied to myself, too. I told myself that you really cared about me and that your lack of trust eighteen months ago was the result of the tremendous stress you were under."

She was afraid to say anything else. He was so serious, so painfully angry.

He clenched his fists and turned away. "We're going to get married as soon as possible."

Chapter Seventeen

"We're going to what?"

He couldn't have said what she thought he'd said. Not after telling her how little he thought of her. No way. A man did not jump from accusations of mistrust to proposals of marriage. Did he?

He spun around to face her again, the tenseness in his body exhibiting the same stress she felt. "You heard me. We are getting married."

Disbelief warred with hysteria as she tried to grasp what could be prompting him to make such a ludicrous statement. "We are *not* getting married."

"Oh, yes, we are. And as soon as is humanly possible."

He sounded so certain, as if she had nothing to say in the matter, as if he took her agreement for granted.

"Marcus, this may have escaped your attention, but we are not living in the Middle Ages and you are not some despotic potentate that can order a woman to do his bidding. This is the twenty-first century and men have to ask women to marry them."

"Like you asked me if you could withhold my son from me for almost the whole first year of his life?"

She didn't want to go there. Too much guilt ran along that roadway and the potential for her defeat. She decided to take a different tack. Logic.

"Why are you saying this? You can't possibly want to marry me. You looked at me like you hated me when you came in here tonight."

"How did you expect me to look?"

She refused to answer that loaded question on the grounds that it might incriminate her, so she remained mute.

His mouth twisted in something that might pass for a smile. "Exactly. My son *will* have my name. He will never doubt my desire to acknowledge him *publicly*."

"You can acknowledge him without marrying his mother."

The blue in Marcus's eyes turned stormy with rejection of that idea. "No."

She felt helpless in the face of his blunt refusal to acknowledge her argument. "But, Marcus, we can't get married just because we have a child together. No marriage based on such a shaky foundation could survive."

His expression made her shiver. "I don't care how long we stay married. All I care about is becoming my son's legal parent, making sure he never suffers the pain of rejection I felt growing up the son of a prominent man and his mistress."

"I'm not your mistress and neither of us lives in a small town like the one you grew up in. No one in Seattle or Portland is going to care whether or not Aaron's parents are married."

"No one? Are you sure about that? Are you absolutely positive that Aaron won't be taunted by his schoolmates, that he'll never overhear himself referred to as an embarrassment or, worse, a bastard?"

"No, of course not. That's not the point—"

"That is precisely the point, Ronnie," Marcus said, interrupting her before she could finish her thought.

"Marcus . . ." Her voice trailed off as she marshaled her defenses in her mind. She couldn't marry Marcus. "You lied to me."

"I never will again." Sincerity rang through the anger still vibrating in his voice.

"How can I believe you?" she asked.

"I guess you'll have to start trusting me," he replied, with biting sarcasm.

She swallowed. According to him, that wasn't a likely possibility for the future.

"You despise me," she said painfully.

"If I despised you, I would be looking at fighting you for full custody of our son, not marriage."

His argument was irrefutable and such a terrifying prospect that she wouldn't willingly dwell on the subject.

"You don't believe in commitment."

"I've changed. I want my son."

"And to get him you have to marry his mother,"

she completed, her heart constricting at the thought.

Marcus shrugged. "Yes."

She wanted to hit him. "This is about more than giving Aaron your name, isn't it?"

He sat down and ran his fingers through his golden hair and then dropped both arms, allowing his hands to dangle between his spread thighs.

"Yes. I want to be a full-time father to my son and I can't do that with weekend visitations and split holidays. I don't want you marrying some other man a year down the road and letting him take my place in Aaron's life."

"So, when you said you didn't care how long the marriage lasted, you didn't really mean it, did you?"

Please say you didn't mean it, she pleaded mentally, still reeling emotionally from that cruel comment.

He turned to face her, reaching out to touch her face. She didn't flinch, but the touch unnerved her.

"No, I didn't mean it. I'm still pissed as hell at you and it just popped out, but I don't want to get married with you thinking divorce is the easy alternative to living with me."

Shaken, she realized that it was on the tip of her tongue to say yes to marrying him. She loved him, even after everything. She couldn't imagine her life without him. The past eighteen months, she had felt an empty, aching place in her heart that had not been filled until he had held her again.

"You really don't hate me?" Even loving him,

she could not stand the thought of marriage to a man who hated her.

"No."

But he didn't love her either. Could she live with that? She didn't know. Her indecision must have shown on her face because he started talking again, saying things to convince her.

"You realize that when we get married, you can move back to Portland. Jenny can go back to her old high school."

She wiped at moisture that had somehow gathered across her lower lashes. "Jenny would like that."

"I'll help you put her through college as well."

She choked out a laugh. He was even willing to buy her cooperation if rational argument didn't do the trick.

"I don't expect that. Jenny's not your responsibility."

His mouth firmed into a now familiar grim line. "When we get married, your sister becomes my sister and since you are her guardian, she also becomes my ward. That makes her my responsibility. You've carried the burden alone long enough."

She swallowed a sob trying to crawl up her throat. How could he be so kind and so cruel at the same time?

"Have you thought about staying home with Aaron?" he asked.

She had and then dismissed it as impossible. The reality of her sister returning to school next year had been weighing heavily on her. She would have to find outside day care for Aaron and she didn't relish the prospect. She just shrugged.

"If you want to work, I'll support that decision, but if you want to stay home either half-time or full-time, I'll support that as well. Isabel went to half-time after maternity leave. She seems to like it."

With each word, Marcus embellished the already tantalizing lure of marriage to him.

He pulled the blue blanket from her nerveless fingers and inspected it. "This is nice. My mom used to quilt. I've still got the one she made me for my high school graduation on my bed."

Remembering the log cabin pattern beautifully done in fall colors, she thought his mother must be very talented. The quilt had looked like the kind that won a blue ribbon at the state fair and got auctioned off later for hundreds of dollars.

And despite his pain-filled childhood, Marcus must still have very tender feelings for his mother to keep the quilt out.

She nodded toward the crochet project in his hands. "I'm making that for Aaron's big boy bed."

For the first time that evening, Marcus's humor shone through in an engaging grin.

"It'll be a while before he's ready to come out of the crib, won't it?" he teased.

She smiled, some of the awful tension of the past few hours draining from her. "Yes, but it could take me a while to finish this. I only work on it in spurts."

"I don't want to be a father in spurts, Ronnie. Please make a family with me."

She shook her head, not in denial, but in helpless confusion.

He was begging. Marcus, the man who had told

her the first time they made love not to get sex confused with tender emotions. He wanted to make a family with her, and Heaven help her, she didn't know if she was strong enough to deny him.

"I need time to think about it." When he looked like he would argue some more, she did her own begging: *"Please."*

"While you're thinking about it, think about this." He tossed the unfinished blanket aside, grabbed her waist in both of his large hands and pulled her with one swift movement into his lap.

His lips slammed down onto hers with passionate intensity, and every thought of protest flew from her mind like a flock of pigeons going south for the winter. She could taste a curious mixture of male hunger and residual anger in his kiss. She pressed her hands against his chest, intending to separate their bodies.

She didn't want to kiss him when he was still angry with her, when she was still angry with him.

But then his tongue pressed erotically at the softened juncture of her lips and she wanted nothing more than to open her mouth to his sensual exploration. Instead of pushing him away, her fingers clenched in the fabric of his shirt, and she met his questing tongue with her own as her anger turned into something far more dangerous—passion.

Her breasts ached and her already hardened nipples pressed against the silky confines of her bra. She rubbed herself against him, wanting his touch. Needing it. Growling low in his throat, he seemed to know exactly what she needed as he let go of her arms to work on the buttons of her cotton shirt. He only undid enough to slide his hands inside and cup her aching flesh. He squeezed gently and rubbed his thumbs over her engorged nipples simultaneously.

Mewling in both desire and frustration because her bra was a thin but persistent barrier to his naked touch, she ground her bottom against his erection and pressed her tormented flesh against his hands.

Laughter rumbled in his chest, but he didn't stop kissing her to give vent to it. She didn't know what he thought was so damn funny anyway. She wanted him naked and in her arms. *Now.* Working with feverish intensity on his shirtfront, she managed to get his buttons undone and shoved the fabric off of his shoulders.

Her hands greedily caressed the curling hair on his chest, and his entire body gave a convulsive shudder as her fingertips found the hardened nubs of his tiny male nipples.

As he pulled his mouth from hers, his head fell back against the couch, but his hands continued to knead her breasts. "You turn me on so fast, baby."

"Good." She'd hate to be this out of control by herself.

Licking a trail from his collarbone to his chin and back again, she stopped to place sporadic kisses against the heated flesh of his neck.

He unsnapped the front closure on her bra with unusually clumsy movements, and then the calloused skin of his masculine hands gently rubbed her hardened nipples and the swollen flesh of her breasts. It felt so good she wanted to cry.

She lifted her head and met his blue gaze, unfocused by desire. "*Marcus.* I want you *now.*"

"*Yes!*"

And then clothing started flying and she ended up on the carpet next to Aaron's toys, while Marcus shucked his jeans. He stood above her, outrageously masculine and so aroused that even knowing his body as well as she did, she felt a frisson of purely feminine anxiety at the thought of taking him into her own.

He must have seen the worry in her eyes because he smiled with reassurance. "You know I'll fit."

"Yes." It was hard to get the one word past the dryness in her throat.

He came down on top of her, letting his hardness nestle in the juncture of her thighs. His thick erection pressed against her swollen flesh.

He groaned and rubbed himself against her. She whimpered and tried to take him into herself.

He held back. "Not yet," he said, as he reached for something in his jeans pocket.

Then he knelt between her legs and tore open a foil packet.

"You brought a condom with you?" she asked, even as aroused as she was, shocked by his sensual arrogance.

He nodded and she saw the calculation in his gaze.

"You planned this," she accused, as he slid the condom in place.

He didn't answer but came back down on top of her, adjusting himself so that his mouth was in line with her breasts. His lips closed over one turgid nipple and her worries burned up in the heat of the response he drew from her body. He suckled her while gently rolling her other nipple between his thumb and forefinger until she was begging him to take her.

"You want me?" he demanded, his face set in the almost cruel lines of masculine arousal.

"I want you. *Now*, Marcus, *please!*"

She didn't care that she'd begged him. She just wanted this burning ache assuaged.

He pushed her thighs apart, almost roughly, and then set his erection against the opening to her flesh. She tipped her body up and groaned as the tip of his penis penetrated her aching body. Then with a feral shout that deafened her, he pushed forward and seated himself in her in one long thrust.

She stopped thinking after that. She could only feel. The rough carpet beneath her. The hard and fast thrust of his flesh inside her, the sensation of his lips on hers, the hot slide of his tongue in her mouth, and then everything began to splinter around her. She cried out against his lips, the sound muffled by the possession of his mouth over hers, and convulsed around him, her body rigid with pleasure that was close to pain.

His muscular body shook against her and she felt him grow even harder, longer and thicker before he came too.

He collapsed, his head falling into the curve of her neck. They lay there panting for several seconds.

"I'm too heavy for you." He sounded exhausted.

"I don't care." And she didn't. This closeness felt too good to let go.

He moved his head and she felt a tender kiss against her temple. It was so gentle, so completely nonsexual even though their bodies were still intimately connected, that she felt tears prick her eyes. She blinked, unwilling to let them fall.

And then her gaze focused on the clock in the corner. Stiffening, she pressed against Marcus. "Oh, my gosh. It's almost nine. *Marcus! Jenny could be home any second.*"

Even though she knew it was necessary, her body rebelled when Marcus withdrew from her. He jumped up, grabbing his clothes as he went. She followed, a slight ache in her feminine flesh reminding her what they had just shared. She swept her clothes up off the floor and stopped with him outside the hall bathroom.

"You use this one. I've got another off my bedroom."

He nodded, his expression going remote. "I guess we won't share a shower this time."

Blushing in memory of what they had done in their last shower together, what she had said, she swallowed. "Not this time."

She turned to go into her bedroom.

"Ronnie."

"What?"

"The sex is good, too."

She spun around to face him. "What's that supposed to mean?"

He reached out and cupped her neck, his thumb caressing the underside of her chin. "It means that our marriage will be a passionate one."

She tried to glare at him but failed miserably. "I haven't said I'll marry you."

"You will." With that, he released her and strode into the bathroom, shutting the door in her bewildered face.

Had it been planned? Had he seduced her to remind her what she'd be giving up physically if she refused to marry him? He should realize that she could never forget. She hadn't forgotten for eighteen long months and she doubted her body was any more capable of forgetting the craving he'd fostered in it now. How could she forget? She loved him.

Marcus returned to the living room ten minutes later, his hair still damp from the shower. There was no sign of Ronnie, or her sister. The living room looked like a tornado had rolled through, though. If Jenny came in and saw the mess, it would embarrass Ronnie.

He had no doubt his little prude would assume her sister knew it had been caused by two adults having just made passionate love on the carpet.

He started picking up toys that had gotten scattered and tossing them into a dark green plastic laundry basket already half full of baby toys. He spied the unfinished blanket on the floor, partially under a chair, and picked it up along with the crochet hook. After rolling it in a bundle, he shoved it into the bag she'd taken it from earlier.

The room looked pretty good. Now, he needed some coffee.

Round one with Ronnie on the marriage question hadn't gone too bad, but now he faced round two. *Getting to know the future sister-in-law.* He had no doubt that Jenny's opinion would hold some sway with Ronnie in the marriage decision.

He could only hope that the teenager wanted to move back to her old stomping ground enough to encourage Ronnie in the right direction with him.

He walked into the kitchen and started looking through cupboards for the coffee. He found it in the shelf above the coffeemaker. Typical. He'd just gotten it going when he heard a key scrape in the lock on the front door.

He turned to watch through the opening over the breakfast bar as the door opened to reveal Jenny. Her hair was the same color as Ronnie's, but cut short. He wondered if that was because of the treatment she'd undergone in France.

She dropped her backpack on the table by the hall closet and then moved toward the kitchen. She stopped when she saw him standing by the active coffeemaker. Hazel eyes went wide as her gaze traveled over him. *What?* Had she expected some kind of monster? It wouldn't surprise him.

Ronnie would have had to explain to her kid sister why she hadn't told him about Aaron. He could imagine just what kind of role he'd played in the story.

"Hi, Jenny. I'm Marcus." Might as well get the introductions out of the way.

She regarded him with a steady gaze, hazel eyes expressing knowledge beyond her seventeen years. "I figured that out. Veronica doesn't date much and lately the only man on the horizon has been the ogre she was terrified of telling about her son."

"*Jenny!*"

Both he and the teenager turned toward the

sound of Ronnie's shocked voice. She stood in the entrance to the living room from the hall, her expression full of chagrined embarrassment.

He looked at Ronnie, though he answered Jenny. "I'm the ogre."

Ronnie's mouth drew in a familiar tight line. "I did not call you an ogre. Not once."

"No, I did," Jenny said, with sassy candor.

He found himself laughing and winked at Jenny. "I prefer Marcus, but if you really feel the need to call me by a nickname, ogre will do in a pinch."

Surprisingly, she smiled. "I'll keep that in mind."

He turned to pour himself a cup of the finished coffee. "Anyone else want some?"

Ronnie came into the kitchen and pulled out the sugar and a spoon for him. "No, thank you."

"I'd love some, but Veronica thinks it's bad for me." Jenny smiled at her sister to soften the complaint and Ronnie smiled back, her face going soft in a way that made Marcus feel protective.

She'd been through hell with her sister and he wasn't going to let her go it alone any longer.

"It is bad for you," he said.

"Then why do you drink it?" Jenny asked, with a superior tilt of her youthful face.

He shrugged. "Because I like it."

"A cup a day is supposed to be good for asthma. Do you have asthma?" Jenny asked, her eyes twinkling with humor.

"Nope."

"Too bad. I guess you just have to call it a vice then."

He stirred a heaping teaspoon of sugar into the steaming liquid and nodded. "I guess."

He took a sip of his coffee. It tasted Puerto Rican and it smelled like Heaven.

"So, what did you think of Aaron?" Jenny asked.

The spoon Ronnie had picked up clattered into the sink.

She'd done it on purpose, the little scamp.

He forced himself to swallow the hot liquid without choking, then turned his head to give Jenny the benefit of his undivided attention and answered her with absolute honesty. "He's completely amazing."

Jenny's face, which had been lit with mischief, sobered and her eyes warmed. "Yes, he is. He's a wonderful little guy, even if he doesn't sleep at night when he's teething."

He leaned back against the counter, crossing one ankle over the other, and took another sip of his coffee. Jenny scooted around the counter and took a seat on one of the stools at the breakfast bar while Ronnie hovered near the sink, wiping a nonexistent spot on the Formica with a dishcloth.

"So, like, are you two going to get back together, or what?" Jenny asked, in another bout of grueling candor.

Ronnie froze and her gaze flew to Marcus, pleading, but for what? Didn't she want him to say anything about his offer of marriage? Too bad. He wasn't going to be the bad guy in everything.

"I'd like to," he admitted truthfully. "I've asked your sister to marry me."

Ronnie laughed at that. "Yeah, right."

"You're saying he didn't ask you to marry him?" Jenny demanded, with avid interest written all over her thin but youthful face.

"Yes."

"Like hell—" he exploded, but Ronnie cut him off.

She fixed him with her librarian look. "You didn't ask. You told. There's a big difference even if you can't see it."

Hell. Is that why she'd balked at the idea?

"It's been a rough day. I wasn't at my romantic best," he admitted, feeling the skin on the back of his neck heat.

She probably thought he'd make a good running for Neanderthal man.

"You're serious?" Jenny asked, all mischief, humor and teenage superiority wiped from her expression. "The ogre wants to marry you?"

Ronnie glared at him as if saying, *look what you've stirred up now*, while nodding for her sister's benefit.

"I thought he was no ties, no commitments." Jenny sounded dazed.

He felt his jaw clench. "Your sister didn't know me as well as she thought she did."

"Excuse me, I *did*." Ronnie slapped the dishcloth into the sink. "You told me you didn't want a commitment, that it was all about sex, and you can damn well accept it."

Jenny sucked in a breath when her sister uttered the uncharacteristic swear word. He was getting used to it. When Ronnie got mad, she lost her grip on the controlled façade she always wore.

He took a deep breath and let it out. He couldn't deny her words. He had spouted that garbage, because he'd believed it. It never had been anything more than sex before with a woman, and it had shocked him that the little automaton could be the one to spark deeper feelings in him, feelings he'd never before believed in.

Rather than try to explain the inexplicable, he focused on something he could get his teeth into. "I don't think we need to discuss our sex life with your teenage sister."

"Why not? I've been living with the results of it for ten months," Jenny quipped.

Ronnie's hands fisted at her sides and her eyes filled with painful confusion before she turned her head away. Marcus had this crazy urge to pull her close and tell her everything was going to be okay.

Instead, he frowned at Jenny. "You've had a privilege I would have given anything to share."

She nodded, sympathy softening her expression for a second. "I bet. I told Veronica that just because you didn't want her didn't mean you didn't want to know about your kid."

Jenny had a point. Even if Veronica had believed he didn't want to make a commitment to her, there was no reason for her to assume that meant he'd feel the same way about a child. Except her fear that he might try to take that child away. Had she told Jenny about that? He didn't think so.

Hell, he bet she hadn't even told Jenny about the fiasco with Hypertron and how she'd managed to raise the money for Jenny's treatment in France. That would be just like Ronnie to hide the ugly reality from her sister and carry the burden alone.

He poured the remaining coffee in his cup down the sink and headed for the door. Ronnie remained in the kitchen in frozen silence while Jenny watched him with assessing eyes.

He stopped at the door and spread his gaze between the two women. "But the point is that I do want your sister."

Chapter Eighteen

"What in the h—e—double toothpicks is this?"

Allison flicked her gaze to the piece of paper in George's hand.

"I believe it is self-explanatory." It was her resignation with a request to be released from employment as soon as a suitable replacement could be found or two weeks from yesterday, whichever one came first.

She'd spent the night before considering her future and coming to the conclusion that it would not include George Kline. She respected herself too much to be any man's sexual fix, and since that was all she was to George, she had to get out of his life.

"You are not quitting over that dumb-ass argument we had yesterday."

"No, I'm not."

That stopped him. "Then what is this about?"

"It's about respect. You respecting me, which you don't, and me respecting me, which I do. Too much to continue working for you."

He crossed to her desk and pulled her out of her chair. His hold wasn't harsh, but it was firm. "I'm not letting you go."

Being this close to him was killing her, but she stuffed her emotions . . . like she always did in the office. "I realize it will be inconvenient for you to hire and train another PA, but it can't be helped."

"Am I supposed to train another lover too?" he asked, his tone biting.

She winced. "Yes."

He shook his head. "It's not going to happen. You aren't leaving me, lady. You belong to me, you got that?"

"An employment contract is not a slave agreement. I can move on to another job if I like."

His face went ashen. "This isn't about your job, darlin'; this is about us."

He'd never called her darlin' in the office before. Why had he waited until today to do it? It might have meant something before.

"My job is the only role you really care about me playing in your life. You proved that yesterday. I'm not staying and you won't seduce me into changing my mind."

"Why didn't you answer the phone last night?"

"I unplugged it."

"Did you unplug the buzzer for your apartment building too?"

She shook her head, her throat clogged with emotion. She'd ignored the multiple buzzes, just as she'd ignored the pounding on her door when he'd obviously gotten another resident to let him in.

"I hurt you yesterday."

"You think?" Sarcasm wasn't her thing, but sometimes it was all that would do.

"I didn't mean to."

"I don't care."

He dropped his hands and stepped back. "I never suspected you of the espionage."

"You didn't tell me about it."

"That was me being independent and dumb."

George admitting fault? Unbelievable. "It doesn't matter."

What they had was over.

"It matters all right. I'm not letting you walk out of my life. I can't force you to work for me, but I'm not giving up on us, and you can take that to the bank, darlin'."

Then he kissed her. Right there in the middle of her office, where anyone could see. And it wasn't a quick kiss either. It was long and slow and sensual.

When he pulled back, she was swaying.

He gently propelled her backward until she landed in her chair. "You belong to me and don't you forget it."

He kissed her again, hard and fast, and walked back into his own office.

"I still can't believe you didn't tell me that you and Marcus were an item." Sandy's voice rose in chagrined condemnation as she walked with Veronica toward the cafeteria.

Coffee had sounded good to Veronica's sleep-deprived brain. How was she supposed to get even a partial cycle of REMs with the prospect of marriage to Marcus dominating her every waking thought, *waking* being the key word?

Still, she almost wished she'd refused the lure of

caffeine if it meant dealing with Sandy in a thwarted mood. And her gorgeous blond friend was feeling very thwarted that morning.

"I mean, can you imagine how I felt when he told me you guys were dating? Here I'd just made a play for my friend's boyfriend? It was so embarrassing." Sandy didn't look embarrassed. She looked aggravated.

"You didn't have anything to be embarrassed over," Veronica tried to say soothingly, but she realized her voice had come out sounding a tad annoyed.

It wasn't as if Sandy *needed* another conquest. The woman had more than her fair share of men.

"You didn't know Marcus was interested in me."

"You could have told me. I *did* ask."

Remembering the message Sandy had left Monday morning, Veronica felt the stirrings of guilt. "I didn't call you back because I got busy. And you asked if I knew if he was involved with anyone, not whether or not he was involved with me."

As explanations went, it wasn't very good.

"Oh, *please*," Sandy replied, with obvious exasperation.

Okay, so she could have called Sandy back. She could have told her friend that she and Marcus had gotten serious, but she'd been so confused and beset by guilt about Aaron that she hadn't wanted to discuss Marcus with anyone, least of all another woman interested in him.

"Look, Sandy, Marcus is . . . He's . . ."

"What?" Sandy asked, her voice impatient. "Are you trying to say the interest only goes one way? If you don't want him . . ."

Sandy's voice trailed off, but her expression turned from one of irritation to pleased contemplation in a heartbeat.

Veronica wasn't sure of a lot of things, but one thing she did know: she didn't want the blond bombshell going after the man she loved. It was time to be honest, with Sandy at least.

"He's Aaron's dad and I think I'm going to marry him."

"Are you serious?" Sandy was almost shrieking. "Aaron's *dad?* Why didn't you say something right away? Now I feel even worse."

Veronica had no doubt her friend felt worse, but she didn't, for a minute, believe it was because Sandy had inadvertently made a play for an attached man. Veronica really liked the vivacious woman, but she wasn't blind to Sandy's faults and she didn't like to be thwarted in her pursuit of the male of the species.

"I didn't tell you because I didn't think it mattered."

"How can you say it didn't matter?" Sandy asked, sounding bewildered now, instead of angry.

"I didn't know he'd be interested in getting back together. I thought he sort of hated me."

She'd actually thought that he despised her and that there was no hope of resurrecting their relationship. Heck, she hadn't thought there'd been much of a relationship on his side to resurrect. Apparently, she'd been wrong.

The man wanted to marry her and if she could convince herself it was as much for her sake as Aaron's, she'd probably agree to do it.

"That's not the way he talked on Monday at lunch."

Walking into the cafeteria, they headed straight for the food and beverage bar.

"What did he say?" Veronica couldn't help asking, as she lifted a brown plastic tray and set it on the metal railings.

"I'd just asked him if he wanted to come to my condo for dinner. He turned me down. You know me, I don't take no easily." Sandy's mouth twisted in a wry smile. "So, I asked for another night and he told me that you would be keeping him busy for the duration of his consulting job up here."

"Oh." Was she just being paranoid, or had there been significance to the fact he'd said for the duration of his time in Seattle?

"You said you might marry him," Sandy added, as she grabbed a tray and set it beside Veronica's.

"It's really iffy." Veronica put a napkin and spoon on her tray. She was just getting coffee and a scone.

"But it is a possibility?" Sandy pressed.

"More like a definite probability," Marcus interrupted from behind her before Veronica could answer.

She turned so fast that her glasses slid down her nose. She had to adjust them. "Marcus, *what are you doing here?*"

How much had he heard?

"Looking for you."

"Oh." Either the lack of sleep had affected her brain, or her conversational skills had taken a major downward turn in the past thirty minutes.

Or the sight of six feet, two inches of sexually devastating male had melted her brain cells. Just looking at him brought feelings from the previous night, when they'd made love on the floor, rushing through her. She had this scandalous urge to wrap her arms around his neck and bring his lips down to her level for a breath-stealing kiss.

He'd probably go for it. The man had no shame. He would also probably think it meant she was giving in on the issue of marrying him.

He frowned and she wondered what was bothering him now.

"So, are congratulations in order, or not?" Sandy asked, batting her lashes in what Veronica was sure was a purely instinctive, flirtatious gesture.

"Ronnie may not feel like celebrating, but we *are* getting married." He smiled down at her and she felt her facial muscles clench.

He could be so darned arrogant!

She drew herself up to her full five feet, four-inches and strove for a cool expression. "We are not decided on this. I'm still thinking about it. Remember?"

Rather than answer, he grabbed her tray and put it back in the stack, tossing her napkin and plastic spoon in the garbage.

Then he favored Sandy with his most winning smile. "You don't mind if I kidnap Ronnie for a while, do you?"

Sandy smiled back—of course. "Not at all, provided I get dibs on first right to know when Veronica makes up her mind to take a hunk like you off the market."

Veronica's teeth clenched and she bit back a scathing comment about hunks and not-so-subtle man-eaters.

Marcus flashed that megawatt smile again. "Thanks. I'll make sure she calls you."

He put his hand out to her. "Coming?"

She wanted to tell him to take a giant leap some-where deep, but she nodded.

There would be enough gossip on the employee rumor mill after the things she had told Sandy with-out adding a scene in the food line to it. Ignoring his hand, she swept by him and out of the cafeteria.

He caught up with her in a couple of steps. "So, what do you say? Should we go to that coffee place down by the water?"

Coffee still sounded heavenly, if not downright necessary, so she didn't demur.

Taking her acquiescence for granted, he led her outside to his car. She let him open the passenger door and help her into the Jag without a word. When he leaned over her to buckle her seat belt it reminded her of his innate courtesy whenever they were together. It made her feel cherished, which was a dangerous way to feel when trying to weigh the decision of marriage with a practical mind-set.

He didn't move right away after clipping her buckle into place, and his masculine scent sur-rounded her as he turned his head so that his mouth was only inches from hers. "You're so damn pretty, baby."

She opened her mouth to reply but didn't know what she would have said, and in the end, it didn't matter. His lips prevented her from uttering a word. They moved sweetly over hers for a brief but devastating kiss and then he stood up.

"You've got the sweetest lips." He winked at her and then walked around the car and slid into the driver's seat.

Sweet lips? Pretty? Didn't the man have eyes? Couldn't he see that she wasn't anything special, just an average, everyday wren type?

The heated look he gave her as he turned the key in the ignition said that he didn't see her as a brown little wren at all. In fact, if she was reading the expression in his eyes and curious tension in his body correctly, he saw her as fatally attractive.

Warmth curled in her insides and she found herself smiling at him.

He muttered a curse and leaned forward to kiss her again, this time hard and fast. "Thank you."

"For what?" For kissing him? For coming with him without arguing?

He brushed the skin of her cheek. "For telling Sandy that I'm Aaron's dad."

She expelled a fractured sigh. "I would have told her sooner, but I hadn't told you yet."

"I can see where that might be awkward." Rather than sounding angry at her admission, his words came out with wry humor and he smiled at her again before putting the car into gear. "I called Alex last night. He congratulated us both."

"On what?" she asked suspiciously.

"Having a son. He wants to know when we're getting married. I told him as soon as I could talk you into it."

"At least you didn't tell him we were getting married as if I didn't have anything to say about it." She could never accuse Marcus of not knowing his own mind, but she wouldn't be at all bothered if he just once acknowledged that she knew hers.

"Do you want me to apologize?"

"To me or to Sandy?"

"Why would I apologize to the barracuda? To you."

He thought Sandy was a barracuda? Interesting. Clearly he didn't think the blonde deserved an apology for losing her coffee break companion or being lied to. Then, Marcus clearly thought he'd been telling the truth.

"Why?"

"It obviously bugs you when I tell people we're getting married."

"Don't bother. You'll probably just do it again."

He shrugged, which she took to mean he agreed with her, and then expelled a heavy sigh. "Believe it or not, I didn't drag you away from Kline Technology to push you into a decision about marrying me."

She snorted. Yeah, right. "According to you, there is no decision to make."

His knuckles turned white where they gripped the steering wheel, revealing that he was a lot tenser about her reaction to his pseudoproposal than he let on. "Let's leave that alone for right now."

Gladly. "Whatever you say."

"So what did you want to talk about?" she asked after several minutes of silence while he drove.

"My investigation. I figure that since you know the suspects on my list, you can give me insights into them."

He had a good point, but it made her feel creepy to be talking about her coworkers in conjunction with an investigation into corporate espionage. "So, who are they?"

He shifted down as they approached a red light.

"Your boss, Jack. Sandy's on the list too. A design engineer by the name of Kevin Collins and an intern, Jerry Parks."

"*Sandy and Jack are on the list?*" Somehow she had never considered such a possibility.

"Yes."

"But Sandy's my friend."

Stupid. Stupid. Marcus wouldn't allow her friendship with the other woman to cause him to take Sandy's name off his list. After all, he'd left *her* name on his list of suspects even though one might term them *intimate* friends.

"That doesn't mean she's not capable of selling company secrets. She fits the profile and she's had access to all the information that's been leaked."

"What profile?" Strain filled her body and leaked out in her voice.

Maybe she would have rather talked about the marriage thing.

"She drives a flashy car, wears expensive clothes and she has contacts with several competitive companies. She could be up to her ears in debt like the rest of America, or she could be augmenting her income as a technical marketing engineer with a little espionage on the side."

It was all so superficial, but she could see how Sandy might look suspicious to him. "But she was the first one to bring up the possibility of a spy to me."

Marcus made a sudden stop as an old woman carrying a black plastic garbage bag stepped out into the street in front of the car. "She could have been feeling you out. Seeing if you noticed the wealth of information about your company on the market."

"Or she could be innocent."

Marcus patiently waited for the woman to move across the street before putting the car into motion again, ignoring the honks of drivers behind him.

"Maybe." He didn't sound convinced. "What about Jack?"

She just could not see her boss selling out his company. "He's a real team player, Marcus. And he's got lots of ideas for Kline Technology's future. I can't see him trying to undermine it."

"That could go hand in hand with his deep and not very subtle interest in Kline's supposed plans for expansion. Or he could be very good at making his interest in information not strictly related to him look legitimate."

"You're so cynical," she accused, as he pulled into a parking spot in a lot near Pike Place Market.

"Kline isn't paying me the big bucks to be naïve."

"No, I guess not."

She climbed out of the car and followed him to the parking attendant.

He paid the young man sporting dreadlocks and a tie-dyed T-shirt with the logo of a man playing the flute and dancing on the front enough to guarantee his parking spot for a couple of hours.

Marcus reached out and casually took her hand as he pulled her toward the market. She thought about pulling away, but it felt remarkably good and, really, wouldn't it be childish to insist on walking alone after what she'd let him do to her the previous night?

* * *

He was making progress.

She hadn't pulled away when he took her hand. Pretty soon she'd realize there was no point in pulling away when he talked about marriage either. Whether or not she realized it, she needed him and he was going to be there for her and for their son. Not like his dad, who had left his mom to face the censure of her neighbors and the pain of loving a man legally committed to another woman.

She'd also told Sandy he was Aaron's dad. He liked that. She'd made a public declaration and she'd admitted she was considering marrying him. All in all, he'd learned quite a bit while he shamelessly eavesdropped on what he was sure the women assumed had been a purely private conversation.

"So, you think Sandy's too nice to be a spy and Jack is too dedicated," he said, reopening their previous discussion as they crossed the street toward Pike Place Market.

She was silent for several seconds and he wondered if she was going to answer. "Actually, put like that, I guess my defense of them doesn't hold much water. I mean, I'm a nice person, at least usually, and I was as loyal as they come toward Alex and CIS until my loyalty to the company came into conflict with my love for my sister."

He didn't like the sound of self-condemnation he heard in her voice. He stopped in the middle of the sidewalk leading down to the market and turned her to face him with the gentle expedient of his fingers on her chin.

"Listen to me, Ronnie. You did what you felt you had to do. Your sister is well again and I don't think you can dismiss that. You'll never face a similar set of circumstances again." He'd make sure of it.

She wasn't alone anymore. She had him, and this time, he'd make sure she knew it.

Her pretty gray eyes widened behind the black frames of her glasses. "Are you saying you forgive me?"

"There's nothing to forgive. You were right when you said that if Alex had gone through with his plans to destroy Hypertron, his marriage would have been in trouble. I don't know if Isabel would have left him, or not. She's a pretty sweet lady, but it would have hurt her and he would have had a hell of a time forgiving himself for doing that."

Ronnie's soft lips parted and she expelled a short breath. "You're right. It's really hard to forgive yourself when you hurt someone you love."

She turned and started walking again, tugging him along.

Did she mean him? He had been ready to dismiss her supposed love for him the day before. He'd been sideswiped by the realization she'd kept knowledge of their son a secret from him, but he'd had a whole sleepless night to contemplate her actions, and he realized that he could almost understand the fear that had motivated her and taken over normally intelligent thought processes.

First, she'd been terrified of losing her sister to disease like she'd lost her parents to an accident. Second, she'd been afraid of losing Aaron to a vengeance-minded father. Since he'd been so vocally supportive of Alex's plans to gain revenge against the man he felt responsible for his dad's death, Marcus could readily believe that Ronnie had assumed his reaction to news that she was pregnant with his child would be less than heart-warming.

It still hurt like hell that she'd never trusted him, but he wasn't going to let that pain get in the way of their present relationship. They walked by a stall of flower sellers. Aging Oriental women arranged bright blooms in oversized bouquets that demanded a second look and he stopped, pulling Ronnie to his side with their clasped hands.

She reached out one hand and touched a calla lily in the center of one particularly eye-catching arrangement. "It's so lovely," she said to the smiling Oriental woman behind the counter.

"Only fifteen dollars, missy. You take home."

Ronnie stepped back, shaking her head with a regretful frown, and Marcus's heart twisted. How many times since her parents had died had she had to say no to her own desires in order to provide for Jenny and then, later, Aaron?

He reached into his pocket and pulled out a twenty. "I'll take it."

The old woman's smile blossomed into a knowing grin. "You like for the missy, eh?"

"Yes."

"You don't need to—"

He cut off Ronnie's protest before she could finish it. "I don't need to, but I *want* to."

The old woman wrapped the stems in wet newspaper and secured a clear plastic bag over them with a rubber band.

"Don't hurt the woman's feelings; take the flowers," he admonished when Ronnie still looked like she wanted to refuse.

She took the bundle with her free hand and then treated him to a truly dazzling smile. "Thank you."

"You're welcome." The words came out a little strained, but what did he expect?

The smile had made him go from the semi-aroused state he was always in around Ronnie to rock hard in the space of two seconds, just like it had in the car.

It was a darn good thing his shirt hung low enough to hide the evidence.

They wandered away toward the fresh-fish stalls. The smell of uncooked seafood assaulted him and he directed Ronnie toward the interior of the market.

"Look, they sell coffee," Ronnie said, as she used her flowers to point toward a small café-style restaurant.

He let her drag him inside, where they ordered coffee and scones before sitting down at a table that overlooked the water. The place was empty except for them and the cashier-slash-cook. Ronnie laid her flowers on the table and took a sip of her steaming latte. Watching her tantalizing lips purse to almost kiss the cup did nothing to help cool down Marcus's libido.

"So, what about the design engineer?" he asked her, to get his mind on something that wouldn't leave him aching in an embarrassing way.

"Kevin Collins?" she asked, breaking off a bite-size piece of her scone.

"Yes. He's worked for four different electronic firms in the last five years."

Ronnie popped the morsel of scone in her

mouth and chewed thoughtfully. "I don't know. He's quiet. He always seems like his mind is on something serious and he's very good at predicting what could go wrong with a project. Other than that, I don't know him very well."

Marcus nodded and took a sip of his espresso. It kicked like a crazed bronco at the rodeo. "What about the intern? Jerry Parks."

Ronnie smiled. "He's sweet."

"*Sweet how?*" he asked, for the moment forgetting the investigation.

He didn't like the faraway look that had come into her eyes at the mention of Parks. She brushed her hair behind one ear and smiled again. He had a totally irrational urge to punch the *sweet* college intern right in the kisser.

"I don't know. He's so helpful and he tells me I look nice. He tries to flirt, but he's kind of bashful and it comes off like a kid trying to ride his bicycle for the first time."

"Inept?"

There went that smile again. "Yeah. In a really sweet way."

He felt like beating his chest and making mating calls. Hell. He was feeling more than a little possessive.

"I remember being a college kid. They're only after one thing, baby."

Her pencil-thin brows rose in unison. "And you aren't?"

"Damn right. I want a hell of a lot more than sex from you." He wanted it all. "And the intern's too young for you."

She laughed out loud. "You're jealous."

He glared at her, not even thinking of denying it. "So?"

What did she expect? She'd just told him the college boy had been flirting with her. It wasn't as if he thought Ronnie would fall for it or anything, but he didn't like the idea that another male thought he had an open field.

"It's not like you met the prospect of Sandy making a play for me with total sanguinity, either."

She frowned at the reminder of her jealousy that day in her cubicle when Sandy had horned in on his lunch date with Jack.

"I've known her since I started working at Kline Tech. She's very determined when it comes to the opposite sex."

"She's a barracuda." Sandy had obviously never heard of the feminine mystique of playing hard to get.

"It takes one to know one," Ronnie said, blowing a very un-Ronnie-like, very sassy kiss across the small table at him.

He wanted to grab her and yank her into his arms and make that kiss real.

"I'm a reformed barracuda. I'm not after all the fish in the sea anymore; I only want you."

George buzzed Allison's apartment, wondering if she would ignore his summons like she had before. Despite the fact that she'd responded to his kiss in the office, she'd kept her distance since then.

Maybe he deserved it. Hell, he knew he did. He'd been an arrogant SOB and she had every right to be angry with him.

The surprise was that she'd put up with his cowardly behavior for so long. He'd been afraid of feeling too much and he'd made her pay the price by keeping her pigeonholed in his life. It wasn't something he was proud of, but he was hurting too much at the thought of losing her to let her go—even if that was exactly what he deserved.

"Yes?" her voice came over the intercom.

"Open up, darlin', it's me."

"I don't feel like company tonight, Mr. Kline."

Mr. Kline? Like hell. Bad temper and fear mixed inside him until he was ready to explode, but he was old enough to know better than to give in to the emotions and act like an idiot again. He'd hurt her and he had to make it right.

"I'm sorry, Allison, please let me come up and talk." They were difficult words to say. Apologies had never come easy for him, but losing her would be a damn sight harder.

There was silence on the other end of the intercom.

He dumped his pride and said, "Please," again.

He could hear her sigh. "I don't think it's a good idea. We don't have anything else to talk about."

"We have a relationship that needs straightening out."

"Our relationship, such that it was, is over."

"I can't accept that."

A young man, looking cocky like he had at that age, came up to buzz an apartment and George stepped back. He wasn't about to share his heart in front of a stranger. Surprising himself, he didn't follow the other man inside when the door unlocked.

Allison had to want to talk to him for this to work and God help him if she didn't.

He buzzed her again.

"George? I thought you left."

"I had to let someone else buzz an apartment."

"You didn't follow them inside," she said, in a choked voice that made him feel like a heel.

"I've acted like an arrogant fool one too many times already. Will you let me talk to you, darlin'?"

She didn't answer and he was starting to sweat when the door buzzed. He yanked it open immediately and strode purposefully inside. He took the stairs to the second floor two at a time, his mind whirling with the things that had to be said, things he should have said to her months ago.

She opened her apartment door on the first knock, but he didn't take that as a sign of eagerness to talk on her part. How could he with the look she was giving him? He might have been a bill collector for all the welcome in her eyes. They were red rimmed, but remote, and her cheeks were dry.

She still looked so lovely to him that it was like getting a kick in the gut to see her.

She stepped back to let him pass, but he stopped in front of her. "You are so beautiful."

"I look like a mess," she said, with a frown that questioned his sanity.

"You never look anything but delectable to me. Every time I see you, I feel like I'm getting an exclusive viewing of the Mona Lisa."

Her mouth twisted in a disbelieving sneer. "Not at the office. You treat me like a stick of furniture there."

"If I didn't I'd be making love to you on every piece of real furniture within reaching distance and the floor besides."

"Sex," she said disparagingly, turning away.

Reaching out to grab her and stop her from moving away from him, he shook his head. "Never just sex. You're an integral part of my life, Allison."

"I'm a very efficient PA who happens to be good in the sack. That doesn't make me irreplaceable, just convenient."

He hated the self-contempt he heard in her voice and the pain. He'd put them both there and it was his job to eradicate them too, but he didn't know what to say. Not with her looking like she'd rather eat a bug than let him touch her.

One thing he knew was that no matter what she might be telling herself, she still wanted him. She wouldn't have responded to him in the office after giving her resignation otherwise. He would take advantage of that fact.

Hell, he'd use anything if it meant keeping her in his life. If he could get her pregnant, he would. His competitors hadn't labeled him *ruthless* for his easygoing nature and willingness to let go of something he wanted.

He pulled her into his body for a scorching kiss, and though her body remained rigid against his, she didn't fight him. He kissed her with all the persuasive passion he had at his disposal, along with all the knowledge he had of what made his woman respond until she finally relaxed into him and her lips went soft under his.

It was hard, but he forced himself to lift his lips and say, "We need to talk."

She ducked her head, not willing to look him in the eye. "Okay."

"Don't be ashamed of responding to something as incredible as what we have between us."

She just shook her head and led him into a living room that had always made him feel warm and peaceful . . . much like the woman herself.

She went to sit in an armchair, but he beat her to it and then pulled her down onto his lap before she had a chance to move to the sofa. He laced her fingers with his. If he didn't keep his hands occupied, he was going to strip her naked and make love to her until she made the noises that drove him wild.

He wasn't ready to resort to that tactic. He would try talking first.

"Look at me, *please*." He'd said that word more tonight than he had in a month of Sundays.

Her head came up and her eyes met his, her expression wary.

He lifted one hand to cup her soft, pale cheek. "You are much more than a body to me, or a superefficient PA."

Pained uncertainty flickered in her eyes and he hated himself for it.

"It's true," he stressed. "You are the woman who made me feel like life was worth living, like there was something besides my business to live for."

"You have your children."

"When Ellie died I shut myself off from everyone, including my children. I told myself that they were grown and had their own lives. Neither of them lived nearby and if you hadn't been there pointing out that my kids were grieving too, that they needed to know Kline Technologies wasn't more important to me than they were, I would have gone right on shutting them out. I love them, Allison, and I'll always be grateful you saved me from hurting them more than they'd already been hurt by their mother's death. I think it's pretty obvious I need you."

"You don't love me."

"I didn't want to, that's for sure, but that doesn't mean I don't."

She stared at him, her eyes wide with shock she should not be feeling. Not after everything they had shared. He supposed that was his fault too. He'd done too good a job convincing himself and her that what they had was only a small part of his life when in fact it was what made his life worth living.

"What?" she asked in a dazed voice.

"It hurt like hell when Ellie died," he admitted. He'd never found talking about his feelings easy and he hoped she wouldn't expect these kinds of discussions every other Saturday. "I promised myself I would never again be in a place to hurt like that again. The only thing that mattered was the company. Like I said, I started to push the kids away, but then you came along and you reminded me about important dates—"

"I'm a good PA."

"You're more than that; you are a woman who understands what it means to be part of a family and somehow you made sure I stayed part of mine. My kids and I both owe the relationship we have today to you."

"You would have gotten back on track on your own."

"Don't count on it. I'm a damn stubborn man when I want to be."

She looked down, acknowledging that there she sat on his lap when she hadn't even wanted to let him in her apartment. "I already knew that about you."

"Then you know I'm not letting you go."

"You can't hold onto me if I don't want to be held."

"I'm praying I haven't destroyed everything between us."

"What us? Your kids have been to visit you several times since I came to work for you, a few since I became your lover, but you never introduced them to me."

"I was selfish. I wanted you all to myself. I needed you to belong to *me,* but if I'd realized how much I was hurting you . . . how devalued you felt, I would have fixed it immediately."

"You wanted to keep me compartmentalized," she said, in a thick voice, her eyes glistening with moisture. "I didn't belong in that part of your life . . . the permanent, important part."

"Bull puckey. You belong there all right. You *are* that part of my life . . . you and the kids."

She shook her head, two tears spilling over, and he swore.

"Please don't cry, darlin'."

"I can't h-help it. You can say anything now, b-but I l-lived it with y-you."

Total honesty was all that was going to cut it here. "Okay. You are right. I did compartmentalize you. I was trying to protect my heart, *but it didn't work.* I love you, Allison, and if you leave me, it's going to hurt as much or more than it did when Ellie died."

"You don't mean that."

"I do. I will do anything to keep you. Just tell me what you want and it's yours."

"All I ever wanted was to be part of your life . . . your whole life, not just the hours at the office and a few stolen moments in bed."

"I want that too, darlin'. I do. Will you give me another chance? Will you meet my children, share my secrets? I swear I'll never hide anything like the corporate investigation from you again. I never suspected you. I need you to believe me about that."

She nodded, tears streaking her beautiful cheeks.

"And you'll let me try to make it up to you?"

Again her head bobbed and a tiny little sob escaped as she buried her face against his neck.

His hand slid down over her collarbone, then lower, and cupped her breast. "We aren't going to be able to maintain our distance at work anymore. I can't do it. It was getting damn impossible before I admitted how I felt about you; now there's no chance. Besides, it hurts you. I see that now."

"It doesn't matter. I gave my notice." The words were muffled into his neck.

"I don't want you to leave." Just the thought of facing a day in the office without her made him break out in a cold sweat.

She went stiff and he knew he would do whatever he had to in order to make her trust him again, to make her happy.

"But if you feel like you have to quit, then you do. Just don't leave *me*. Please, Allison."

"I don't want to leave you, or Kline Technologies, but I won't tolerate you treating me like a stick of furniture or a simple PA ever again."

"There's no chance of that."

She lifted her head and met his gaze, her mouth creased in the prettiest smile he'd ever seen. "Oh, George, I love you too."

Then she kissed him and the tight rein he'd had on his libido slipped.

He cuddled her to his body much later that night, listening to her sleep, and thanked God for her gentle, forgiving nature. His kids were going to love her. He already did.

Chapter Nineteen

Veronica tried to concentrate on the report she was generating for Jack, but her mind kept sliding into the murky waters of her personal life. She just couldn't get Marcus's words to stay where they belonged, in her subconscious.

I only want you played like the most persuasive and enticing of litanies in her head.

Mr. No-ties-no-commitments wanted her and only her. And according to him, he wanted her for a lifetime.

Marriage.

They simply were not the sentiments of a man who had lured her into bed as part of an investigation. He'd accused her of not trusting him, of never trusting him, and she had to acknowledge that he was right.

She hadn't trusted him to want something more than sex from her during Jenny's illness.

To be fair to her, he had to take at least partial

responsibility for her misguided thoughts. After all, that's what he *said,* that all he'd wanted was sex. Yet, according to him, he'd been thinking in terms of commitment even then. Long before he knew about Aaron.

Could she believe him?

Other than his guise as an investment consultant, he had never lied to her. Why was she so sure he was lying now?

What if everything he said had been true? What if he really wanted her for herself, even before he knew about Aaron? What if he *hadn't* confused their personal relationship with his investigation? What if he *had* wanted her to be innocent?

She weighed the knowledge she had of his actions against his words and her heart lifted. If he'd truly believed she was guilty, he wouldn't have opened an investigation into anyone else, but he had. He would have told Mr. Kline about her past and gotten her promptly fircd, but he hadn't.

So, if he hadn't slept with her in order to further his investigation, then he must have done it because he needed her, like he had said. Need wasn't loving, but it was a lot more than just physical desire. If that were all he felt for her, he could have slaked it elsewhere in the last eighteen months, or more recently with Sandy, but he hadn't.

Everywhere she looked, she saw actions on his part that indicated a deeper commitment and care for her than anything she ever could have imagined him feeling. And wasn't that partly her own fault? Marcus never called her a little brown wren. She did that.

He acted like she was the sexiest woman alive

and she'd always discounted that reaction, but why?

He could have any woman he wanted, but he wanted her.

I only want you.

But he didn't love her . . . did he?

Was it possible that with Marcus's pain-filled childhood, he had as hard a time recognizing love for a woman as she did recognizing dedicated desire in a man? Could he love her and not realize it?

The idea seemed fantastic, but considering the things his mother and father had done in the name of love, she could see Marcus hesitating to label the emotions he felt toward her with the word.

He needed to learn that loving meant a lot more than pain and sacrifice. It meant joy and caring, wonder and commitment.

And who better to teach him than the woman who loved him like crazy?

She certainly didn't want one of his former beautiful bimbo girlfriends taking on the task.

Marriage meant a lifetime in which to teach Marcus these important concepts. A lifetime she had every intention of sharing with him.

She didn't know why it had taken her so long to come to terms with the idea. After all, the prospect of a future without him held no appeal whatsoever.

Setting the report aside, she stood up. She'd tell him now and then maybe she could keep her focus on her work.

The phone rang just as she was going to step out of her cubicle.

Impatient to be with Marcus, she picked up the headset. "Veronica Richards here."

"Miss Richards, this is Allison. Mr. Kline would like to see you in his office immediately."

Her discussion with Marcus would have to wait.

Veronica was shown into Mr. Kline's office as soon as she arrived on the top floor and she couldn't help comparing today's visit with her last one. Clearly being in the loop on a corporate espionage investigation gave her a certain amount of clout.

Mr. Kline didn't smile when she approached his desk. Nor did he stand, or indicate that she should sit down.

With his mouth set in steely lines and his green eyes emotionless pools in the mask of his face, he said, "Miss Richards, I've come into possession of some very disturbing information regarding your past."

Miss Richards? What had happened to Veronica? And then his other words sank in. "My past?" she asked, faltering.

"Yes. It has come to my attention that you left CIS under a cloud, that cloud being the speculation that you had sold company secrets to a firm by the name of Hypertron."

Feeling all the blood drain from her face, she concentrated on remaining standing on legs that felt like the pins had just been knocked out of them. "I . . ."

What was she supposed to say? She couldn't

deny it. That would be lying and she'd promised herself she would never compromise her personal integrity again.

The price was too high.

"How did you find out?" she asked instead.

If anything, Mr. Kline's countenance turned grimmer. "Are you saying it's true?"

"Yes," she practically whispered.

She wished she could have said it with brazen confidence, but she just didn't have it in her to be brazen about admitting to acting as a spy.

"You'll understand, I'm sure, that I have no choice but to terminate your employment with Kline Tech. If you leave without making a fuss, we will provide the usual severance package."

And if she made a fuss? Would he terminate her without severance pay? Looking at his emotionless features, she didn't doubt it for a second.

"I'd really like to know who told you."

"I'm not at liberty to say."

And that was that. But then who else could it have been? Marcus and Alex were about the only two people on the face of the earth who knew about what she'd done. And she couldn't see Alex calling Mr. Kline with the news.

She turned to go but stopped and faced him again. "I'm not your spy, Mr. Kline. If you make the mistake of believing I am, you'll be putting your company at further risk."

"I will, of course, share your denial of any involvement in the current situation with our corporate investigator."

* * *

"You fired Ronnie?" Marcus's voice rose in disbelief as he took in what George Kline had just told him. "Why the hell did you do that?"

Kline expelled a deep breath. "I know it's rough, but once she admitted she'd sold company secrets at CIS, I couldn't keep her on."

Marcus jumped from his chair and leaned over Kline's desk, his knuckles resting on the glass-covered polished wood. "Cut the crap. You wanted to set our perp's mind at rest and make him believe you trusted him."

Kline did not lean back in his chair but met Marcus's glare head on. "Hell, yes, I wanted to leave him with the impression that he's safe. I don't want him taking a runner before we get a rock solid case against him. I want that bastard nailed to the wall."

"So you sacrificed an innocent employee."

"She's not innocent. I told you she confirmed she'd sold company secrets."

Marcus spun away from the desk. "It was a one-time deal, damn it. She needed money to save her sister's life."

"Are you saying she couldn't have gotten the money any other way?"

"She didn't think so." And that was all that mattered.

"I don't employ corporate spies, former or otherwise."

Marcus turned around to face Kline again, his every protective instinct urging him to exact retribution for Ronnie's loss. "It's my investigation, damn it. You should have talked to me first."

Kline laughed, surprising Marcus with the genuine humor he read in the other man's expression. "You know, you're like a hired gun from the Old West. You don't acknowledge anyone else's authority, even the man who hired you."

"I'm not trying to discount your authority."

Kline smiled. "I know. It's instinctive. I realized that from practically the moment I met you. You probably felt perfectly justified in not telling me about Veronica's past with your company as well."

"I would have told you if it had become an important factor in my investigation."

"In other words, if you thought I needed to know. And here I was under the mistaken impression that only the FBI operated on a need-to-know basis."

Marcus felt a reluctant smile tug at the corners of his mouth and sat down. Kline was right. He ran things his own way and trusted his own judgment. Those qualities made him a damn good investigator. On occasion, they also made him every bit as arrogant as Ronnie had once accused him of being.

"I was trying to protect her job. She's had a rough time of it the past few years."

Kline sighed, regret apparent in the uncharacteristic sag of his shoulders. "I know. Her parents died, leaving her custody of her sister, and then she had a baby."

"How the hell do you know this stuff?" Kline had once told him he didn't have time to read all of his employee's files.

"I read her file after Jack Branson came to me with his *concerns*."

The bastard. Marcus agreed with Kline on one issue at least: he wanted to see Jack's hide nailed to the wall, after he got a chance to muss it up a little.

"I also talked to Allison about her." Kline leveled a piercing look at Marcus. "She keeps up on company gossip with astonishing efficiency."

"Is that right?" What else had the personal assistant told Kline about Ronnie?

"Yes. You can imagine my shock when she told me that she'd heard from one of her coworkers that Veronica's baby just happened to belong to my hot shot consultant and said consultant had asked her to marry him."

Sandy hadn't wasted a second spreading the news. What had she done? Sent out a broadcast e-mail?

"Ronnie hasn't decided."

"Well, I've done you a favor, then, haven't I? Not having a job to hold her in Seattle should make it that much easier for her to come up with a favorable answer."

Kline was right, but that didn't make Marcus feel good. He didn't want Ronnie coming to him because she didn't have any choice. What kind of marriage would they have if she felt pressured by circumstances into agreeing to it?

He wanted her to want to marry him.

"Don't try to justify your indefensible treatment of a loyal and dedicated employee with that kind of garbage."

Kline laughed again. "You've got the whole code thing down, don't you?"

What was the man talking about?

"Code?" he asked, with barely concealed impatience.

"That Old West thing. Not only are you a law unto yourself, but you've got the whole honor and integrity thing going too. You probably think it would be taking unfair advantage of a woman to use financial pressure to get her to marry you."

"And you don't?" Marcus demanded.

Kline shrugged. "Hell, I don't know, but if it's the best thing for her, then maybe I wouldn't worry too much about my methods in getting her there."

Marcus didn't feel like arguing the merits of that kind of cold-blooded pursuit, because maybe if it had been any woman but Ronnie, he would have agreed. It wouldn't have mattered how he got the mother of his child to marry him if he didn't care about her personally, but loving her meant he wanted a hell of a lot more than grudging acceptance.

Loving her?

Hell, yes. Loving her. Just what did he think he'd been feeling for the last almost two years?

He needed Ronnie more than he needed his job, his lifestyle or any of his friends, including Alex.

Only love could explain his unshakable desire to make a life with a woman who had once abandoned him and caused him more pain than anyone had been allowed to since his parents.

Well, one thing was certain: he wasn't going to use this situation to force her into the marriage.

"When did Jack bring his concerns to you?"

"He came in first thing this morning."

"How did he find out?" Marcus knew Jack hadn't gotten the information from anyone at CIS.

That left the company Ronnie had sold the secrets to, Hypertron. But, frankly, he couldn't see the guy talking. It would damage his own reputation in the industry.

"He said an old friend from Portland told him. He worked down there at one of the high-tech companies before coming to Kline Technology."

Marcus didn't buy it, but he'd have to wait until they brought their accusations against Jack before getting the truth about who had ratted Ronnie out from him.

"Listen, Marcus. What I learned today goes no further. I didn't even tell Allison. She thinks Veronica resigned because of her plans to move to Portland. I also told Jack I didn't want the word getting out. I said it would look bad for the company image and I wanted to keep it under wraps."

That was something at least. He didn't know how much comfort it would be to Ronnie, though.

"So, we know who our spy is." A certain amount of satisfaction sizzled through him even amid his concern about how Ronnie was handling the latest upheaval in her life.

Kline smiled a predator's smile. "Now, you just need to build a case against him."

"I'm already working on it. I've got a tracer program on his e-mail that records the IP address of every outgoing and incoming e-mail, even anonymous ones. I've also got your internal security going over his regular and cell phone logs."

Alex was also running discreet inquiries at Jack's former company in Portland.

"It shouldn't be any time at all before we know who he's selling the information to. From there, it's a cakewalk setting him up to take a fall."

"Good." Deep satisfaction vibrated from the single word.

Kline had his own Old West code and it clearly encompassed getting his own back at a betraying employee.

After leaving Kline Technology, Marcus ignored speed limits on his way to Ronnie's apartment. When Kline had told him what he'd done, Marcus had been gutted. He could only begin to imagine how Ronnie felt. Damn. He hoped she wasn't crying. Her tears tortured him.

She had no way of knowing that Kline's giving her the axe was the man's idea of *activity to set the bad guys at ease.*

He slammed into a parking spot outside Ronnie's apartment. Not bothering with his usual ritual of turning off the Jag, he jammed it into first gear to keep it in place and was out of it without a backward glance. He didn't bother trying to look cool as he sprinted across the pavement and up the stairs to the hall outside her apartment.

He rang the bell and waited. Nothing. Damn it. She had to be home. Even if she wasn't, shouldn't Aaron and Jenny be there? He pounded on the door. Where was she?

He pounded again. "Ronnie, baby, open up."

The door swung inward, revealing Ronnie, her eyes swollen and her cheeks damp. Damn. She *had* been crying.

"Marcus. I shouldn't be surprised."

Of course she shouldn't be surprised. Had she expected him to do anything else but come over to offer comfort once he realized what had happened to her that day? She might not know he loved her. Hell, *he'd* just figured it out, but she knew he cared. A lot.

He stepped inside, closed the door and pulled her into his arms all in one movement.

"It's going to be okay, baby. Trust me," he said into her hair, as he placed a reassuring kiss on the top of her glossy brown head.

"T-trust you?" she asked, her tears making her stutter.

He closed his arms more tightly around her and groaned as she shuddered with a small sob. "Yeah, baby. Trust me. You aren't alone anymore. I'm here for you."

She went stiff against him and tried to pull away. It was just like her. She was too damn independent, but he wasn't going to let her face this alone.

"It's going to be okay. Kline promised to keep what he knows to himself. No ugly shadows are going to follow you to Portland."

"Follow me to Portland?"

He sighed. "Honey, I know you're upset, but do you need to repeat everything I say?"

She shoved against him, this time hard, and he stepped back a little so he could see her face but kept his hands locked reassuringly on her arms.

"You'd like that, wouldn't you?" she asked, her pretty gray eyes going squinty.

He wasn't going to lie and he didn't know why the idea that he wanted her to move should upset her. "Yeah. I like the idea of living in the same city as my wife."

Her glare turned sulfuric. "I just cannot believe you!"

"Damn it, baby. I thought you understood. I want to be married to you. I want to be Aaron's daddy. I'm not ashamed of those two facts." He had hoped that from the way she had responded to him earlier that day, she was beginning to see things the same way. She'd said she loved him, damn it.

She yanked herself away from him and backed up until she was clear on the other side of the room. "How dare you stand there all smug and satisfied when you've ripped my life to shreds?"

He didn't feel smug and he sure as hell wasn't satisfied, and he wouldn't be—not until he had her agreement to marry him. So, he didn't see where she got off accusing him of feeling either emotion, especially in the face of her devastating news. He reined his temper in, though.

She wasn't thinking rationally. She was still reacting to what had happened at Kline Technology.

He tried a tentative smile on her. "Your life isn't ripped to shreds. You've got to believe me, honey."

"That's easy for you to say." Taking off her glasses, she wiped furiously at her cheeks. "You've got everything the way you want it. I'm out of a job and you think I don't have any choice but to marry you and move back to Portland now."

He was trying really hard not to let her ridiculous accusations get to him, but for her to accuse him of being glad she'd been fired was pushing him to his limits.

"I am *not* glad you got fired."

"Right." Enough sarcasm dripped from that one word to drown him.

He felt his body tensing with anger, but he refused to give vent to it.

"I won't deny that I want you to move back to Portland with me, but I'd rather you did it of your own free will than feel pressured because you'd lost your job," he told her in all honesty.

No man wanted to feel like nothing more than the only port left in the storm of his lover's life.

"If you were so high-minded in your ideals, then why did you tell Mr. Kline about what happened at CIS?" she asked, her voice breaking on a fresh sob.

She turned from him and this time he felt more than gutted; he felt like death had come knocking on his hopes and dreams.

"You think *I* told Kline about Hypertron?" His voice sounded hoarse to his own ears, but maybe that was because his throat felt tight enough to choke him.

She didn't bother to turn and face him. "Are you saying you didn't?"

On another day, he might have thought that was hope he heard in her voice, but now he knew better. *She still didn't trust him. She would never trust him.* Just how had he thought they could build a life together with that lack lying between them? The pain of loss ripped through him.

He loved her, but what good did it do?

She might love him, but she was never going to trust him enough to marry him. Even if she did, her lack of trust would destroy any happiness they could hope to have. He saw the years stretch out bleakly ahead of him, years of being a weekend dad to his son, years of watching Ronnie probably fall in love with someone else and marry him, years when that man would squeeze Marcus's role in Aaron's life to the side.

He turned back toward the door. The last thing she needed was to have him around her right now. He'd come to give her comfort, to stand by her, but his presence was obviously just a source of pain for her. He felt like he'd gone climbing and taken a free fall on a hundred-foot-high ridge only to discover that his safety rope was frayed.

He put his hand on the doorknob. "Why bother saying I didn't do it?" he asked, the bitterness he felt heavy in his voice. "You're going to believe what you want to believe anyway."

Chapter Twenty

Veronica watched as Marcus's hand turned the knob as if it were in slow motion. He'd said *trust me* over and over again since walking in the door and she'd done everything but that. She'd made accusations. She'd demanded answers, but she hadn't once just trusted him.

She loved him.

That truth blazed through her like a search-light, exposing all of her faulty thoughts. So what if she couldn't think of any way besides Marcus betraying her for Mr. Kline to have learned about her past? Trust by its very nature implied belief in the unbelievable sometimes. It also meant taking risks and putting your life, or parts of it, in another person's hands.

How could she have said she loved Marcus and never trusted him?

Galvanized into action by the sound of the tumbler clicking on the door, she flew across the floor and literally threw herself at Marcus's back. "You're right. It wouldn't matter either way, because I already know the truth."

He was rigid beneath her grasp. She wrapped her arms tightly around his midsection as if she could keep the blond giant in her apartment by sheer force of will.

"Let it go, Ronnie. We'll work out some kind of visitation thing with Aaron and I'll help you find another job up here, if you'll let me, but right now I need to leave."

He didn't want to marry her anymore, but why should that surprise her? It would be an act of criminal insanity for a man to want to marry a woman who didn't believe in him.

She hugged him with all her might. "No. You can't leave. I won't let you. I know you didn't tell Mr. Kline about my past. I'm sorry I ever thought you did. I was thinking with my head, not my heart. But I've got my priorities straight now."

He was so stiff, not reacting at all.

"I trust you, Marcus. With my secrets, with my past, with my present and with my future."

He leaned his head against the door, his body emanating masculine defeat. "That's not what you said five minutes ago, Ronnie. You don't need to lie to me."

She felt the tears start again. "I'm not lying, Marcus. I love you and I can't lose you. *I can't.*"

Pressing her cheek against his back, she absorbed the warmth of his body through his shirt. She'd shrivel up and die inside if she could never feel that warmth again.

"Please forgive me, Marcus. You have to forgive me. I can't live without you anymore."

His chest expanded as he breathed in and held his breath for a second before letting it out. "You did pretty well for eighteen months."

"I was miserable."

He peeled her hands away, gently but firmly.

He was going to leave. He wouldn't forgive her. She'd lost the man she loved for the second time because she hadn't trusted him. Choking on a sob, she fell back a step as cold misery enveloped her.

Then the world tilted on its axis as Marcus lifted her high against his chest, one arm under her knees and the other against her back.

Blue eyes filled with tenderness gazed down at her. "Stop crying, baby. I really can't handle your tears."

She took a shuddering breath, trying to do as he'd asked, but fresh moisture dampened her eyes as she locked her hands behind his neck.

"I decided to marry you this morning, just before Allison called me to Mr. Kline's office. Now you don't want me and I can't blame you," she wailed and buried her face in his neck.

Soft lips caressed her temple in a fleeting touch. "Where are Jenny and Aaron?"

"Aaron's in a baby play group and Jenny's at an afternoon show with a friend from down the hall. Today's her afternoon out or I wouldn't have come home to cry," she admitted, in a soggy voice.

Marcus didn't say anything. He just carried her through the living room, down the hall and into her bedroom. He laid her on the bed as if she were a one-of-a-kind Lladro figurine, breakable and very precious.

Standing beside the bed, he took her hand and

pressed it against the unmistakable hardness of his arousal. "Does that feel like I don't want you?"

She felt her cheeks heat. "I d-didn't just mean in bed."

He smiled and her heart felt like it stopped beating, that smile was so full of tenderness and warmth.

"I didn't either. My physical desire for you is just one of the things that makes your presence in my life as necessary to my happiness as the air I breathe."

She sat up and stared at him with eyes she knew mirrored her hope. "Does that mean you still want to marry me?"

Dropping to his knees on the carpet beside the bed, he took her left hand in his. The image of her once commitment shy lover on bended knee in front of her literally stole the breath from her lungs.

"I love you, Ronnie. Will you marry me?"

There were no fancy words and she found that she didn't need any. That simple, straightforward question was filled with all the romance her heart-hungry soul could desire.

"You love me?" she asked, needing confirmation of the fulfillment of her dearest desire. Maybe she was hearing things.

"Yes. I didn't realize how much, or what that really meant until Kline told me that he'd fired you today and why. It hit me right away that his actions would work in my favor as far as convincing you to marry me."

"But you said you didn't want me feeling forced."

"That's the conclusion I came to, and when I did, I realized that I loved you too much to take you as anything other than a willing partner in marriage. So, are you willing?"

She had to swallow twice before she could answer without squeaking or crying. "I would be honored to become your wife."

He slid the most exquisite diamond ring on her wedding finger and then yanked her into his arms for a victorious, joy-filled kiss. After which, he set about expressing his happiness at her acceptance in a very tangible way.

A long while later, her body exhausted but satisfied beyond her wildest imaginings, she snuggled into his side and reveled in the feel of his naked body against hers.

"So, do you want to hear who ratted on you to Kline?"

The question startled her because once she'd accepted it wasn't Marcus, she hadn't cared. "I guess. Does it matter?"

He kissed her. "Yes, it matters. You see, when this person came to Kline with the information, he tipped his hand as the corporate spy."

She sat up. "He did?"

Which he? "Was it Jerry?" He was such a sweet kid she really hoped he hadn't done it.

Marcus crossed his arms under his head. "Nope."

"Was it Kevin?"

"Wrong again."

"Jack? The all-around team player and corporate go-to guy? I can't believe it."

"Well, believe it. The bastard went to Kline this morning and told him he'd learned about how you had left CIS under a cloud; then he hinted about information leakages that might have been going on since you started working for the company."

"And Mr. Kline thinks I'm innocent?"

She didn't understand. Why should her former employer trust her over Jack, and if he did, why had he fired her?

When she asked Marcus, his entire body tensed with anger. "You were the sacrificial lamb, sweetheart. Kline wants time to put together a rock-solid case against Jack. He thought firing you would make Jack feel safe enough to stick around and take the bait on one last big information deal."

She stared at Marcus, unable to take it in. "You can't be serious."

"As a heartbeat, baby. I gave him hell for it, but the bottom line is, he owns Kline Technology and can pretty much do what he damn well pleases."

"You yelled at him?" On her behalf?

Marcus's gaze wasn't on her face. It had drifted downward and she felt her nipples hardening under his hungry male scrutiny.

She crossed her arms over her chest. "Stop that and answer my question."

His expression turned harsh. "Yes, I yelled at him. He's lucky that's all I did. All I could think about was how you must be feeling and I wanted to kill him."

"And then you came here and I accused you of telling him," she said, feeling stricken.

He reached out and tugged at her wrists until she fell across him. "But you trusted me in the end, before you knew about Jack. I'll never forget that."

She leaned on his chest, her face an inch from his. "I love you so much, Marcus."

"I love you too, baby. Forever."

He kissed her breathless, but before she lost her

ability to think at all, she asked, "How soon are we getting married?"

He brushed a possessive hand over her outer thigh. "If we wait until the investigation is over and get married in Portland, Alex and Isabel can be there. I'd like that."

She didn't know how long the rest of the investigation would take and she wanted to make him hers as soon as possible. "They could always drive up."

He chuckled. "Impatient to stake your claim?"

"Yes."

"Me too. I'll call Alex in the morning. I don't know what the waiting period is in Washington, but it can't be more than a week. We'll plan the wedding for a week from tomorrow."

She bit her lip. "I'd like it to be in a church."

"You sound like Isabel."

"I don't know the pastor from the church Jenny, Aaron and I attend very well, but maybe he would marry us."

"We'll look into it tomorrow. Okay?"

Relieved that he wasn't going to go all blank male on her and insist that a courthouse wedding would be more efficient, she caressed his cheek in approval. "Okay. Marcus?"

His hand had wandered to her backside, his fingers going to dangerous places. "Mmmm?"

"I don't want Aaron to be an only child."

His hands stilled on their sensual exploration. "You want to have more children with me?"

"At least one more, maybe two. Would you mind?"

She found herself flat on her back with Marcus

looming over her, male hunger and satisfaction etched in every line of his face. "That's not a problem."

She laughed at his enthusiastic response and that was the last sound she made besides moans for the next forty-five minutes.

Once again snuggled against him, this time her body draped over his, she said, "You are officially retired as a male barracuda."

"Do I get to collect retirement?" he asked.

"I mean it. No more lunch dates, even for the job," she said, in case he didn't get the message.

He rubbed the base of her spine with small circular motions. "It goes both ways, baby."

She laughed at the idea of her being a man-eater. "That's not a problem," she said, repeating his earlier answer.

"That means no flirtation with sweet college interns." He sounded very happy about that limitation.

"I'm not working at Kline Tech anymore. There are no college interns on my horizon," she reminded him deflatingly.

"Well, the university is bound to be full of college men, if not interns, and I don't care how sweet any of them are; your study partners are all going to be female."

"University?" she asked.

"I thought maybe you'd like to go back and finish your degree. You could do it part-time at first, get the hang of being in school again."

She could spend more time with Aaron that way as well.

Tears in her eyes, she hugged him tightly to her.

"You really are the most wonderful man in the world."

"It may have taken you eighteen months to get there, but you've finally got it right," he teased.

She didn't laugh. She agreed. It had taken a while. But she'd finally gotten it right.

She'd gotten Marcus.

"You could have worn something a little more conservative. It *is* your wedding day."

Marcus glared at Alex Trahern, his best friend and partner in CIS. "Hey, I wore a tux."

He'd even traded his loafers for a pair of expensive black dress shoes. What more could Alex want?

"Yeah, well your cummerbund and tie are bright enough to make Veronica wish she'd worn sunglasses."

Marcus looked down at the tropical birds covering the cummerbund and matching bow tie and saw nothing wrong with them. He'd seen them in the tux shop and had known immediately that Ronnie would appreciate them as much as he did. He'd been right. She'd smiled when she saw him standing next to the minister.

He'd wanted to kiss her, but had been forced to wait until after exchanging vows that made her his wife.

They'd gotten married in Seattle as planned, but his mother had insisted on throwing a reception at a downtown hotel and had asked them to wait one more week so she could do it. He had grudgingly given in, not wanting to hurt her feelings.

She and Mark had been both shocked and surprisingly pleased to learn they were already grandparents. Marcus would have thought the offspring
from his half brother and half sister would have
been enough for them.

Ronnie had laughed when he expressed as
much to her and informed him that grandparents
never felt they had enough grandchildren. He
guessed he'd have to spend more time visiting them,
so they could get to know Aaron. The prospect no
longer held the old specters it used to, not when
he'd have Ronnie by his side.

Mark had abdicated his role as father a long
time ago, but he would make a terrific grandfather
and Marcus could live with that.

"Ronnie likes the way I dress," Marcus informed
Alex, with arrogant satisfaction.

According to his new wife, she liked pretty
much everything about him.

Alex smiled, his gaze wandering to where his
wife, Isabel, stood talking to George Kline's personal assistant, Allison. "And here I always thought
she had better taste than that."

"Hey, she's crazy about me. What can I say?"
Marcus took a sip of his champagne and caught
his wife's gaze across the room.

She smiled and blew him a kiss before turning
to say something to her sister.

Jenny had been the maid of honor and very
happy that Ronnie and he had gotten back together. She had gone so far as to plan their new
life in Portland with typical teenage enthusiasm.

"Her taste has never been in question. Unlike
Isabel, she wasn't willing to settle for a man who

thinks the only colors appropriate for male attire are black and shades of gray."

Alex's dark eyes glittered with humor. "Isabel hasn't complained."

"But she bought you a pink polo." Alex had worn it twice.

"She likes me to try new things."

Knowing Alex and knowing Isabel, who had shown up at the office on more than one occasion with a picnic basket and a wicked little smile, Marcus had no doubt Alex wasn't just talking about his attire.

"Nice party," George Kline remarked as he stopped beside Alex and Marcus.

"My mom makes a good hostess." She also made a very sweet and supportive mother-in-law, according to Ronnie.

Still, he wouldn't have minded skipping the party. He just wanted to get Ronnie alone. Consummating his marriage sounded like a lot more fun than celebrating it with champagne, food and a bunch of chitchat.

"You did a damn fine job with your investigation. My lawyers assure me that Jack's hide is as good as nailed."

Marcus had finished the investigation two days earlier, turning in a report with enough evidence to guarantee a conviction against Jack Branson for contract violation and industrial espionage. He probably wouldn't do any jail time—most white collar criminals didn't—but Marcus would be willing to bet that all of the man's ill-gotten gains would end up paying for court fees and fines.

"It gave me a lot of personal satisfaction," said Marcus.

Alex's eyes turned serious and he inclined his head in male understanding. Jack had hurt Ronnie, and at that point, Marcus would have nailed him even if Kline had pulled the financial plug on the investigation.

"Did you ever find out who told him about Ronnie's past?" Alex asked.

"Harrison had told his personal assistant. Jack knew how to grease the wheels of the rumor mill and got the story out of her. He has a pretty fine knack for putting two and two together. It's helped him in his sideline of selling corporate information to the highest bidder."

"But why look into it all?" Kline asked.

Marcus took another sip of his champagne. "He didn't trust me. The idea of Kline Tech expanding through investment didn't sit right with what he knew of your business style."

Kline frowned. "Damn. The man saw too much, but I still don't understand why he researched Veronica."

"As her supervisor, he would have known about her having worked for my company and leaving it. He probably noticed she hadn't put anyone from CIS down as a work reference and decided it was worth investigation."

Alex nodded. "There'd been speculation about a takeover of Hypertron after Harrison and St. Clair made their deal. I don't know how Jack figured out CIS had a role in it, unless he just took a stab at it after finding out I was married to Harrison's daughter."

"Whatever the reason, he figured there was a story in there somewhere, and he went looking for it." It would be a long time before Marcus would forget the desolation in Ronnie's eyes when he'd shown up at her apartment after she'd gotten fired.

"It looks like your wife is trying to get your attention."

Marcus liked the sound of that so much it took him a second to glance where Kline was pointing. Ronnie balanced on a chair, her smile radiant, her delectable little body outlined in every curve by the crinkly, clingy ivory fabric of her short dress. She was getting ready to toss the bouquet.

Afterward, he was supposed to remove her garter and sling it to a crowd of single men.

He didn't need further urging. The idea of putting his hands on her silky thigh, if only temporarily to get the garter, had him wishing he was wearing a Hawaiian shirt, not the black tuxedo pants, which did about as much to hide the evidence of his arousal as a pair of boxers would have done.

He reached Ronnie just as she threw the bouquet over her shoulder.

Allison caught it with a totally bemused look on her face. George Kline walked right up to her and pulled her into his arms for a kiss that left no one in the room in any doubt about the relationship between the two of them.

Then, he watched with amusement as the older man slid a ring on Allison's left hand and the PA started to cry, her smile as wide as the outdoors.

Marcus's smile was pretty big too as he turned away from the sweet tableau to face his beautiful wife. He knelt in front of Ronnie, now seated on the chair she'd been standing on.

Her smile melted his heart and he forgot about Allison and Kline's happy ending in favor of his own. "Ready?"

He slid his fingers just under the hem of her dress and encountered the satin garter. "More than you know."

Her gaze dropped to the front of his pants and then flew back to his face. "I guess you are."

The room faded away as he slid the garter down her leg, centimeter by centimeter. By the time he'd removed her pump and slid it over her sexy little foot, she was breathing in shallow little pants and the shouts of approval around them had grown deafening enough to pierce his desire-filled brain.

He leaned forward and gave her a kiss filled with promise of things to come before standing up and slinging the thing over his shoulder. He didn't bother to see who caught it.

He'd waited long enough.

He swept her out of the chair and started carrying her out of the reception room. His mother tried to stop him and ask a question, but he walked by her with a promise to call her later.

Alex wolf whistled and someone else yelled something about them not being able to wait to get alone. He didn't bother to agree; he figured his actions spoke for him.

He pushed the button on the elevator. It had been smart to get a room in the same hotel as the reception for their wedding night. It saved travel time.

They were leaving in the morning for their honeymoon. He was taking Ronnie to Paris. She'd been miserable before in France and he wanted to give her some very good memories to make up for the harsh ones.

Jenny and Aaron were staying with Alex and Isabel while he and Ronnie were gone. The babies already played together like they'd been doing it since birth.

Ronnie's arms locked around his neck as he stepped onto the elevator.

Once they were in the suite, he laid her on the bed and stood above her. She was his; this beautiful, enticing, strong-willed, bighearted woman was his. He almost couldn't take it in.

"I love you, Veronica Danvers."

Her eyes glistened and her mouth curved. "I love you, Marcus Danvers. Forever."

He had always believed that love made you weak, now he knew better. His love for Ronnie made him strong and complete. He looked forward to a life filled with love, joy and the occasional squinty-eyed wife intent on having her own way.

It just couldn't get any better than that.

Don't miss Lucy Monroe's
WILLING,
available next month from Brava

Josie's heart fluttered in her chest as Daniel unlocked the door to their hotel room. Facing armed guerillas was not as intimidating as the unknown beyond that door.

She'd known soldiering her whole life, but the man—woman thing and sex were all a complete mystery to her. Other women started heavy petting when she'd been busy learning how to build and dismantle car bombs. The only orgasms she'd known had been of the self-made variety and while they made pretty good battle-tension relievers, they weren't anything to get excited about.

Not like the way she felt when Daniel kissed her.

Which was why she was here, ready to make love for the first time to a man who until that very morning, she'd been convinced didn't even like her.

He'd acted like he liked her in the park. He'd played with her and she had a feeling their tussling had been as new an experience for him as it had been for her, but the desire they felt was not.

He knew so much more about this than she did.

"My dad wouldn't have taken you on as a partner if you weren't a pretty good teacher, would he?"

Daniel turned his head to look at her, his hand on the doorknob. "What?"

"Your method of teaching isn't tossing someone into a river and seeing if they learn to swim before they drown, is it?" Her voice was high-pitched and her breathing had turned ragged at the edges.

He winked, shocking her to her toenails. "Don't worry, Josette. I won't let you drown."

She swallowed and tried to believe him. He pushed the heavy, ornate wooden door open and indicated she should go in first, but her legs refused to cooperate.

His dark eyes narrowed. "Are you okay?"

"Yes, but I can't seem to get my feet to move."

"You're nervous."

What had been his first clue? The way she equated making love for the first time with death by drowning, or the deer-caught-in-the-headlights look she knew was in her eyes? "I shouldn't be. I'm not a child."

"But you are innocent."

"Only physically." She'd heard and seen things women married for forty years would never experience.

He shook his head, his mouth twitching at the corners. "Your heart and your mind are still very innocent, no matter what you think you know."

"Oh really?"

"Yes."

That sparked another set of worries that kept her feet firmly glued to the floor outside their room. "Won't you be bored making love to me, seeing as how I don't know anything?"

"Josette, I could spend the entire night just looking at you and not get bored." His tone wasn't reassuring so much as bewildered.

Contemporary Romance By
Kasey Michaels

__Can't Take My Eyes Off of You
  0-8217-6522-1 $6.50US/$8.50CAN

__Too Good to Be True
  0-8217-6774-7 $6.50US/$8.50CAN

__Love to Love You Baby
  0-8217-6844-1 $6.99US/$8.99CAN

__Be My Baby Tonight
  0-8217-7117-5 $6.99US/$9.99CAN

__This Must Be Love
  0-8217-7118-3 $6.99US/$9.99CAN

__This Can't Be Love
  0-8217-7119-1 $6.99US/$9.99CAN

Available Wherever Books Are Sold!

Visit our website at **www.kensingtonbooks.com**